Photography by Patrick Hemingway

BetsyLulu has always loved the written word. As a young child, make believe became her world, with all the characters she created within it. Daring to dream bigger, she branched out and turned her love of writing into a steady stream, reaching into several outlets. BetsyLulu has had her work published on several online publications and local newspapers.

Her travels over the years to different countries, have inspired her in much of her writing. Working and teaching English in a kindergarten in post-Soviet Russia led her to an eye-opener of a culture.

She has been involved in many creative conferences, able to judge and give valuable insight to up and coming writers.

Her love of the ocean has led her to think, she really is a mermaid. Perhaps, in another life, or story.

Always on the lookout for inspiration, the next place you may find her is lying on a beach, with a cool drink in hand, pen in the other.

BetsyLulu

Russian Love Spell

Olympia Publishers
London

www.olympiapublishers.com
OLYMPIA PAPERBACK EDITION

Copyright © BetsyLulu 2023

The right of BetsyLulu to be identified as author of this work has been asserted in accordance with sections 77 and 78 of the Copyright, Designs and Patents Act 1988.
All Rights Reserved

No reproduction, copy or transmission of this publication may be made without written permission.
No paragraph of this publication may be reproduced, copied or transmitted save with the written permission of the publisher, or in accordance with the provisions of the Copyright Act 1956 (as amended).

Any person who commits any unauthorised act in relation to this publication may be liable to criminal prosecution and civil claims for damage.
A CIP catalogue record for this title is available from the British Library.

This work is inspired by a true story. The events are portrayed to the best of the author's memory. While all the stories in this book are true, some names and identifying details have been changed to protect the privacy of the people involved.

ISBN: 978-1-84897-946-8

First Published in 2023

Olympia Publishers
Tallis House
2 Tallis Street
London
EC4Y 0AB
Printed in Great Britain

Dedication

"Life is not transferred to fiction but transformed."

The involvement of your mind is far greater than your words, alone.
Digging deep down into the depths of your soul, forming and writing every word and scene until you reach the last set of words, that is when you know you have conquered and reached the final writing stone.
Dedication to the craft is an ongoing perseverance, you must always strive and reach for the stars.
The destiny of your book finally comes full-circle when you finish writing that last and final page.

Send it out into the world, your readers are waiting....

To David and Norma,
Enjoy the read!!!
Beth
xx

Russian Love Spell

One man's destiny would become one woman's ultimate fate. Their first encounter was short like a dream; it seemed too good to be true. Oceans parted them and yet love stood the test of time.

Love can unexpectedly touch the heart, but can break you in the least expected ways.

Katie was from the Western world. Halfway across the world, in faraway Russia, a young man named Max stirred her soul. Love knocked on both of their hearts when their paths crossed on a fateful winter night. This Russian boy captured Katie's heart.

But I am not of his world.

Even so, his language was to become her own. Walking across that forbidden soil, it knew her destiny, a land far away that seemed hidden from the rest of the world.

Who could overlook its beauty or vastness? In the core of its awakening she was the girl it captured.

To cross over from her own culture into another one, it truly was something Katie never saw coming on her horizon. Unlocking the key to her heart would ultimately be up to one young man, who held her fate in his hands.

To become one of them, a foreigner among Russians, would be part of her final destiny. To leave being one of them would shatter what she thought was her life and all she knew it to be. In her mind, Russia was to be her home, forever...

~Russian Memories~

I suppose the picture in Katie's mind of the train on its way rolling, will be with her always. Perhaps haunt her forever? The sound of it making its way on its vast journey. The memories remain, due to visions of that train in faraway Russia. Not just because of one boy, yet for many things buried deep down in her past. Always to remain, there to stay, forever and always.

When you hear the sound of a Russian train, remember me always.

~ BetsyLulu ~

Chapter 1
Distant Memories

Max walked the familiar path on that snow-frosted February morning. Pulling off his thick black gloves, he took a seat on the trolley, the usual commotion around him. He loosened the scarf that kept him from falling ill in the harsh Russian winter. His bright emerald eyes gazed out the icy window. A smile spread across his lips. He saw her in the reflection. It had only been five days, yet he yearned to see her, to look upon the face that had taken his world by utter surprise. He didn't think his heart would be full of change like this, each and every time he ran into that Canadian girl, a person he had known a mere three weeks. Someone not of his own culture.

With each passing day, his heart grew a little fonder. Distance had a way of doing that to a person, yet he had no idea these feelings would overcome him. Take over his thoughts each new day. Katie was far away now and he needed to move on. Easy to say yet hard to do. Max missed the intense excitement in his body each and every time he saw her. All those rare moments they shared, each time fate brought them together. Chance meetings. Looks of love passed between them.

All his efforts were not in vain. For he did tell her, yes, he loved her, when she left him and journeyed back to Hawaii. It was unexpected the way she had come into his life. The way Katie left him was heart breaking. He knew she longed to run off the train and into his arms, staying with him forever. Max could still see her sweet smile every time they met, how her eyes sparkled with excitement. He kept the hope in his heart that one day she might return to him. To him, alone. It seemed impossible at that moment, but his heart kept her memory well alive.

When they had said goodbye at the railway station, Max wanted to take Katie and keep her with him forever. Such nonsense! At that moment, his breath had already misted on the window pane of the tram. He jerked back and looked again, thinking he saw Katie's figure pass by outside at the bus stop.

"Stop daydreaming, Max," he mumbled in Russian. *"What are you even thinking?"*

He did have his life, after all, in this country she knew so little about. How could he possibly think Katie would ever fit in among the place he had known as home for most of his life. He knew this Canadian girl loved his culture and the people there. Yet it would be hard for Katie to fit in among the Russian society for a long time. The mentality was so different than the western world. How could she ever be one of them? I mean, he had seen the way she had interacted in amongst his people. Katie seemed so sweet, yet naive, as if she could be taken advantage of perhaps?

Los Angeles / LAX Airport - Christmas Day, 1992 - Two months previously

Tilting her head, Katie held a firm grip on the handle of her grey suitcase. It was just the right size for her to carry, the winter clothes packed inside would surely be enough for the journey ahead.

Through the bay window her eyes caught a plane soaring as it made its way off the runway. She held a steady gaze as excitement filled her heart, eager for Moscow. Travellers swarming in the airport that morning trying desperately to reach their destinations. Couples, families, children, babies in tow. Happiness filled the air on that Christmas morning, in sunny California. Katie was grateful for this chance, a once in a lifetime opportunity that awaited her on the other side of the world.

What would fate hold for her, she thought to herself smiling. Never mind, Kate let's just get to Russia and explore and enjoy every moment. She let out a chuckle, going from hot Hawaii to a cold foreign country would certainly be a change.

Tossing her cardigan over her shoulder, she walked on towards to the rest of the group.

A card sized envelope halted her in her tracks. It fell to the ground. Katie picked it up in a hurry. The blue writing simply read— *"Merry Christmas Katie."*

Smiling with profound joy, Katie secured a spot on a nearby bench and opened the card.

Swirls of red and green danced out at her, the wonderfully displayed Christmas scene popping vividly across the card.

"My dear Katie, we send you happy Christmas wishes. Hoping that your time in Russia will be full of adventure and you will see many exciting things. All of our love, Mom, Jake and Ellen"

"Oh!" Katie said out loud as her spirit was filled with

joy. Her family was far away, yet close in heart. Her eyes twinkled with excitement as she began to recall how this journey had all begun.

A group of six young people from all over the world had stood in hot 100° weather only a mere twelve hours before. Inside the Honolulu airport. Boarding the plane that Christmas Eve, their lives would be changed forever. They were to meet their youth leaders from Switzerland, Marty and Shara Anliker, in Moscow within a couple of days. Then journey on by train to southern Russia – Krasnodar, to visit the orphanages of Russian babies and children.

They would be the second group of missionaries allowed past the iron gates of post-Soviet Russia.

Six weeks before the trip, a bright sun streamed through the window of the classroom that morning in Honolulu. All of the students were told to go to their rooms, and choose a place to visit for two months, from the list.

She wrote down all the locations; India, Taiwan, the Philippines and Russia on a separate piece of paper, folding each one into a tight square. Holding all the squares in her palms, she threw them into the air. The first to land on her desk, was to be her fate.

Opening the paper, Katie smiled to herself, seeing that Russia was staring her right in the face. Bold and clear. It would be the country that she was destined to head to in a matter of weeks. Six short weeks. Glancing outside the window at the palm trees swaying, knowing that cold Russia was a complete contrast. She warmed to the excitement exploring a new land with great eagerness.

Chapter 2
Journey to Russia

Moscow- 9:21 am, December 26th, 1992

The vastness over the skyline that morning was a glorious dusty blue; birds soared overhead, circling and greeting the warm yet cold day ahead of them. Bursts of sunshine surrendered to the impending grey clouds that scattered across the Russian sky. Terrain capped with a sheer blanket of snow on that cool December morning, forlorn in the beauty of her capital – Moscow. Breathtaking.

Katie smiled, looking out of her window on the airplane, sweeping down-ward like an eagle landing in the nest of its familiar life. The beauty engulfed Katie instantly. *"Oh my!"* she thought. The landing strip came up with a thump. Having just left the brightness of L.A., it was quite the change in climate for her. Knowing this, she was well prepared.

Feeling the cold against her cheek, they definitely had come from paradise. Minus eighteen-degree weather greeted them as Katie bundled her scarf tighter around her neck that morning. Shivering, she momentarily second guessed her present location, but this was quickly dismissed.

Katie slept most of the way to Moscow. It had been a long journey, despite the stopover in Amsterdam. She had felt the heat change to cold.

It was then that she knew they had crossed onto foreign soil. Peering out of the tiny window, her impression of Moscow was now forever set. *"Wow, so this is what I have seen in all the history books. It truly is remarkable."* As the plane taxied into the Sheremetyevo International Airport, Katie looked out at iridescent white snow that had begun to fall lightly onto the runway.

Stepping off of the plane, carrying her back pack, she followed the others. *"Okay, guys, let's go... follow me."* Joe, the oldest of the group said, *"Let's head through customs."*

Clutching her passport tightly, Katie glanced at the people around her, primarily various generations of families. Walking into the dark passageway, plastered all around were old torn posters in writing Katie had never seen before. Deep silence echoed from the concrete walls, as if the Soviet era still remained and encased all who moved and still lived there. Her eyes widened in curiosity at the new surroundings that had just greeted her coming off the plane from the western world. In awe of everything, she wanted to grasp this whole new culture around her to the highest degree possible.

Katie walked down a dimly-lit hallway into a waiting area with other Russian citizens, ones who clearly knew this was their home and they just wanted to get back to business.

Masses of people crowded in, speaking an unknown language. Katie hoped to learn it rather quickly.

She was eventually funnelled through a crowded, cold,

steel walled corridor. Every step seemed to be darker.

When her turn came, Katie reached up to the window as a young Russian soldier motioned for her passport and stared back right through her. *"No older than eighteen,"* she thought looking away. *"He is not that much younger than I am,"* a mere twenty years old. *"How can he be so young and be in a position of authority at his age?"* Staring under the bar, his boyish hand reached for her Canadian passport. In the exchange, their fingertips slightly touched, she felt the soul of this Russian boy. It gave her chills as he stared stone-faced at the document she had just presented to him. Nerves all in a bundle now, she felt the boy before her stand completely still. Frozen. Katie looked away, as the Russian official stamped her passport firmly and threw it back to her under the bar.

"Oh," she thought, *"such a different world."* Still feeling, without question, the tension between her and this foreign boy. Cautiously Katie stepped over to the rest of the group and helped them as they began to look for her luggage at the nearby carousel.

Looking around at the line-ups of people, Katie hoped to blend in and get settled on the train to their final destination – Krasnodar.

Curious with delight, Katie wondered what this country would bring over the next two months, what she would see and experience; she promised herself to keep a mental diary.

"Come now, we need to catch our train to Krasnodar," Joe said sternly. Following his lead, the group headed out of the terminal.

In a hasty pace, the group followed Joe to the taxi stop. Fumbling with his mini translation book, he managed to speak the driver's language.

Brilliant! In a matter of minutes, all six squeezed into the warmth of the cab.

The taxi moved effortlessly and swiftly through the city. Immediately they were heading to the downtown core of Moscow. Looking out the window, Katie saw various buildings flash by. The signs with unusual wording in different shapes and sizes. Newness to her all around, the culture that had welcomed them would have a lot more to give over the coming months. Katie looked forward to every adventure that was to come.

*

Approaching the Moscow central train station, it was massive and swarming like a bee hive. One could almost get trampled in there. Katie followed quickly up the ramp as her head began to spin. People around her packed in and pushed without hesitation. As she tried to pull her heavy suitcase up the stairs to the train platform, Katie was shoved suddenly, causing her to gasp in the cigarette smoke filled air.

"*Katie, hurry.*" Jenna waved to her at the top of the stairs.

"*I am trying,*" Katie said as she felt tears well up in her eyes. Suddenly she felt a strong hand on her back, and then an older gentleman began to lift her heavy suitcase all the way up the stairs. It was as if he was guiding her along with his arm. He smiled at her and spoke in soft Russian, as he helped her to the top of the scuffed up set of stairs. He gingerly patted her shoulder. This stranger, in that moment became her angel. Then the man disappeared as fast as he had come into sight.

"That was so nice of that Russian man to help me," Katie thought to herself. On the side of the platform, she looked for the rest of her group. Then saw Jenna running ahead of her, and people began to scatter and run towards the train doors, as the train whistle blew loud and clear.

Marty came towards Katie. *"It's okay, come, we are over here."* He grabbed her hand and they ran towards the train. *"Just jump,"* Marty said.

Katie looked down at the space between the train and the platform. It was cavernous and dirty. *"No!"* Katie screamed. Fearful that she couldn't bound the gap, her body halted.

"Hurry, the train is going to leave!" Marty shouted. This was the point of no return. Katie closed her eyes as she grabbed Marty's open hand and leaped onto the train as it rolled away from the platform. She fell to the floor and took her scarf away from her face, catching her breath. As scared as she felt, Katie was glad to have caught the train before it headed on its journey to Krasnodar. Katie did not want to think about what would have happened if she had been left in Moscow alone.

Walking down the train corridor, Katie heard the familiar voices of everyone from her group. She felt so happy inside. *"Katie! Sweetie!"* Shara ran to her and they hugged warmly. *"Are you okay?"* Katie nodded.

"We made it," she said calmly. Katie excused herself, shimmied past the others and went to her compartment to rest on the bed. Soon she began to unpack, occasionally peeking out into the corridor. A familiar face of an older man passed. *"Wait,"* she thought to herself, *"he's my angel, the kind man who helped me with my luggage."* Returning to her unpacking, she drew the moss green

curtains and watched the scenery roll by. Curiously, she looked out into the corridor again. Her angel walked by, this time smiling at her. Katie smiled back, closed the door and sat down. She felt the most amazing sense of relief inside. She had made it safe and sound.

*

The train droned on to its final destination. They were to meet their leader from All Saints Church who would be their guide for the next two months. The world was here and now in magical Russia.

Sounds of Russian people speaking all around rocked Katie out of her sleep; the language was so distant and foreign to her, she had to learn it, she must, and she would.

Stretching her arms above her head, she opened her mouth and said a quiet *"Da."* Smiling she knew in no time the language would be fine-tuned through her mouth. Moving the half-tattered curtain, she looked out in awe. Fields passed by with old crumbled buildings, misshapen. Clearly from the Soviet era. The images flashed over her young blue eyes. In all its glory this was the Russia she had seen in the media growing up in the Western world. Even so, it was a bit of a shock to behold. It was like stepping back in time, falling into all the history books she had ever read.

Everything around Katie looked stereotypical. It was like being in a 1960s spy film. Never in her lifetime, did she envision herself here.

Grateful for the chance, the opportunity to explore and embrace this diverse culture. Katie knew she would see much in the next few months and would learn even more than she had ever imagined. What memories would she take home? It was all in the eyes of the beholder and she was the girl it would capture.

"*Katie, good morning,*" Shara interrupted her thoughts, peeking into the cabin.

Nervously picking up her translation book she began to speak in Russian. *"Pre-vyet,"* Katie said, practicing her precious new word she had picked up the day before.

"*One minute, I will be out soon and get some breakfast with you.*" Shara smiled in approval.

Holding the book in her hand, Katie skimmed over the words unknown to her, saying them out loud to herself again she smiled. *"I will get this right one day,"* she whispered. *"Da!"* Happy with her newfound language, she took a navy blue cardigan out of her luggage that lay beside her, and went to join Shara for some breakfast.

The smell of eggs and fresh bacon enticed Katie towards the dining car. Stepping inside, she joined Shara. Men and women gathered. Some holding their offspring. The sound of this new language was all around her and it became clear to Katie, she needed to learn more of it. And fast.

Several hours later caught Katie reading in her compartment, softly turning the pages of her translation book. *"I will learn this language,"* she whispered, *"and I will learn it well."*

The bumpy train ran its course over the tracks as the sun appeared to shine brighter and hotter that afternoon. Despite it being a bitterly cold Russian winter. Katie could feel the warmth of the brief rays, yet she was reminded of the sunshine in Honolulu, that had sun kissed her face days before.

Pushing the scrap drapes aside, exposing a window view, Katie peered outside. *"Wow!"* The glorious countryside. Beauty all around. Basking in the momentary warmth, Katie started to daydream. What would her new living quarters be like? Would she meet new friends?

"Katie!" Shara called as she knocked on her cabin door. This brought Katie back to reality.

"*Yes, Shara?*"

"Katie, we are approaching Krasnodar, we will be there in about twenty minutes, please prepare your luggage." Katie nodded in agreement standing up and grabbing her big grey suitcase. It felt heavy with every lift Katie took, yet she managed.

Walking out of her compartment, Katie followed the rest of her group and stepped off the train into her new hometown.

"Katie, make sure you don't get lost this time." Jenna smirked as she patted her back. Katie smiled.

"I know; I am so glad I was not left in Moscow alone."

"Okay, everyone, let's grab some taxis and head to our hotel," Marty confirmed.

"This is going to be such a great trip!" Olivia squealed in delight. *"I know how much you have been looking forward to coming to Russia."*

Katie smiled to her friend.

The InTourist hotel was a mere fifteen minutes by car and once there, the young group of missionaries quickly settled into their rooms. Opening the door to their room, Katie was in awe. Post-Soviet style wallpaper graced the walls, displaying a colour of deep burgundy with plush velvet embedded into it, flaunting a design of exquisite flowers, it felt like crepe paper. Katie traced her hand over it, feeling in a sense she had just stepped back into a time zone, a very backwards kind.

The roommate assigned to her was Jenna, an American girl from Chicago. *"Wow, Katie, this is really back in time, look at our room, old wallpaper and old furniture. There is even just a drain in the ground to take a shower? Gee, we are really getting a taste of the old old Russia,"* Jenna offered.

Katie closed her eyes. *"Yes, and that is really our mission, isn't it? To be among the poor and help them the best we can."* Jenna nodded in agreement.

"We best go to sleep now so we can get up early for our first real day in Krasnodar," Katie said.

"Yes, Katie, that is a wonderful idea," Jenna agreed. Soon the girls were under the covers and fast asleep for the night.

Chapter 3
Krasnodar

Preparing for the first full day in Krasnodar brought much anticipation to Katie. Pulling on a pair of long johns was not something she would have imagined a few months ago living in the hotness of Hawaii. She chuckled as she pulled her blue jeans on next and then the pair of thick wool socks that she had pulled out of her suitcase.

"Katie, are you ready to go?" Jenna asked her friend.

"Yes, I am and warm enough I think."

The girls made their way down to the corridor of the hotel where they would be meeting the rest of the group that morning. After a quick instructional plan from Marty, they all made their way into the dining room.

Hot blini were served as well as toasts with various meats and cheeses. *"This is sure different,"* Olivia declared. Katie laughed.

"Well, my dear, we are in Russia, not Hawaii."

"Da," Olivia confirmed. Katie giggled. Learning the Russian language was already starting to show amongst them.

Olivia was a dear friend to Jenna and Katie. Upon first meeting in Hawaii the girls knew they would become close over the next few months in Russia. These three girls had their whole lives ahead of them and travelling to post-Soviet Russia would bond them forever.

Next, a beautiful samovar was brought out and piping hot chai was served all around. It warmed Katie's soul that winter morning.

Happily finishing up breakfast, the group of eight headed out into the crisp, late December air of Krasnodar. Soft, fresh snow was around, tracings from the previous day. Katie pulled out her black gloves and put them on as she wrapped her blue scarf closer around her face.

Walking to the nearby tram was only about ten minutes uphill. Stepping onto a Russian tram for the first time was done with only a little bit of ease. Crowds pushed and shoved onto it. Katie was speechless. Looking all around her, she felt trapped in another world. Almost as if people were looking at her and thinking why are Western people here among us. This awkwardness silenced her as she kept to herself in the corner seat. Looking around she saw the young and old and feeling slightly overdressed, Katie knew, I am certainly not of this culture.

The orphanage was a building, made of a dark stone structure. Outside various pictures, cartoon-like were displayed across the doors leading inside. Bunny rabbits, chickens, and little gophers holding handkerchiefs vibrantly displayed.

"Come now, come." An older lady, the headmaster spoke in quick Russian.

Walking into a room full of babies, no older than ten months, Katie slowly took off her scarf as her mouth gaped open. Look at that little sweetie. Her eyes were drawn to a small boy about six months old. He rolled back and forth in his crib over and over. Katie felt the tears well up in her eyes. Placing her hand on her cheek, she whispered, *"Oh, no, dear one, I wish I could take you home with me. I will never forget this sight; it will be in my memory for-ever."*

As the weeks passed, the young missionaries explored Krasnodar with eagerness and zest. Meeting all kinds of young people, vibrant Russian youth who were curious to learn about life in the West. Arriving in the former Soviet Union, at a time when these up-and-coming youth craved freedom and newness after being under oppression for so long.

"I am sure going to miss this culture," Jenna declared.

Katie was writing a letter to her family back home, as she listened to Jenna speak about their time in Krasnodar. American music softly played in the background of their hotel room. Katie smiled.

"I know, it is such a rich and lovely culture. We have been so lucky to come and experience it, I feel like I am at home already."

Jenna laughed. *"Well, I can see how you would love it here, you have a heart for kids and the Russian children adore you, Katie."*

Beaming, Katie agreed. *"Who knows maybe one day I will return here, to this wonderful country and explore some more,"* Katie whispered.

"I can totally see you doing that, Katie... I really can. You're picking up the language quite nicely too, I heard you speaking it to the children." Katie winked at her friend and ended her letter, sealing it and placing it on her desk.

Falling asleep that night, she had visions of little Russian children in the orphanage, with their arms wide open, calling out her name.

Chapter 4
Max

Snow fell lightly on the ground as a bright moon followed Katie's moves that night. Walking at a brisk pace it was bitterly cold and the sooner Katie got back to the hotel, the warmer she knew she would feel.

Looking down at her gloves, she let out a short laugh. She had been here in cold, faraway Russia for the past six weeks. Now soon she would return to wonderful warm Hawaii. No more scarves or warm sweaters. Soon she would be in sunny paradise admiring the beauty of the islands. It seems like such a long time ago. Coming to Russia had been an experience in itself, what with the new culture and meeting so many different people.

Katie felt happy in this place, where a new adventure was around every corner. She had picked up the language easily, as Russian words surrounded her daily. The Russian language was not as hard as she thought it would be, in fact Katie had adjusted to the way of life here and the language barrier seemed to lift the longer she was in Russia. She felt like she truly belonged. She wanted to learn everything she could about the culture that she began to fall in love with, something she never expected. It was now natural to her, as Russian words were ringing in her ears constantly.

As the coldness began to set in, Katie pulled her scarf

tighter around her face. She had already mastered the skill of keeping warm, living in this frigid Russian winter. There are so many wonderful people here in Krasnodar. All the friends she had made. And soon this group of young missionaries would leave Krasnodar.

Katie had mixed feelings about leaving the city. Her thoughts became interrupted by the sound of footsteps. Behind her someone crunched the new snow intensely. Looking over to her left side, she stole a glance at the stranger.

The boy was much taller than her five-foot-three-inch frame. With him he carried a black knapsack over his back. He was lost deep in thought. Sporting jet-black hair, the young man was strikingly handsome to her on that moonlit night. His gentle smile caught Katie a little off guard.

This unexpected visitor on the same path as her, walking, surprised, yes. Startled, no. The elegance of his chiselled jawline drew her in rather quickly. Very European-looking and handsome in all ways. Katie felt something like a swarm of butterflies well up in her stomach. A nice feeling indeed. She stole a quick glance at him, as he caught her stare briefly. His gleaming emerald green eyes pierced through Katie's. He sort of made her heart do a sudden flip. They turned in unison.

"Hello," he said, smiling at her. Katie returned the smile. *"What was your name again,"* the boy asked?

"Katie," she quietly replied. *"Katie Steele actually."*

"My name is Max," he spoke softly.

Wow! Katie smiled. *"He is so very handsome,"* she thought to herself, *"I love the sound of his voice, such a thick foreign accent, oh, so sleek and warm to my ears. I feel so drawn to him. This young boy beside me."*

Suddenly, like in a trance, Katie listened more eagerly to this Russian boy walking in close beside her on the snowy path. They continued on down the hill together towards the hotel. The winter sky was lit with bright stars that night, as they became their guide.

The Russian boy began speaking to Katie again. *"Do you know much of the Russian language?"*

"A little." She smiled shyly up at him. Max returned the smile. His face became clearer now to Katie as the moonlight enhanced his features. She thought she had seen him before at the university Bible studies?

His piercing green eyes were sparkling and so alive reflecting in Katie's very own. She felt like she was drawn in by his strong glance at her alone. *"English with a foreign accent, now that is different."* Katie smirked. Adorable, simply sweet ... The sound of this young man's voice made her practically weak in her tracks, the warm insides of her whole body lit up. If she wasn't too careful, Katie would give away her bundle of nerves at that very moment. *"Yes, Katie,"* a little voice said, *"mind your feelings please, and thank you."* Like an orchestra playing, Katie was drawn and mesmerized to his voice making her want to hear more and more.

Eyeing Max out of the corner of her eye, Katie admired his well-defined cheeks that stood out with sheer definition. *"He is so handsome."* Katie giggled inside.

They walked on together, approaching the hotel entrance. Max opened the door for her, his smile mimicked her own. Thanking him, she quickly walked to her room. Taking off her coat, Katie looked forward to resting and keeping warm inside. Turning off the lights, she was fast under the covers and ending her thoughts for the day.

Except her thoughts kept racing. Pictures of the previous encounter kept spinning in her mind. His face. Max. She could not shake their meeting.

Katie had grown accustomed to the culture around her. It had become like her second home. She felt like she had begun to fit right in place. Russia was a country that seemed to be isolated from the rest of the world. Katie closed her eyes. She loved being here, all the great friendships made in the country that had been forgotten. So it seemed.

My little Russia. Katie intended to take every memory home to Canada with her, whether it would be in her suitcase or in her heart. She would always hold Russia and the people dear.

In a silent room, far from home, Katie yearned towards sleep, thinking of Max. She had met so many wonderful people in Krasnodar. It was natural that night, part of her usual routine. *"Just another wonderful Russian,"* she thought to herself. Soon enough the wonderful two-month journey that had started in Moscow, would be ending in the south of Russia. The world was here and now in magical Russia. How those few months had flown by before her eyes in so much amazement.

"Who was that young boy anyway?" Katie contemplated, lying in her bed that night. He was different, soft-spoken and pleasant. *"The way he looked at me and smiled did catch my attention,"* Katie pondered as she drifted gently off to sleep, the angels above stroking her eyelids and dusting her thoughts with only one Russian boy, by the name of Max.

Chapter 5
World Forgotten

Katie's nose scrunched up wildly, her eyes scanned the outside of the hotel. Another frosty morning in Krasnodar. Cool snow graced the main entrance as the sun dazzled across glistening white powder. Winters in Russia were bitterly cold, and one had to dress very warm to bear them.

She made sure to wear her favourite navy-blue sweater, a present from her grandparents for her trip to Russia. Though she was far, it made her feel close to them. They had worried about her, who wouldn't? Russia seemed to always be in the news and papers. This terrible, forsaken, poor land – Russia, as some people viewed it. A place that seemed so hidden from the rest of the world. Certain Russians Katie met were happy in life, even though they didn't have many things. Meaning, in a sense they longed for things that the Western world promoted, and that was surely appealing to them.

In her letters to family and friends, Katie wrote about the tender-hearted people and the beauty of Russia. How every day was a new and interesting adventure. Katie loved this country, but soon she would have to leave. She did not ever expect to return in her lifetime. There was no reason to really, nothing held her there. Her love of Russia began to transport her back to the place of fond memories.

Taking a walk into the neighbourhood with nothing but happiness in her heart.

The displays in the various magazine-stores stood out to Katie. Appealing to her own eyes. One thing that truly commanded her attention in particular were the fancy Russian nesting dolls. Matryoshka dolls as they were called. How she longed to bring a set home in her suitcase. Colours of red, blue and green were everywhere; they showcased in the most unique designs, decorated with various swirls and past designs of old Russia, Katie had always been fascinated especially by the era of Anastasia. How she was drawn to the dolls. *"Oh, I would love to bring some of the dolls home to display proudly."* Stopping in front of the window, she glanced inside. The ladies were putting out new dolls, enticing her inside. So many designs, so many choices. What would she pick?

After looking in the hotel lobby mirror one more time, Katie sat down and waited for Olivia.

Soon they would leave and return to Hawaii. Living in Russia, Katie felt happy to have made new friends, visited the sick, and cared for with young children. Now the mission was coming to an end. She looked forward to a future of hopes and dreams with much more to see and do. Being only twenty years old. Life was good, and Katie was glad to move on. She didn't worry about what the future held.

Olivia came walking down the stairs. *"Hi, Katie, are you ready?"*

"Yes, I am," Katie told her.

The two young girls wrapped their scarves around their heads and walked to the trolley stop. *"We are the true little babushkas!"* Olivia giggled as they walked arm in arm.

"Da!" Katie shouted. They had been given this name by many of the older ladies they had met. It was a personal joke. They were just young foreign girls who wore their scarves around their heads, and this helped them really fit right in. Indeed, they had many looks given to them by curious Russians. It was the way the Russians treated any foreigner who passed through their country. While on public transportation, they kept their voices low when they spoke in English. Being a foreigner was kind of a curse, in that Russians became curious if they heard English spoken.

Strangers might approach the girls, or worse, steal from them. Sadly, in the former USSR, a foreign contact was often a secret way to escape the country. It was one of the harsh realities Katie had learned during her stay in Krasnodar. And yet not everyone was like that. There were Russians who truly loved their country, and only wished to take joy in friendships with people from the Western world. Katie could understand that. She had seen the poor, had touched them, and given them all she possibly could.

A sense of fulfilment captured Katie as she smiled through the thick wool scarf that kept her warm. The trolley came fast. Olivia and Katie scurried inside only to be pushed aside by an oncoming horde of old-school Russians.

It was like going back in time. It had been a long seventy years of communism, and it was as if an entire generation of Russians still lived in that cold dark past, ignoring the new emerging Russia. Their eyes stared through everything; no smiles, just dark, vague bitterness over the new system and the new generation: their children, the future. New styles and attitudes were developing throughout the former USSR on young people, and Katie felt proud to be in Russia at this moment in history, observing this culture and learning their way of life.

In her heart she would cherish the memories, and yet Katie also looked forward to going back to her sheltered lifestyle. She was more thankful now for all she had back home in the Western world.

At their stop, Olivia grabbed hold of Katie's knapsack. She wasn't about to lose her, especially in a foreign country. Katie led the way, and they walked toward the Russian orphanage.

"I can't wait to get back to warm weather," Olivia declared.

"I know! Won't it be wonderful?" Katie smiled to her friend.

"You are getting homesick here, aren't you, Katie?"

"I do miss Hawaii. That's for sure."

Ahead of them, a group of boys were talking rapidly in Russian. Katie turned her head sideways to get a better look at them. One of them looked familiar. The boy turned around, sadly, he was someone else. Katie was sure it was the Russian boy, Max, the one she had met the previous night. His black coat triggered a memory of last night's encounter. Suddenly this mysterious new boy came to her mind. *"Was it Max or Maks?"* Katie pondered.

"Hello? Katie?" The sound of Olivia's voice jolted her back to the present.

"Yes, Olivia?"

Olivia lifted her eyebrow. *"Are you okay?"*

"Yes, I am just deep in thought, about this new culture."

"Well, we are here, my dear." Olivia chuckled.

The girls smiled and chimed, *"Da. Da!"* Oh, the times they had in Krasnodar. It had become their world, and they loved each and every moment in this country of secret despair and forbidden dreams.

Kids were running and jumping all around, full of excitement in the playground on that winter day. The orphanage intrigued her, it was an older building, inside, the walls were plastered with pictures, reminders of the past Soviet era that surrounded the Russian people. Katie felt as if she was going back in a time zone from so long ago. The nurses were orderly in fashion, wearing big, white, scarf shaped hats on their head, and nursemaid type aprons as they scurried the children into their rooms for nap time.

"Katie! Katie!" a young girl called, her Russian accent obvious to Katie's ear.

She turned and saw the face of a familiar young Russian girl. The girl wore a dark red dress, years of wear apparent, and Katie's heart warmed to her instantly. *"Privyet Darya!"* Katie said in broken Russian.

Darya squeezed her arms tenderly around Katie's neck. Katie's heart melted, such a sweet little girl. What would become of her and her life in Russia? Katie wanted to scoop this little love up and take her back to Canada. Wishing she could have a brighter future, Katie paused and smiled to little Darya. *"Ya tebya lyublyu,"* (I love you) Darya whispered in soft Russian. Her golden locks of hair gliding softly over Katie's cheek.

"Da," Katie offered. "I do too, little one."

After the class and meeting with the children, Olivia and

Katie caught the trolley back to their hotel. This had become routine for them and they loved every minute in the foreign setting. In just a matter of weeks they would head back to beautiful, sun-drenched Hawaii. Katie just wished she could have more magical times, to spend with all of her dear Russian friends. Secretly she wished to meet that Russian boy again. *"Nonsense,"* a little voice whispered. *"If it is meant be, you will see him yet again."*

Chapter 6
Love for Two

Opening her eyes the next morning, Max played on Katie's mind. She turned over as the softness of the pillow squished her nose. *"Just how do I get this boy off of my mind?"* She contemplated.

*

In the afternoon, Jenna, Olivia and Katie were excited as they were going to visit some local Russian teenage youth at a wrap up party for the Hawaii group. They had become good friends with the girls during their stay in Krasnodar. The party would be held at their friend, Megan's. All of the girls from Hawaii spoke about what they learned during their stay. Katie sat and looked at the different faces of the young Russian girls.

When it was Katie's turn, she stood and began: *"I look at each of you and think of such warm hearts and great potential. I have learned the value of true friendship and that it is rare. It was so good to meet and know all of you. Even though we speak different languages, we share a bond of love and faith in God and that can break all barriers. I pray for all of you to continue to keep your faith and strive to stay strong in your country, where even just two years ago, Bibles were barely able to pass through to you. I will miss you all and hope to write and continue our wonderful friendships."* Finishing, she took her seat as the next girl spoke.

After all of the comments were made, Megan stood. Her small frame, and sure smile lit up the room. *"Let's have some chai and tort,"* she announced.

Megan was an American girl who had lived in Russia for three years already. She was so well adjusted, speaking fluent Russian, and helping this group from Hawaii feel at home.

It was almost nine o'clock, when Jenna, Olivia and Katie left the party for their InTourist hotel. *"Goodbye, Megan,"* they said, leaving in the lift.

"Bye, girls! Keep safe."

"We will," they shouted. Down they went into the night. A broken-down, worn out, rusty door opened as they stepped out into the winter air.

A sudden and bitter wind blew with a strong force, as the girls clutched on to one another. While Olivia and Jenna talked about the upcoming days, Katie glanced around her at the many apartment blocks. Looking up into a nearby window a low light flickered as Katie saw a couple, with their arms wrapped around one another, slow dancing. The young man had jet-black hair and smiled deeply at the young lady. *"Almost like."* Katie smirked – *"Max."*

He came to her mind yet again. It had only been two days, yet she wondered about this mysterious new stranger and their meeting on the snow-covered path a few nights before. *"His life, one I know so little about. Who is this mystery boy? I wonder what will become of his life here in Krasnodar. He seems well versed to everything around him, despite living in this country. Almost westernized, something about him was very different."* Katie smiled. She was curious to find out more.

*

The next afternoon, Katie decided she needed fresh clothes. So she prepared and did the same thing she had done for the last two months: washing them by hand. It would take two or three hours to finish. Katie put her clothes in the basin to scrub and turned on some American pop music. It seemed to set the mood.

A short time later, someone knocked on the door and Katie answered. Olivia stepped in. *"What are you doing tonight?"* she asked. Katie laughed and pointed to her laundry project for that night. Olivia smiled. *"I see. I just wondered if you wanted to come down and have some chai?"* Olivia laughed.

"Oh, da! Chai! Sounds good. Besides, I can finish this later," Katie agreed, as both girls laughed. They had learned some good words during their stay in Krasnodar. This was one trip they would remember for years to come. Katie left her clothes and followed her friend, key in hand.

Opening the lounge door, the girls were suddenly bombarded. *"Hello, ladies!"* David said, almost knocking them down.

"David!" Olivia exclaimed.

"Are you trying to scare us?" Katie said, only half joking.

"Hi people, chai is in my room," John declared laughing behind David, acting his usual jolly self. Katie

looked past John, to another boy standing behind him.

"What? It can't be him."

Max, her mysterious boy, was right there before her very eyes. Katie felt her cheeks give off a rosy glow. Looking over them, she smiled and greeted Max, still surprised.

"Katie?" John said, staring at her stunned face.

"Okay. Let's go," she said, not wanting the obvious to be seen.

As they all walked to John's room, Katie wondered what was going on. *"I feel so strange around this boy, I can't feel like this, not now. I will be leaving soon."* She silently prayed. *"What is happening to my heart?"* Katie continued to walk beside Olivia, unable to look at Max.

Descending into the stairwell, the group made their way to a place in the boys' quarters where soft music played. Katie spun around to see Max behind David. Something about this Russian boy kept Katie constantly wondering. She grew more and more curious. Katie found a place at the table in John's room and sat down. Max came up to Katie. *"May I?"* he asked, pointing to the chair next to her.

"Of course." Katie smiled. Inside she felt full of joy! Feeling like she had just been given the best gift of all, standing right in front of her, her heart melted. Literally, warm feelings that were deep down now shone all over her young face.

David lit a candle and placed it between the two of them. Katie lifted her eyebrow at him *"What is that for?"*

John winked. *"For a pleasant night. Enjoy."* Katie was glad her beaming red cheeks could not be seen in the dim light.

Max warmly smiled. *"How are you enjoying Krasnodar?"* he asked her.

"I love it!" Katie exclaimed. *"It's beautiful, and the people here are amazing."* She continued to tell him about her feelings for the city, Max stared at her, and Katie felt her heart leap. Their conversation flowed and in some moments all they did was look at one another.

"Well, Katie, we best be going now. It's getting late." Olivia walked towards her and Max.

"Yes, let's go," Katie said. She got up from her chair as Max placed his hand on her arm.

"It was so nice to see you again." He winked.

"I feel the same, when will I see you again?" Katie said, as she walked out with Olivia.

Max smiled. *"I'm staying the night with the boys, and going with the group tomorrow morning."*

Katie shyly put her head down as a huge smile spread across her lips. *"Unbelievable, we meet again. I will always treasure this moment and night. Oh Max,"* she whispered.

At her door, the girls parted ways and Katie got dressed for bed and was soon under the covers. She turned over, thinking how Max made her feel inside and of the happiness every time she saw him. *"Russia, here and now. Will I ever return, to this magical place?"* Katie thought drifting off to sleep.

Chapter 7
Krasnodar Winter

Waking up the next morning, Katie felt as if she'd been aroused from a wonderful dream. As she dressed for breakfast, she remembered Max. They were having a guest today. Hoping to look extra special, she applied a little more makeup than usual. Her face had always had a youthful look. She was grateful for that quality. Making sure her hair was in place and looked just right, Katie headed downstairs to breakfast.

The familiar Russian breakfast was on the menu once again: buterbrody (open-faced sandwich) with kolbasa, or smoked sausage, and various types of cheese. Including an array of syrniki pancakes, and fried or boiled eggs, all of which were becoming Katie's favourite. The very first time Katie tasted the pancake she was pleasantly surprised. Biting into it, the cottage cheese filling left her wanting more. As she entered the room, her eyes searched for Max, and found him sitting at the table with all the other men from the group.

Katie hoped that he would notice her as she walked by. He looked up from drinking his warm sweet chai; their eyes met just before Katie shyly looked away. She sat down and tried to eat, barely able to finish her breakfast. She took another bite of her eggs, but decided she was done and took one last sip of her warm tea, so soothing on a cold morning. The group was dismissed and Katie went up to her room to dress for their outing to the local children's hospital.

The sun made its way out that day as Max and Katie ended up walking beside one another. *"Katie, it would be great if you came back to Krasnodar in the summertime. It's so pretty and warm here,"* Max told her as a small bird flew above them.

"I hope to return one day to this place," she said, smiling at him. It was as if the bird was a sign saying indeed Katie would be back. A silent message of hope for the future. Katie beamed up at Max as they neared the hospital.

In all her twenty years, she had never felt so magical around any boy. *"I've only read about a heart skipping a beat, now I feel that for real."* Katie turned to Max, He looked perfect to her, his face fresh and alive in the sunlight. They continued the last few steps of their journey, toward the final destination.

There it was again. Her heart. She could hear it. His name leaped off of her very soul. The way Max smiled, walked and talked made her more and more curious with delight over him. When he opened the door for her she felt like a young girl being completely cared for. He seemed so different from any boy she had ever met. Her heart wasn't the same since she had met Max. Katie felt warm and tender like she never had before.

Once inside they sat opposite one another. Every now and then Max would steal a glance at her and Katie would return it, smiling tenderly.

Songs were sung as the children joined in and clapped vivaciously. The Russian children were joyful in the presence of these young people. It was hard to believe the group would be leaving this faraway world soon and return to their previous lives in Hawaii.

In the middle of the meeting, Max stood and stated his regrets about having to leave. Then he turned slightly and caught Katie's glance and winked at her. Her eyes followed him as he walked out the door. She had already began to miss him. How she wished they could talk further. The love Katie had for him seemed to grow by the minute. By now, she was smitten with this Russian boy.

*

Tuesday was suddenly upon her and Katie knew there was a possibility she would see Max that night. She was almost too anxious to finish her dinner. The Bible study at the local university began at 7:00 p.m. Making her way over there on the local tram got her there much faster than she expected. Katie looked at her watch, perfect timing. She stood by the window in the classroom and heard the wind howling. Then she spotted Max coming into the room. Dressed in a blue jean shirt and black vest, looking as handsome as ever.

Walking past his desk, she turned and smiled, he grabbed her hand, with a squeeze and said, *"Hi, Katie, how are you?"*

Her whole being warmed up. *"I am good."* Taking a seat, Katie had the perfect view of him. Her handsome prince.

After class, Max caught up to Katie, and on this night

they exchanged addresses so they could keep in touch. *"How are you enjoying the last week of your stay in Russia?"* Max asked her as they made their way down the corridor.

"I love Krasnodar; it's such a beautiful city," Katie replied, her voice cracking a little. She felt nervous and did not want Max to notice anything unusual.

"I wonder if I may show you some more of Russia," he offered, placing his hand gently on Katie's arm.

Taken aback, she said, *"Maybe one day,"* knowing the rules, no romance or close contact was allowed. They were on a mission, and that kind of relationship was not appropriate. She only wished that was possible. Knowing there was only one week left made it all the more difficult for Katie to imagine leaving her new friend. All their time together was always met with such sweet pleasure and unsurpassed magic. They walked out together into the air of Krasnodar, the soft snow beneath their feet.

"You're leaving soon," said Max.

"Too soon," Katie replied quietly.

He let out a laugh. *"I know what you mean."* With these words, he left the rest of his feelings to Katie's imagination.

"Hurry up, you two!" Marty called as the tram door began to shut.

"I see we are holding them up." Max smiled at her as he gently guided her up the steps. The swift-moving tram went along its way as Katie stood at the door pressed against a small huddle with Max right behind her.

Reluctant to turn around she spotted his reflection in the window. The shy Katie became more bold at once. *"He looked so at peace and happy with himself. Perfect* view." Katie smiled. *"He is amazing, and in all my life I have never felt this way, especially not toward someone not of my own culture."* Katie closed her eyes. *"But I will be leaving Krasnodar soon. And I will be leaving him."* Max, this Russian boy, had already stolen her heart.

In the sudden commotion to get off the tram, Katie suddenly felt other bodies pushing hers, shifting her forward, and she fell onto the floor with a bang. Blushing like nothing she ever felt, Katie hoped Max did not take notice in that moment. On her behind, she managed to get up slowly and grab onto a nearby bar, more angry than hurt. She felt strong hands with thick gloves and knew Max had come to her aid. Being lifted up she turned to see the kind gentleman who had helped her in the Moscow train station. *"My angel!"* Katie mouthed in surprise. She thanked him in Russian, then found Max.

"Hi," she said, half laughing and looking into his eyes. Max's emerald-green eyes looked at her in disbelief.

"That was a hard push and yet you seem fine?" Katie tried to steady herself between the bar handle and now Max's firm grip on her hand. *"No, please let me help you,"* Max said.

"Yes, thank you," Katie said as she became steady on her feet. As a stranger pushed them together, Max's strong arms reached all the way around her.

"Oh," they said, looking at one another without a further word. Katie felt that strong sensation in her heart again.

Max smirked, stepping away from her. *"Katie, this is my stop. I will see you soon."*

"I hope so." Katie smiled up at her new friend. He

placed his hand on her arm, and was gone fast into the night.

Katie felt as though she was in a trance. *"Katie! Katie!"* Jenna called. *"Over here."*

Waving, Katie made her way to her, already missing Max. Giggling all the way to the hotel, questions were raised. *"So did you have fun talking to Max?"* Jenna teased.

"It was just for a few minutes," Katie said, unaware people had been watching them. *"Oh, yes."* She smiled to herself, feeling her whole body warm up to his face flashing before her eyes, she knew she had to conceal her feelings for the time being.

Going to bed that night, Katie began to think more and more about this boy and his behaviour. He felt something too, she was sure of it. *"But it's too soon... too fast."* Katie's thoughts about Max continued as she drifted off to sleep in southern Russia, far away from her native Canada.

Katie smiled as she gently closed her eyes, thinking about these growing feelings in her heart and how her life had already changed because of one Russian boy she hardly knew. A deep and new love began to form in her heart that winter night.

Chapter 8
Winter Love

Early the next evening, Katie heard knocking, the beat on the door louder and louder. *"Coming!"* Katie called as she finished twisting and turning her wet sweater in the basin.

"Hey, Katie!" John said as she opened the door.

"What's happening tonight?"

"Well, Max and his friend Dmitri are going to be here soon and we're going to have a little party at eight. Max is working all week, and we want to say goodbye to him ..."

"Tonight?" She asked inquisitively. Katie felt tears begin to well in her eyes.

Unaware of her true feelings, John did not catch on to her shock. *"So come over around eight o'clock, okay?"*

"Yes, I will be there," she assured him.

Once John had left, Katie turned the lock, her whole being could not face this sudden farewell. Hot tears began to trickle down Katie's cheeks. *"Tonight is the last time Max and I will see one another."* Their time together had gone so quickly and now all this magic would be lost forever. Slumping down on her bed, Katie placed her head on her pillow. She turned and stared out the window. *"I have to be strong, I can't show Max how I truly feel. We may never see one another ever again. How can this be?"* She stopped trying to reason. Katie stood up. Looking outside at the snow drifts, she bit her lip down. *"Oh Max, I can't bear to say goodbye to you. Not just yet."*

*

Everyone was gathered in Joe and John's room. The big guest was waving her over. Katie felt her insides turn with emotion, and sadness. *"Enjoy your last time with Max,"* a voice told her as she made her way towards him.

"How have you been?" he asked warmly.

"Very good thanks," Katie said. The night was filled with laughter. Katie still felt the strong connection between them.

"Hey, Max and Katie," Joe called. *"Look over here!"* He took a photo of the young couple sitting on the couch.

"Our first picture together..." Max whispered shyly. Katie looked at him and returned the smile, her face flushing bright red.

"It is time for me to go," Max announced, rising to his feet. At that moment, the party broke up and everyone began to shuffle to their rooms.

Knowing this was the last time for her to say goodbye to Max, Katie felt a wave of sadness pass over her. *"I have to be going too."* She smiled up at Max. They slowly walked down the hallway turning and looking at each other, without any words passing between them. Katie wanted to tell Max how much he had meant to her during her stay in Krasnodar.

She quietly whispered *"Goodbye."*

He placed his hand over hers, as if to say it was not yet their final farewell. Max stepped inside the elevator.

"Goodbye for now," he mouthed as the door began to close.

"Max!" She blurted out. It was too late. It had to be this way. She had let Max go without saying how she truly felt and maybe now she really had lost this wonderful Russian boy forever. Only time would tell.

*

On the way down, Max closed his eyes. To let her go, the girl he felt was changing his heart into a burst of something he never knew possible. Love?

As she passed Shara's room, Katie decided to say goodnight to her. Knocking softly on the door, Katie waited. Silence. No answer. She shrugged her shoulders and began to walk to her room. Moments later, Shara's head peeked out of her door. *"Katie?"* she called out.

Turning around Katie's eyes widened, *"Shara! Hi... I thought you had gone to sleep."*

Shara motioned her over. After she was let inside, Katie heard Marty continuing his conversation with his wife – telling Shara, *"I don't know where we will find anyone; it is too short notice."*

"Find someone to do what?" Katie asked. Shara explained to Katie that Alexi, their regular translator, was sick and they were unable to find someone to translate for tomorrow's Bible study at the local university.

Katie shut her eyes for only a second. This could be her only chance to see Max yet again. *"I think that maybe Max might be able to do it. But he just left,"* she said with hope. As Katie's words trailed off, Marty grabbed his coat and headed downstairs. Katie and Shara looked out the window and saw several people in the dimly lit entrance of the hotel.

"I hope Max can do it. That would be just the answer we need," Shara said to Katie.

Through the foggy glass, the girls saw the faded shadow of Marty and two other figures. Within ten minutes, he returned with a smile. *"He's going to do it. Max will be there tomorrow night. We have a translator."*

"That's great, darling!" Shara said to him.

Saying goodnight, Katie let herself out of their hotel room and once in the hallway, she placed her hands on her cheeks, letting out a quick laugh. Her prayers had been answered. *"I am going to see Max yet one more time! We are going to meet once again."* Katie silently thanked God for her precious friend and the time they had together. Looking out the window of her room, she hoped her time with Max the next night would be heart-warming. Katie might be able to say how she felt in a subtle way to this Russian boy.

*

The next day could not go fast enough for Katie, who eagerly waited for the night ahead.

At five minutes past seven, the teenage youth were gathered around the classroom, but there was still no sign of Max. Katie wondered if something was wrong. *"We need to begin,"* Marty told them. *"Dmitri will translate for now."*

The first speaker went up to the podium. Katie fiddled with her sheet of paper. A few minutes later, someone knocked and she heard a burst of cheers. Katie felt her stomach turn as her eyes fell on Max.

Sitting in the third row from the front, Katie had the perfect view of him. She rested her hands on her cheek and watched his every move. The green dress shirt and grey tie he wore made his appearance even more attractive to her and she thought about all that he meant to her.

Afterwards, Max tried to make his way to Katie, but they got lost in the shuffle of others. *"Never mind, it probably would not be the wisest thing to speak with Max. I do not want people suspecting anything. It is perhaps just a little crush, I am sure."* Katie smirked. *"Or maybe more,"* she thought, making her way out into the bitter winter night. Coldness enveloped her on the street of Krasnodar.

Sitting on the tram back to the hotel that night, Katie stared out the window and sighed. *"It just wasn't meant to be, for now."*

The next morning after breakfast, Shara made her way to Katie's table. *"You don't look very well,"* she said.

"I'm actually feeling sick," Katie declared as she took her seat. Her pounding headache that morning was followed by a sore throat that felt painfully raw.

"We are going to just one school today to talk about the upcoming new orphanage being built. Do you think you can make it?" Shara asked her with a worried look on her face. *"I am even thinking you should go see a Russian doctor, that would be the best thing to do."*

Katie nodded in agreement. *"I will try my best, Shara."* Closing her eyes, the pain increased.

Katie did not see how she would bear the day ahead. Walking out of the orphanage, they all decided to take a taxi back to the hotel. The meeting at the school went fast at least. Katie sat with the others on a nearby bench as they waited for their ride. She felt too hot and then too cold, as she tried to tighten her scarf. Feeling helpless, the waiting seemed to take forever. Even so, catching a taxi was easy to do in Russia, for many people wanted to earn money and this was one way, quick money in the pocket. It was a cool winter afternoon and streams of children flocked around the group of young people as their day of school had just finished. Katie looked at each passing tram, wishing she could get on one before she felt any worse. Not noticing, one stopped. She placed her hand on her head, and felt the heat of her fever.

Ding, the tram door opened. Katie felt stunned as she realized Max was walking off it. He walked toward the group, and headed straight to her. *"Hello, Katie."*

"Hi!" Katie smiled shyly, knowing her face had turned a bright red at that moment. The cold wind blew against her face, as she continued to look into his eyes.

"Let's go, guys." Dmitri, their new translator motioned as the taxi waited. Reluctant to leave, Katie rose and slowly walked to the car, just so Max could catch up with her. He followed her every move. She purposefully fell behind the group, so they would have another chance to talk.

"I'm going to a Russian doctor today," Katie whispered to him.

"What?" Concern crossed Max's well-defined face.

"I feel just terrible," Katie continued.

"No, I have medicine. It's a good kind and I will bring it to you tonight."

She heard the love deep in his voice. *"Thank you,"* Katie replied softly and half fainted. He held her up and lifted Katie into the car, as the bitter February wind blew softly against her face. His black glove shielded her from the cold, so tender, as he waved goodbye.

Once more fate, was on their side. Katie did not want to read too much into anything, yet inside her heart was screaming and dancing with joy. They would meet yet again in a few hours.

When they returned to the hotel, Katie was nearly at her room, when she heard a voice calling out, *"Katie! Honey!"* She spun around and faced her friend, Shara. She looked lovingly and concerned at Katie. Who she thought was so young and full of life. Shara knew and saw what was happening between Max and Katie, the obvious love that surrounded the couple. *"Katie, I see the twinkle in your eye."*

"What do you mean?" Katie whispered.

Half-smiling, Shara placed her arm around Katie. *"Honey, listen. I know. I see how you are each time Max is around."*

"Oh, Shara, he is so nice!" Katie burst out laughing. *"I think I really like this Russian guy!"*

"Just remember it is not long until we will be leaving Krasnodar." Katie closed her eyes. The girls walked down the hall, as the gornichnaya looked on out of her quarters.

That night as she waited for Max, Katie hoped they would share yet another special moment together. What she felt now was stronger and more real, perhaps because their time in Krasnodar was about to end. A sudden knock on the door rocked Katie out of her thoughts. When she opened the door, Katie saw Shara in front of her, her eyes were shining with delight. *"Here's something to make you feel better."*

Standing behind her was Max. Katie could not believe her eyes. Shara smiled leaving the couple alone.

"*Hi,*" Max said. *"How are you feeling?"*

Katie, pulled her scarf closer. *"A bit better. Thank you so much for bringing this for me."*

"This medicine will help you. It's a really good Russian cure," he promised. *"And tomorrow I will bring you a tasty Russian jam that my grandmother makes. I must go, but see you in the afternoon."*

"Thank you for coming to see me." Katie smiled as she looked up at him.

He turned and gently kissed her on her left cheek. *"Goodbye – until tomorrow."* Katie didn't say a word, but managed a bigger smile.

Still in awe, Katie nodded, closing the door. She couldn't believe it. *"He kissed me!"* Not wanting to see this kiss as anything more than just a friend helping her, she gave a thank you to God above. So tender and sweet had this young Russian boy become to her over a matter of weeks.

Going to sleep that night, Katie was undecided on whether or not to write to her mother about her new friend. Instead, she decided to call her from Amsterdam the following Tuesday night.

*

The next day, Katie stayed behind when the others went to the school, knowing she needed rest and Max would come to see her. After looking in the mirror and brushing her hair once again, Katie looked out the window, and waited. Anticipating what he would tell her, she didn't want to get her hopes up yet, but deep down Katie felt that the unspoken words were there. She knew little about Max really and the life he led. But the thought of him made chills rush through her entire body.

Katie walked to the nearby window. She placed her hand on the window pane. Feeling the cold, her heart warmed at the thought of him. *"Oh stop, Katie, you hardly know this boy."* It was not only snowing, but it was also getting dark. But then, on the path where they had met only weeks before, Max appeared. Katie watched him enter the hotel.

After a few minutes, she heard him knock. *"Who is it?"* Katie asked mischievously; then answered the door, already knowing.

"Hi, Katie, how are you feeling today? Did the medicine help you?" Max asked.

"Yes, it did, I'm feeling better. Thank you."

"Here is the jam I have promised you. It will soothe your throat. Drink it with tea."

"And, oh yes..." he added, *"this is what teachers eat."* He handed a pastry shaped like a bun to Katie. Max had shared his dream of becoming a teacher with her, and now he was starting to make his dream a reality by translating for foreigners. This made her smile. She hoped to support him in all his dreams and future aspirations. *"I must be off now, to my work. Take good care,"* Max offered.

After he left, Katie lay down on her bed, feeling lifeless. As she looked out the window, thinking about Max, she fell into a deep, deep sleep.

Several hours later she was awoken by a soft voice: *"Katie, wake up now, dear."* She felt a small shake rock her out of her dreams, one of many about this raven-haired Russian boy.

Chapter 9
Russian Eyes

Opening her eyes, Katie saw Jenna standing by her side. *"What time is it?"* Katie murmured. She was clearly still half-asleep.

Rolling over, Katie listened as Jenna continued speaking in a hushed voice. *"Time to go to Alexi's birthday, remember? It's already six o'clock. We do have some time, but need to hurry. How do you feel?"*

"Much better," Katie replied. *"I must have fallen asleep."* In the bathroom, the last thing Katie remembered, Max had been there.

Sitting on the tram on the way to the birthday party she wished it wasn't yet time for them to leave this world, where she had met someone more magical than any place or dream she had ever known. If only they would see each other one more time.

At Alexi's place, the table was wonderfully decorated and many different Russian dishes had been spread out: pirogies, potatoes, carrots and sour cream cradled in an ornate Russian bowl. Various meats were also on display and in a chilled bucket, a beautifully shaped bottle of Russian champagne with a silver cloth adorning it. Everyone began to enjoy the lavish spread, lively talking amongst themselves.

"Katie, can you please pass the caviar?" Shara asked,

gently leaning over her. Katie nodded reaching for the gold flecked dish that held one of the delicacies she now enjoyed. Krasnodar had opened her heart in so many ways, Russian food being one of them. How she would miss the delicious tastes that she had enjoyed the last few months.

Suddenly a knock could be heard in the corridor. Looking up from her dinner, Katie could not believe her eyes. Max. A smile spread across her lips as she felt love once again, reigning around them. Katie's heart skipped a beat. He sat down across from her and gently searched for her eyes. When he met her gaze, Katie's heart beamed and she felt her entire body warm.

How could she not feel such tenderness around this one boy, one who was now part of her present life.

Max began to enjoy his dinner and in between bites glanced over at this Canadian beauty. Katie caught his stares, shyly looking away, then giggling to release any nervousness. *"Let me,"* Max offered, reaching over, holding a newly opened champagne bottle. Smiling coyly, Katie nodded with approval.

Yes, they were allowed to celebrate this night with champagne, that was the word given before the party started. Katie felt she would need just a little more bubbly to help with any future butterflies.

Sitting on the couch, Katie listened to the laughter around her and felt content in that moment. *"May I?"* Max asked. Sitting down beside her with a sparkle in his eye. *"Katie, I wanted to surprise you and come to the party tonight."*

"You indeed did that Mr. Anchov." Her face said it all, in that moment Max held her heart.

Remembering… Katie and Olivia had made a special

poem for Alexi. After they recited it, everyone clapped and then burst into laughter. The champagne was flowing, but not so much that people were unaware of what was happening around them.

"*How are you feeling?*" Max mouthed to Katie across the room.

"*Good,*" she blurted out loud. Feeling herself blush fully and awkwardly. The sound of classical Russian music drowned out everyone else that surrounded them.

Katie and Max laughed together throughout the night and stole occasional glances at one another.

"*It's time to go, everyone,*" Marty said. The clock read ten o'clock.

Katie went to take her coat. "*Allow me,*" Alexi smiled at her.

"*Why, thank you,*" Katie told him.

"*Thank you, everyone, for making my birthday extra special as well, a night I will never ever forget.*"

"*Oh, Alexi.*" Katie smiled inside. "*I am so happy ... your party was a success,*" she silently whispered.

Saying their goodbyes, the group gathered round and went out the door. It was a cold winter night in Krasnodar and only mere hours before they would be leaving for Moscow, and head on their journey back to Hawaii.

Stepping outside, Katie and Max ended up walking together once again. The moon perched above them that winter night as they walked down the path to the trolley stop, just as it had on the night they first met. With butterflies bubbling in her stomach, Katie held on. Hoped. Dreamed a bit that Max may kiss her just once.

"*You are not too cold?*" Max asked Katie.

"*No, I am fine. Thank you,*" she said. Katie's heart fluttered. At the same time, she did not want to think about leaving him.

Silence only held the footsteps crunching the fresh snow beneath their feet, as each was lost in their own thoughts. "*Will you ever return to Russia?*" Max asked.

"*I do enjoy this place and the people here are wonderful,*" Katie said. "*What did he mean? Does he want me to come back to him?*" Feeling shy in his presence, Katie turned away from Max, wrapped in her thoughts.

A cool wind blew softly against her cheek. Gently moving the hood away, the soft fur grazed Katie's hands, it covered her eyes for a moment, as she lifted it off, now it was out of her way and Max was in full view.

He turned, as her glance was more than obvious. Winking at Katie, she knew, it was here and now. Them. Two worlds, one love. Almost set on fire, without any doubt. Except, that fire would have to wait for another time and place.

As they boarded the trolley, Katie took a solitary seat quickly and then almost lost her balance. Behind David, in the back, Max stood watching her with content and admiration.

Feeling shy and caught off guard, Katie felt reluctant to respond to Max. "*Why do I feel this way? I am so caught up in this boy yet I hardly know him.*"

Over and across the railing, his eyes met hers. Like a slow soft love melody, his glance made her warmly melt inside. Katie smiled and turned her head, as if the curtain had lifted.

"*Hi!*" Max said, quickly swinging over a seat and

standing next to her by the window.

"*You scared me!*" Katie said, half smiling.

"*I just wanted to get a closer look.*" Katie felt a deep blush.

"*Look at what?*"

"*You, dear girl.*" Max took her hand and guided her to the rear of the trolley.

"*Very funny, Mr. Anchov,*" she said coyly.

"*Isn't Krasnodar beautiful in the moonlight?*" Max whispered and pointed out the large window close to them.

"*Yes, it is.*" Katie smiled as she felt shivers glide down her spine.

He leaned against the railing, while staring into her eyes. "*You will miss it here. I can see it in your eyes. They tell me all.*" Max spoke in a faint voice so only Katie would hear.

Nodding, Katie turned to him. "*I will miss everything here; it was the best time.*"

Again he began to stare deep into Katie's blue eyes. "*When you leave, I hope you will continue your study of Russian. I will send you some books, so you won't forget the language,*" Max offered, as the trolley sped into the night.

"*That would be really nice and helpful,*" Katie replied, hoping the darkness hid the sudden nervousness in her face. Her heart warmed her whole body as she stood by him. The lights of Krasnodar sprung out at the couple as they journeyed into the night.

"*Oh, no!*" Max's eyes widened. "*I've missed my stop!*" He looked at Katie and they burst out in hysterical laughter. Another chance to see him a little longer. He grabbed her hand and squeezed, before stepping out at the next stop. *"See you soon!"* Max blurted out in his thick Russian accent as he jumped off, into the snowflakes that welcomed him.

Away he went into the cold winter night. Katie watched Max walk towards his flat and his life.

"Yes, I have love to give, but would it ever be enough? We are truly from two different worlds." Katie sighed and smiled, the warmth of her breath surrounding her. Yet, it was as if first love had already caught her now, in Russia. There really was no denying it.

Crawling into bed that night, Katie said a prayer hoping they would meet one more time. Perhaps tomorrow when we leave Krasnodar...

Chapter 10
Farewell my Love

They say that all good things must come to an end…

Music played sweetly that evening, the sounds of it soft to Katie's ears as she hoped, and wished, her dear Max may see her one last time. It could happen.

That night Katie went and said goodbye to Valentina, the hotel maid, who had been a dear soul and happy face to Katie during her stay. Often waving to her as she came back to the hotel after a cold and tiring day out. Both of them trying to converse, Katie tried her best to speak Russian, while Valentina gently nodded and tried to speak English to Katie. Between the both of them, although the language barrier was apparent, affection and smiles were a given.

It was her last shift in the hotel before Katie would head back to Honolulu. The reality was, she was leaving. Tears of sorrow mingled as they embraced and in broken Russian Katie promised to write to her. It was past two in the morning when Katie finally went to sleep after some packing and wondering if she would ever meet Max again. If only.

The next day passed quickly. The team met for a short late afternoon meeting. Lukas, the main leader from Switzerland, began speaking to the young people, *"I want* to thank you all for your hard work in Russia, and for meeting and forming friendships with so many of the Russian people."

After Lukas's speech, the group broke up and headed back to the hotel to prepare and do their last-minute packing for Moscow. Then they would be bound for Hawaii.

Sitting in the back corner of the trolley, Katie looked out the window into the bleak darkness and wondered how Max was doing. A young Russian girl, from the regular circle of Krasnodar youth came up to her.

Zoya placed her hand on Katie's arm. *"Katie, you look so sad,"* she said in broken English.

"Do I?" Katie replied. *"I just don't want to leave Krasnodar. It now has a very special place in my heart."* Zoya smiled and hugged her friend.

Katie did not know how she would make it through the night. In only a matter of hours, the train would take them back to Moscow then flights on to Honolulu. Her experiences here in Krasnodar felt like a book about to be closed, but with all the chapters perhaps not ever written in full. Her emotions ran high.

Russian youth were everywhere at the hotel, gathered in the hopes to say farewell to the young people. Taking a seat in the hotel lobby beside her friend, Olivia sensed Katie felt a strong connection to Krasnodar, and it seemed like she was lost deep in her own thoughts. *"Was there something more? Was she missing a key point in their stay."* She shook her head. *"No, she was like the rest of them, and of course had fallen in love with Russia and nothing more."*

"Hi, Katie," Olivia said. She placed her hand on her

arm affectionately. *"Only two hours till the train leaves."*

"That soon?" Katie said, her eyebrow half-raised.

"I know. I am sad, too," Olivia said.

If she only knew. Katie's heart was now forever in Krasnodar. The girls parted and Katie went out into the hall to get a cassette John had borrowed earlier in the day. Turning the corner by the elevator, Katie almost fell on her own weight. For there in the corner, sitting in a chair, was her new friend. Max. Why was he there?

He seemed to be in deep thought, writing something on paper intensely. She didn't want to bother him, and tried slipping past him in the corridor. *"I can't let him see me, not just yet. Not now. I can't bear to let Max see or feel how I am so drawn to him; I fear my own emotions and thoughts deep inside right now. I don't want to take the chance that he will not feel the same. Although I am sure he feels something, he is thinking deeply about us."*

Katie was careful, so Max did not see her, as she went back to her room. That was a close call. She decided to get the tape later. Instead, she started to go upstairs to say goodbye to little Nadia and her mother. Nadia's mother, Olga, was a housekeeper at the InTourist hotel and often brought little Nadia to work. Katie had befriended them during her stay.

Suddenly, Katie saw Max heading straight for her. *"How are things?"* he asked politely.

"I am sad about leaving Krasnodar," she told him.

"I wish you could stay longer." Max winked tenderly. Katie felt her stomach turn in a twist of knots that very minute.

"Oh, dear boy, how you mean the world to me," Katie said internally, as her hands became clammy, then she

shoved them in her pockets. *"I won't let Max see how I really feel around him."*

"Yes... well... I was going up to say goodbye to Nadia and Olga," Katie told him. *"Why is he here now?"* Katie thought, as she felt nervous suddenly knowing her love was the only one next to her at that moment. How could she ever let Max go? *"Oh, dear, my sweet boy."*

"May I come with you?" he asked Katie. She nodded and they made their way up the stairwell.

"I didn't think you would be here tonight?" Katie said.

"Of course! I would not miss saying goodbye to you." Max smiled at her.

After saying goodbye, with translation assistance from Max. Nadia and Olga hugged Katie, as they stepped into the hall.

Katie encouraged Max. *"I have to get my tape from John, come with me."*

There was silence between them. Yet, she felt magic in the air. Would Max say something or just leave it? Walking towards John's room, neither spoke, yet there was a feeling of love and admiration.

Max knocked on John's door as the couple walked inside. Max by now had placed his hand gently on Katie's back. She felt his complete protection over her as she smiled deeply. Inside she was beaming. This time, life right now. Pure bliss.

Inside John's room, Max and Katie enjoyed some nice warm chai, soothing to both. They counted down the time before Katie would be leaving. Eventually Marty approached. *"We are leaving soon,"* he told them.

"I want to stay," said Katie. She looked lovingly at Max.

"*Okay, Max, you may keep Katie here forever,*" Marty joked.

"*I will,*" Max said, nodding at Katie.

Turning her head to the side, Katie bit down on her lip, now she knew. The confirmation, Max's love and for her alone! Taken off guard she smiled warmly, looking over at her Russian prince. Max winked at Katie as he placed his arm around her and held her just a little closer that night.

In her heart, she knew his true feelings toward her. "*He loves me!*" Katie knew then and there. It was real. Just that very feeling and sense from Max put her thoughts at ease.

They soon excused themselves and left. Alone, knowing the hours were indeed getting shorter and there was no sense in withholding their true feelings from one another any longer. Max turned to Katie. "*You are thinking about leaving. Am I right?*"

"*You read my mind.*" Katie touched his arm gently as they reached the end of the hall. He held the door for Katie. Katie imagined how she would feel with her heart left behind in Russia. Max took Katie's hand and clasped it in his. "*I want to tell you something.*"

The sound of footsteps interrupted Max and he pulled back from Katie. What was he going to say?

Valentina walked toward them. "*Oh, my dear girl,*" she said in Russian, as she embraced Katie. "*We meet again, one more time.*"

"*Da!*" Katie said to her, smiling at Max and hoping his language sounded fine coming from her lips. Katie turned to him. "*Can you please tell Valentina that I am so happy to see her again?*"

"*Of course! In fact, it's my pleasure.*" Max touched her arm slightly. "*But, Katie you should try your Russian first."* Katie tried her best. Valentina's eyes brightened as she smiled at Katie, showing her gold- lined teeth, which Katie was used to seeing during her stay in Krasnodar.

A sense of sadness overcame Katie. She loved this culture, and her first love stood right beside her.

"My girl, I will miss you so," Valentina told Katie. Speaking in Russian to her, as Max translated.

Valentina parted as Katie turned to Max. *"Thank you for translating."*

"You are welcome. Let's go and have some more chai." Max led her to their friend Jafar's room.

Jafar was with a group of pleasant young men from the United Arab Emirates. They had befriended the group from Hawaii and often had dinner with them in the hotel. Once inside, cheers rang out. They clapped as loud Arabic music was playing, happy spirits were gathered all around Max and Katie. Katie felt her cheeks flush again, to a slight red colour.

"Hey, Katie and Max! Come in. Join us." Jafar extended his arms to the young couple.

Max sat on the empty bed, and Katie took her place beside him. Jafar spoke in Russian and Max translated for Katie. *"They would like the two of us to come and visit them in the Emirates one day."*

"That would be fun," Katie told him.

"Yes!" Max agreed.

Overwhelmed, Katie just-smiled and tried to live in the moment. After saying their goodbyes to Jafar and his friends, it was time for them to leave. Max led Katie to a nearby elevator, stopping halfway. *"Please, Katie, take this, treasure it and remember me, always."* Max placed an envelope in her hand.

She stood before him, nearly speechless. *"Yes, thank you, I will."* The couple walked on towards the elevator, but once they got there, it was so crowded that they lost one another. *"Where did Max go? Have I really lost my Max forever?"*

Making her way to her room, Katie inserted the letter Max had given her safely in her Bible. It was the most precious thing to her at that place in time. She wanted it to be her special letter, untouched until she had left Krasnodar. *"Should I read it now?"* Katie pondered what to do. *"No. Best to have some special words from Max after I leave his city."*

Several hours later, the moment had arrived, the mission was over and Katie was on her way back to Hawaii. What had started out as an extraordinary journey, ended with a new love now in her heart. Such a bittersweet moment, she half-smiled.

As luggage was being loaded, Katie could only stand and look outside into the snowy darkness of the winter evening. She found herself torn between these deep new feelings for Max and the fact that she was really leaving his country.

Katie silently prayed. *"There seems to be no way for us to ever meet again. It is such a forgotten dream, a wish, my hope. We didn't even have a proper goodbye."*

People were everywhere pushing and calling, the next thing she knew, Katie was being shoved into her cab and next to Olivia. *"Hi, Katie! What a commotion, I'm ready,"* Olivia said to her. *"I just hope we make it to the station on time."* Katie was not thinking about the station, just Max. Rain drops spilled ... and separated into streams on the sloped glass. Katie placed her glove on it, the coldness strong.

"Dear God, please find a way for Max to be at the railway station. I want to see him one last time. These last three weeks have meant more to me than anything and I know Max understands my heart, as I do his." It would be less than one hour before they would leave Krasnodar forever.

As they passed the flats and headed to the station, Katie looked outside to get her last glimpse of his city. Interrupted by her own thoughts, Katie blinked back the tears and hoped to see him one more time.

"Katie, look, we are nearly there," Olivia told her, pointing out the window. *"There is hope. Don't worry, we won't miss the train now."*

Katie lifted her eyes from the window, wondering if only Olivia knew what she was thinking. *"No, she couldn't possibly."* Katie turned to her friend and just offered a smile.

When they arrived, thick diesel smoke had already filled the air and a large crowd had gathered outside the train station. The girls stepped out of the taxi. *"Over here!"* David shouted, waving to Olivia and Katie.

Disappointment rose in Katie as she did not see Max anywhere in the crowd. *"Where could he be?"* Katie thought, as she moved past people hugging and shoving all at once.

"Hi!" John greeted the girls.

"Are we ever happy to be on time!" Olivia told him. Katie kicked the soft snow slightly. Now, there was no going back.

*

Max knew time was precious now. He sat in the taxi, anxious to see Katie once more. *"Please hurry,"* Max told the driver, his words lost in the blare of the radio.

"Someone special you want to see, boy?" the driver asked, his cigarette hanging halfway out of his mouth as he picked up speed.

"Yes, actually. Very special. She's leaving for Moscow tonight, and I wish to see her one last time. What a girl, so unique and I had to let her go. I just hope I am not too late."

The car swerved sharply, and Max clasped the door. The cab came to a halt, and stopped near the curb. Max sighed. *"There you go, son. Hope you catch your destiny!"*

"Oh, yes, me too." Max jumped outside and into the crowd. He walked as fast as he could to find Katie, the one girl who had stolen his heart. Yet he wasn't sure at this point if she felt the same way.

*

Katie looked down at the train tracks as the others laughed and joked around her. Her sadness was apparent to Shara, of course. She had gotten to know Katie well over these two months together.

"Katie, honey." Shara approached her. *"He's not here and the train will be coming soon."* Katie nodded to Shara.

"I am ready to leave Krasnodar, really. I promise." Katie bit her lip, feeling the pain. *"I do know one thing, that boy will now always play on my mind forever."*

"Be strong, my sweet girl," she whispered to Katie,

giving her a hug.

Knowing the future was not in her hands, Katie knew she would go on, but Max would always remain forever in her heart.

Chapter 11
Train to Moscow

Katie placed her hands over her face, the warmth of her wool gloves keeping her toasty warm.

"Hey, Max!" Katie heard Alexi say. *"What was he talking about?"* Laughter erupted and the voices of young Russian men were heard.

"Oh, da!" a voice spoke, it was full of soft laughter. A voice that Katie knew all too well. Out of the corner of her sad yet now happy eyes, Katie saw him walking through the crowd, toward her. Feeling the warmth of his sudden presence, Katie's heart suddenly leapt. *"He is here, it's not a dream."* At once she felt complete. On the outside, Katie couldn't help but smile, and inside she was dancing with joy. Katie felt caught in a sudden trance. *"Was this for real. My Max, here and now?"* His familiar voice, music to her ears.

"Am I too late?"

"You made it." Katie's voice rose even as she smiled shyly, feeling alive and beaming with happiness.

"I wouldn't miss saying goodbye to you for anything in the world," Max whispered to Katie, his eyes unable to turn from hers. He glanced at his watch. *"And we only have about thirty minutes left until the train leaves."*

"Please don't remind me," she told him softly. *"I wish I could stay here."*

Max swung his head back letting out a small laugh. *"Well, then why don't you stay? I could show you all you haven't seen here in Krasnodar. You would be amazed."*

"That's teasing me, Mr. Anchov."

"I'm sorry." He smiled. *"I know one day you will be back."*

"I hope you are right," Katie replied.

"He feels something for me. It's in the air." The night lights shone all around them as they made their way toward the platform. What a beautiful place and now she was leaving it. And worst of all, she was leaving Max behind.

"Come on, guys." Alexi motioned as everyone gathered around, the stars still bright and Katie's heart full of love.

She wondered if the time would ever be right? It was the way he looked at her that gave her hope, wishing that he had the same deep feelings.

"Lost in thought?" Max asked Katie.

She could only look away, her whole being a bundle of nerves. *"I just know how much I will miss everything."*

"I can see that in your eyes," Max said.

Katie stood in the middle of the group with her knapsack, her breath blowing mist, almost half-frozen into the frosty night air. Young people surrounded each other in little circles. Hugging and saying goodbye to them, Katie smiled, appreciating one last time the warm kindness of people in Krasnodar.

It was bitterly cold. She pulled her scarf tighter around her neck, and then Max took both her hands in his. His eyes met hers and she felt completely safe. *"It's a wonderful Krasnodar night. Look at the stars,"* he offered.

"*I know. It is so pretty tonight.*"

"*It was all planned.*" Max smiled. "*This night, our meeting.*" His eyes gazed into hers.

Katie smiled shyly. "*You are right, my dear Russian boy.*" He winked and Katie knew he would always have her heart.

A sudden, strong gust of wind startled Katie and commanded her to push her hands deeper into her pockets.

"*I guess we are heading to the tracks now,*" Max told her.

"*Okay.*" Katie nodded. She could feel sadness creeping over every inch of her face.

"*Let me help you,*" Max whispered, looking her tenderly in the eye and taking her knapsack.

He carried it over his shoulder, once again becoming the prince of her dreams. Katie did not want this night to end. How could it when everything was so perfect between them? It was pure magic as they looked at each other with hearts full of love.

The smell of smoke was so strong in the railway station, that Katie almost could not bear it. "*It's so hard to breathe here,*" she said, looking up at Max.

He placed his arm around her. "*Katie, come here.*" He drew her close to him and held her inside his coat, protecting her from the industrial transportation air. Even so, Katie caught the aroma of cheap perfume mingled with the smoke.

She saw Russian gypsies and their children standing nearby, occasionally glancing at the young people. A common sight to behold in Russia. Typical garb was worn by the gypsies as they kept watch on their offspring.

Katie and Max were standing on the platform at the edge of the tracks. He gently placed his hand on her shoulder. *"You know, I wish you could stay."* His eyes sparkled with love and mystery.

Katie was taken by surprise and hoped he would say more. *"I know. I feel the same way."*

"Let's make a run for it," Max joked.

"I wish." Katie loved his bright spirit and kind heart. She smiled and tried to savour these last minutes they had together. People around them were still saying their goodbyes. They wanted to avoid anything like that. Max's eyes widened as he saw the oncoming headlights of the train approaching.

At that moment the group of youth had an opening and they quickly ran to board the train. *"Goodbye, my friend,"* Alexi said to Katie as she was pushed away from Max and toward the door.

"Goodbye, Alexi. I will write soon."

Holding back the tears, Katie decided it was better to just leave it. The commotion made it all the more difficult to see Max, and then a figure appeared once more in the crowd.

"Well, Katie, I guess this is goodbye," he said sadly.

"Goodbye, Max," Katie declared, hugging him, as she was pulled up into the train with the others. The scent of him caught her up in that moment. In that second, her heart was left behind, to a boy who had become her world for only a short time.

Katie made her way onto the train reluctantly, wanting to fall back into Max's arms and stay with him forever. The warmth of the train enveloped her, yet she wanted to rush back to him. Too late now. She parted the velvet crimson curtains and hoped for one last look at her Russian dream boy.

At that moment, she remembered every time they had ever met and every emotion that had passed between them. An overwhelming sense of sadness welled inside, shaking the very core of her being. *"No, please. I can't. I won't feel this way."* Katie set her knapsack down and placed her hand on the nearby window.

Looking through, she saw Max standing in the moonlight, striking and handsome as ever. Katie smiled. *"My sweet boy."* He seemed to be searching for her too. They caught each other's gaze. Katie waved to Max, and he smiled up at her. She smiled back as she mouthed to him, *"I will miss you."*

Knowing he was the only one there, and had eyes only for her, cheered her heart. Even though she had to leave, Katie was glad for all the times they did share and for Max's kindness when she was sick. That act alone had truly touched her heart.

Looking from side to side, the train horn announced the impending departure. Max looked up, the beautiful night his background. Stars were sprinkled in an array of designs. Scattered high and low, decorating the winter sky of Krasnodar.

He could see Katie clearly now; she was searching for him. He knew it was now or never. He looked up at Katie through the train window, and in an intimate moment, with love shimmering in his eyes, he stared adoringly through the misty glass.

His lips moved, slowly and sincerely, *"I love you,"* he mouthed, searching for a response.

Katie couldn't believe her eyes. *"Max?"* Her heart did

a complete flip. Those words would now change her life forever. She felt a powerful surge run through her body, unlike anything she had ever known.

Overwhelmed by his declaration, she quickly ran down the carriage, passing a group of Russian soldiers, as the others were still saying goodbye.

"*Miss! Miss!*" The train master yelled in thick Russian. "*Come back here now!*"

"*Wait!*" Katie said in English.

She tumbled into sheer darkness and ran down the train stairs into Max's arms. He held her so she wouldn't fall.

"*What you just told me... I feel the same way,*" Katie said breathlessly as Max gently smiled. Love filled his eyes, as if they were the only two people in the whole world standing there. In a whimsical trance Katie felt the love of Max encase her-whole being.

"*I believe God brought us together,*" Max whispered to Katie, placing his hand on her cheek. "*I feel we were meant to cross paths. He planned our meeting. But now you must go.*"

Katie nodded. Max gently helped her up onto the waiting train just as its wheels began to turn and steam rolled from the tracks, beginning her journey back to Moscow. Katie ran to the window to catch one last glimpse of her prince. He waved and pretended to run slowly with the train. Now Katie was laughing. She would never forget his, "I love *you.*" That phrase would be her promise now; hope she would need for the future. He did love her, despite the many miles that would keep them apart. Her heart ached. "*Dear Max, please know how much you are loved, despite the distance between us. You are so deep in my soul, as are those three words you shared with me."* In her dreams, she knew she would run back to him, fall into his arms, as he gently kissed her.

In reality, she was startled by small voices...

Katie lifted her head and looked at her watch. It read five a.m. She must have fallen asleep thinking about Max. And now it was still so early. She left her compartment, careful not to wake anyone still sleeping. Katie remembered Max telling her he loved her. She had been right about his feelings all along. Her heart jumped and she felt butterflies flutter in her stomach. *"Max, you silly boy, why didn't you tell me earlier."* She smirked.

Shara sat near the window, engrossed in a book. *"Hi, honey,"* she said, as Katie approached in the dim half-light of the moving train. Shara suddenly frowned. *"Why do you look so sad?"*

"I just wish our stay in Krasnodar was longer. The past two months were over so fast." Katie was still half-asleep and didn't want to explain the entire truth, not yet anyway. The Russian boy was still in her heart.

"I know. It was a wonderful experience, wasn't it?" Shara looked into Katie's eyes questioningly, as if to see if that was the only reason for her unhappiness.

"I'm going to try to go back to sleep." Katie went back to her compartment, and lifted her pillow, where the precious letter from Max was waiting to be read. *"I didn't forget,"* Katie said to herself as she picked up the envelope. It was still very early. Should she read it or wait? She hoped to find something in it, and perhaps understand Max's feelings better. Taking her knapsack and fumbling for a flashlight, Katie propped the pillow against the window and sat up, anxious to read every word Max had written.

Holding the envelope in her hand, she could almost feel

his tenderness. Turning it over, she saw a tear stain on the front. Katie felt another surge of emotion, as though in a dream. She bit her front lip slightly and closed her eyes. The tear stain must have been from her, when she stared at it last night. In her mind, Katie saw Max, so vivid and clear as she replayed his words of love over and over.

Carefully opening the envelope, Katie unfolded the letter and slowly took in every word.

> *"Katie, there are so many things I want to tell you, but it is really hard to find words (the right, proper words) to convey my feelings ...*
> *I want you to know that I consider myself blessed to have met you here. You were so awesome and encouraging. You are the most amazing person I ever met. One never knows, only God, what will happen with each one of us. Maybe my future will be somehow connected with teaching! It was you, by the way, who made me think of it seriously.*
> *Whatever God will let me be, that is his will. I only wish I had met you sooner. During your journey, make sure you look out the train window. Russia is beautiful and I know you love this country! I am looking forward to seeing you here again ONE HAPPY DAY. I know it will be soon.*
> *I will finish for now. May God bless you. You are always in my prayers. Max"*

On the back of the letter, Max had outlined his left hand, a symbol of his affection for her. Katie placed her hand on the drawing, and closed her eyes. After a moment, she withdrew her hand and fumbled around in her knapsack, searching for a new piece of paper so she could reply to her beloved. She began to write.

"Feb. twenty-first, 1993

Dear Max,
Hi! It's Sunday night and the day after we said goodbye in Krasnodar. I am on the bumpy train back to Moscow.
After we left the station, I didn't fall asleep until about three a.m. I was tired and yet I could not sleep. You will be so proud of me; I read your letter this morning! I am glad I waited for today to read it, because it would have kept me awake the whole night! Every word you wrote touched my very heart! It mesmerized me beyond words! I WILL NEVER BE THE SAME AGAIN. Thank you!
It was so wonderful to meet you in Russia. I know we only began to know each other near the end of my stay, but I still feel that our time together was a true blessing. You were an encouragement to my life as well. Thank you, Teacher, for caring for me when I was sick. It meant so much to me. I keep you in my prayers, now and always.
Seven thirty a.m. Krasnodar time March first, will be your twenty-first birthday. How could I forget? And on that day especially, I will remember you fondly.
Always pray to God, to guide you in your life. Since He brought you into my life, during my short stay in Krasnodar, I know He will reunite us one happy day. It would have been awesome to have met you sooner,

but at least we were close in the end. Does it sound crazy to you that I feel like we share a special bond? I pray you will understand. Even though I am leaving now, I know I will be back one day.

I will always think of our times together. Thank you for your prayers. I feel them. I know there are great plans in store for the future.

Love, Katie."

Placing the letter in her Bible, next to his, she smiled and her heart leapt with the joy of knowing that even though they were apart, Max loved her! She lingered in his heart and soul just as he lingered in hers.

Moscow was fast approaching. In the early hours it looked bleak, yet her heart held on to her joy.

He is of this world. I am of my own.

*

That night, in the Moscow Aerostar Hotel, Katie thought of Max. She loved him more than life itself. Many changes had taken place in her heart over the last few weeks.

"Kate, are you feeling okay?" Jenna asked as they unpacked.

"I just miss Krasnodar."

"I know what you mean," Jenna said, smiling.

Someone knocked on their door and then they heard Shara's voice. *"Jenna and Katie, dinner will be ready in twenty minutes. We will meet down in the lobby."*

"Thank you, Shara," Katie told her.

Jenna turned to Katie. *"I wonder what kind of food this hotel serves?"*

Laughing, Katie replied, *"I am sure it is better than in the InTourist hotel in Krasnodar, but I was actually thinking the same thing. I mean, this is Moscow."*

Jenna laughed. *"Yes, the capital of our Motherland, right?"*

"Da, da," Katie said. *"Let's go and see the others."* Katie locked their door and they headed to dinner in the elegant Moscow hotel.

Downstairs, John had already saved the girls two seats. *"Thank you, John,"* Katie said.

"No problem. I didn't want you guys to miss out. We are having borscht."

"Oh, that sounds so good," Jenna said.

"I heard the food is really delicious here," John said, taking a piece of hot bread.

"Yes, please. Anything to get us through until we get home to Honolulu." Katie reached into the basket on the table taking a slice of bread. It was warm, and so tasty. The warm butter melted the insides of her mouth, it left her craving just a little more.

Decorative paintings with fine details covered the walls of the dining room. Gold and crimson coloured leaves adorned the entrance to the restaurant. Katie was in awe of the beauty that surrounded her. *"I love the artwork in Russia. It's so beautiful."* The others agreed.

"I know, Katie, I like it too," Olivia said.

Marty brought over a tray. *"I hope you guys will try this different caviar. It's scrumptious."*

"Oh, you're kidding, Marty." Olivia smirked.

"You know I'll try it," Joe said.

"I will try as well," Katie said.

Katie had wanted to try anything and everything she

could that held a part of Max close to her, more so in his land. *"I want to learn and know everything I can about the Russian culture. So I can be a part of Max in a way, be close to him and know all about where this boy has grown up."* Katie felt herself blush slightly.

"Olivia, please go ahead and have a small bite too."

"Okay, Kate, but you go first," Olivia said.

Her friends had sometimes referred to her given name, Kate, and she did not mind this coming from Olivia at all. It was rather cute, she thought.

"It's not so bad, is it?" Olivia laughed. The flavour was salty yet not too much, and the little bead-like bobbles felt like a smooth flutter on Katie's tongue.

"I quite like it," Katie said, in between bites.

Soon, everyone had tried the caviar and found it a nice change from the food in their last hotel. Finally, they were served hot chai accompanied by sweet cakes, the last part of their meal.

"What is the plan for tomorrow?" David asked, as everyone finished dinner.

"I want to go to Red Square and pick up souvenirs," Marty said.

"That's a great idea," Joe told him. Everyone joined in agreeing.

"I have a few letters to mail," Katie said.

"You can do that from Amsterdam," Joe told her.

"I actually wanted to do it here. "They are going to... ummm... Krasnodar." Katie didn't want to divulge the truth. Her precious letters were going to Max.

"I see." Joe ended the conversation with a sly wink. "Tomorrow we will meet at eight a.m. for breakfast and then go from there."

Everyone agreed to this plan then shuffled out of the restaurant and back upstairs to their rooms.

"*Goodnight, Katie.*" Jenna smiled, as Katie entered her room.

"*Goodnight,*" Katie said, planning on writing another letter to Max, once she was alone. "*I think I might take a bath; those big Russian tubs are quite interesting.*"

"*I tried one earlier and, yes, it was so relaxing. Enjoy it. Goodnight.*" Jenna went off into her bedroom.

Stepping into the bath, the water felt perfect. The warmth seemed to release her of worrying thoughts about the future. "*Now what is going to happen? We met and he loves me! Oh! Max truly loves me!*" It was a silent secret she carried with her, what would the future hold now? Katie threw some bubbles over her shoulder, laughing out loud.

"*Kate, is everything okay?*" Jenna called to her from the other room.

"*I'm just great!*" Katie replied. Her soul was happy, and her heart felt complete.

Chapter 12
Hawaii Bound

"This is your captain speaking. We will begin our descent into Amsterdam at Schiphol airport in about ten minutes. Thank you for choosing KLM and enjoy your stay."

The pilot's voice snapped Katie back to reality. During her return flight, she had been hoping and trying to go back into the past, to her time in Krasnodar.

"I must forget Max." For a person who was brought into her life so quickly, then taken away just as fast. And it had only been a few, rare times that they even saw one another, as if in a wonderful dream. *"I will go on."* Katie reminded herself. It was a surprise meeting anyway; she would leave the past alone, even if her whole being was crying out for him. Everywhere she went he was in her utmost thoughts, where couples walked and lovers kissed. In her reflection she saw Max.

After stepping off the plane, Katie went to the main gate and collected her bags; there she met the rest of the group. As she boarded the bus to the hotel, deep down she knew she needed to call her mother.

Once she was settled in her hotel room and dialling the numbers, Katie anticipated her mother, Sarah, would give her confirmation and understand the way she was feeling. She had always been there for Katie, encouraging and listening, in her happiest and saddest moments.

Katie had not seen her mom in six months and she was

missing her dearly. Sarah was back in Katie's homeland, Canada, missing her daughter as well.

Deciding right after coming back from Russia, Katie would not be seeing her mom for another six months. She would remain in Honolulu to volunteer in the kitchen for another upcoming school of young people.

A familiar voice answered on the other end. *"Hi, Mom!"*

"How are you?" Sarah asked her daughter.

"I'm great!" The excitement in Katie's voice said it all. *"Our time in Russia was incredible. We made so many new friends, I will send you some wonderful photos. I guess in many ways I am still there. I only wish..."* Katie's eyes turned to the photograph of Max she'd stuck inside her Bible.

"It sounds like you had a really good time in Russia," her mother said gingerly.

After a pause, Katie continued, her voice quieter now, *"I've also met someone and he's Russian."* Katie waited quietly for her mother's response.

"Really?" The pause was a bit awkward. *"You did?"* Her mom said quietly. *"It seems sudden, Katie. How serious is it between the two of you?"* Her mother's reaction was not quite what Katie expected.

"I know this Katie, you sound very excited and so happy!" her mother remarked.

"Oh! Yes, I am, really, well you would just have to meet Max for yourself, he is incredible. I am so happy." Katie could feel her love for this boy burn across the miles. Knowing her mom was a bit hesitant, she felt her understanding a bit more with every praise Katie spoke about this Russian boy.

"*Don't worry, Mom, we have just begun, I mean, our lifelong friendship. He is very sweet.*" "*Really? Do write and tell me more,*" her mom replied. "*I mean ... Katie, I just want you to be cautious as well.*"

The silent pause in her voice was obvious. "*I will,*" "*I miss you, Mom. Say hello to everyone.* "*Goodbye, I love you.*"

After hanging up, Katie felt a strong surge. She sat on the bed, a slight chill rushing through her body as Max returned to her thoughts. From the moment they met, he was constantly there, a part of her. Katie had come to Russia alone, yet she had left with Max in her heart.

The call home made Katie feel happy that she had shared news about her Russian boy. She always felt better after she spoke to her mother. They had always had a close relationship. She had just needed to hear her voice, and it had been so fulfilling to relay her newfound feelings to her. Katie smiled and closed her eyes. There Max was, right in front of her, just as when they had said goodbye at the train station in cold surroundings, but warmed by love.

*

A month had passed and still nothing from Max. Being back in Hawaii was paradise, yet not seeing or hearing from her Russian boy was difficult. Her heart remained in Russia as she replayed the train scene, their parting, over and over in her mind.

The day began on the islands as a typical sunny one as the stunning, hot sunlight streamed through Katie's window. She turned over on her side, entangled in her blanket. Her dream had been so real and pleasant. But. Max was running to her on the train platform past everyone.

"You must stay with me." He kissed her lips and she felt so strong and full of love. Holding her in his arms and not letting go, he whispered, *"I will never let you leave this place."* Then a fierce wind began to pull Katie back and then a smashing of the train door clamped her inside.

Eyes wide open now, Katie put her hand on her forehead. It was the same vision of Max she had many nights in a row, as though she could never reach him. Wrapping her blanket over her, Katie turned over and thought about how very far Max was from her.

There was no sense in being upset. She had to continue with her life. Maria, her roommate, entered the room at a fast pace. *"Hi, Katie. Good morning. I have got to make the mail delivery and I need to send a letter to Taiwan."*

Katie's face perked up. Maria had always been a wonderful and loyal friend since they had met nine months before, at the school where several groups of youth had gathered from around the world to head out on their different missions.

When both of the girls had gone on separate trips, it was a sad goodbye, even though it was only going to be two months apart. While busy prepping her winter clothes for cold temperatures in Russia, the day Maria departed. Katie had said to her friend before she jetted off to Taiwan, *"Don't worry, Maria, the time will fly, and we will have lots of stories to exchange."*

Katie chose a light blue sundress to wear that day. Her blonde bang fell over an eye as she applied the last bit of her mascara. *"See you after breakfast,"* Katie called to Maria.

Opening the door to the kitchen, Katie let the aroma of fresh coffee rouse her. It helped her look forward to another day of hope and expectation for any word from Max. She felt that a word would be coming soon ... "it had to be."

No matter what Katie tried to tell herself, deep down she knew she was not about to give up on the Russian boy who had stolen her heart. Back in her room now, Katie could easily read his letter over and over again. It was memorized in her heart. She knew without a doubt, he loved her in his own world.

"*Kate, Kate. Can I come in?*" Olivia asked her as she opened the door and peeked inside.

"*Hi,*" Katie greeted her.

"*Are you all ready for the trip to the North Shore?*" Olivia asked.

"*Yes, and I am really looking forward to getting away for the weekend.*" Katie's eyes twinkled with enthusiasm. Olivia went to gather her bags while Katie finished her packing. She took out Max's photo once again as the memories began to flood her mind. She saw herself with him and no other.

*

Max gripped the cold bars and railings that morning, leading up the pathway to the flat on the corner, where Andrew and Linda Rigley, a missionary couple from Canada, lived. They had been in Russia for two years now. Their wish was to come to Krasnodar hoping to fulfill the lives of young people. They were their light in the lost forgotten world of southern Russia. Max had gotten to know them well. He loved their company.

Stepping up to the front door, Max raised his hand to the bell. Signs of the new season were everywhere. April had made her appearance just days before.

"Max, welcome!" Andrew exclaimed, opening the door. *"Well son, how are you?"* Max removed his scarf.

"Hi, Andrew. I am good. It's still cold outside... so nice to be in here."

"Come in and have some warm chai."

"Thank you," Max said, taking off his shoes.

Linda entered the hall. *"Max, so good to see you."* Hugging the young boy made her feel more at home. Being far away from Canada, she had become accustomed to meeting and spending quality time with young Russians, the youth of Krasnodar, that were thrilled to spend time with the couple, which helped her when she missed her own sons.

"It's so good to see you too."

"I will put some tea on," Linda told them.

"Let's go and sit down." Andrew motioned him into the living room.

Max followed Andrew, taking a seat when asked. *"What is new with you?"* Andrew asked, smiling. He had known Max for about two years and had enjoyed visiting with him. He found him to be a very interesting and a pleasant young man. Max's face turned into a bright smile.

"I have been working a lot lately."

"Is there anyone new in your life?" Linda asked inquisitively as she joined them in the living room.

Max felt his face flush. *"I do have a special friend. And by the way, she's Canadian."*

"Canadian girls are truly sweet," Andrew said, taking Linda's hand and winking at his wife.

"She is great," Max blurted out, smiling and sipping his tea.

"Where did you meet her?" Linda seemed to grow more curious by the minute.

"This winter she came to Krasnodar. She was here with a group of missionaries."

"I can see that you really miss her. Let God take care of the rest." Linda smiled. *"He knows what is ahead for you and maybe your special friend."*

"Thank you, both of you," Max said.

"We will be flying home this summer, son, and it would be wonderful if perhaps you could join us?"

Andrew looked at Max with curiosity. A smile spread across Max's lips as he nodded, taking another sip of his tea. *"I do thank you for the invitation and it could very well be a possibility,"* Max said.

"Yes, and of course there is always your special friend, she could be a very short visit away, once you are in Canada." Linda smiled with a twinkle in her eyes. She loved playing matchmaker and had a feeling this could be one made in heaven.

*

It was great to be back in Hawaii of course. And yet it was an entirely different world now, compared to when Katie was with Max.

Olivia came around the corner, interrupting Katie's thoughts. *"Dreaming of Russia again? I know. I miss it there too."*

"I miss that country but someone very special is there and I am here. That's the real problem," sighed Katie.

"Kate," Olivia said, surprised.

"Do you mean Max?"

"Yes, I do," she confirmed.

"How come you never said anything before? Why didn't you tell me this sooner? I am so happy for you!"

Olivia's eyes widened as she looked skyward and was pleased for her friend. Seeing Katie's face and how it shone at the mention of Max's name.

Previously that day Katie had sent two copies of her precious letter from Max to Canada. One copy was for her mom and another copy was for her grandmother. Katie anticipated how they would enjoy the read. The words from her dear Max, would bring smiles to their faces.

"You are blushing," Olivia said, giggling. Katie placed her hands on her cheeks and smiled back to her friend. Katie went into her room, and opened up a letter she saw resting on her pillow.

"March thirty-first, 1993, Rainy Vancouver,
Hi, darling! How are you doing in sunny Hawaii?
Oh, sweetheart, I am missing you so. Lots of news coming out of Russia these days. Tell me everything that you hear. I have been wondering what plan that God has for you. He does all things well. When I look at your baby pictures, I say to myself, God had a plan for you twenty years ago and He must have a plan for Max too. Well, sweetie, I'd better mail this letter. Grandpa is waiting to go to the post office. So I'll say to you as I always say: you're my Love and for the time being we can pray without ceasing.
Love, Grandma
PS – Love your letters. They always have some news that brightens me up."

A second letter was in the envelope, much to Katie's delight.

"Hello, darling, I am trusting you are well at all times. I just get lonesome for you at times. I don't let Grandpa know or else he'd worry I was sick! Well, sweetheart, I just wanted to send a little extra note for you. I'd better sign off. I'll write again, and you keep us posted on all your news. Tell Max we love him already. We want him here! Dear God, please keep Katie under thy wings and Max too.
xoxoxo"

*

Max made his way to the Krasnodar State University that April morning, wondering if Katie received his recent letter. He picked up his pace. Unable to shake the memories of her, especially since time had marched on for both of them. Any thought of her made him smile deep inside.

Max stroked his hand over his hair, the gentle wind caressing his face. It was a beautiful spring day in Krasnodar. He wished Katie were there to share it with him. He would show her the parks, the city, and the true beauty of his hometown.

He had been happy, living in various locations around the former Soviet Union, finishing high school, and traveling. Max's father had been a pilot in the Soviet military, before he became a police officer, so one could say he had an advantage over other Russian boys. When his parents decided to settle in Krasnodar he had been thrilled. *"I will show Katie everything here. The girl of my dreams has left my country. Somehow one day, I know she will return."* He could always hope ... Max smiled upward.

*

Katie headed on her way to check for mail that summer day in Honolulu, the hot sun scorching her face. Windblown and sun-kissed, she felt energetic and hoped this was the day, he would pour out more of his feelings.

She could easily replay the last look of love between her and Max over in her mind. It made her happy inside. More confident of his love for her always. Like an old dream left solely in the pages of her diary.

Peeking inside her room, her pillow was empty, no letters today. Katie went on her way in search of solace.

She had to put the past winter behind her. She needed to move on, worlds apart from Max.

Chapter 13
Missing Max

Returning to her room, Katie passed the others, avoiding their eyes. She did not miss the headlines. They were on every newsstand in Hawaii, impossible not to see. Russia was in trouble. There was brewing political strife, bubbling over. Katie cried even harder.

Russia was so far away. Max still meant so much to her. She fell for this boy from another culture; now she had to pay the price of love, only hoping and praying he was safe and protected. Perhaps their experience had been just a one-time passing of feelings, between two strangers, never to be touched by that moment in time again. Or could it be that one day their souls would meet again? Max had become a constant part of her.

Those cold winter nights were so far away now, but played like a broken record in her head over and over again. The way he cared for her, loved her, it felt so right.

Going to sleep that night, Katie and her roommate Maria talked of future plans.

Katie lay on the top bunk, listening to her friend. *"I don't know what LA will hold for me. I want to go home, and just get back into the real world; Taiwan was such an awesome experience,"* Maria told her. *"How are things for you?"*

"*At this point, I am just waiting for a letter,*" Katie said, deciding to share a little bit about Max. "*He was just so different, Maria. So amazing.*"

"*Do you think you have a future with Max?*" Maria whispered. Shivers came over Katie, and surprised, she said,

"*I'm not sure if we will even see each other again. Only if it is our fate,*" Katie whispered.

"*I will say a little prayer for you both,*" Maria offered.

"*Please dear God, if fate brought Max and my friend Katie together, Godspeed them back to one another.*" The two girls said goodnight, as geckos sang outside of their window that summer night.

Katie's eyes instantly began to close, as the feelings overwhelmed her in that moment. Tears were just about to begin as she drifted off to sleep, with only one last thought – Max, her Russian boy, kissing and loving her in her dreams.

Daybreak came and Katie turned over on her pillow only to see a tear stain from the previous night. "*Max, my boy, how I miss you.*"

She looked at the clock and counted. He's getting ready to go to sleep now. For Krasnodar was thirteen hours ahead. Katie climbed out of bed and made her way into the bathroom. Looking in the mirror, she turned away. "*Oh Max, why are you so far away?*"

Then she heard a silent voice. "*Trust Max, as you trust me, that he still holds you in his heart.*"

A feeling of comfort swept over Katie at that very moment. Knowing that the future was not up to her. Feeling reassured by that voice, she knew she could carry on even without Max by her side.

Heading to breakfast, she sent a prayer upward for her special friend far away.

Katie sat down in the kitchen and stirred her coffee, tired from last night's late conversation. Maria had been very inspirational, and all in the name of love. *"I know we will see each other one day, I have to have faith and believe,"* Katie affirmed.

Janet, the kitchen supervisor, walked into the kitchen. *"Good morning, girls! I have some mail today."* She turned to Katie and smiled. *"A letter has come for you,"* Janet said handing it to her.

"What?" Katie said in disbelief. Katie recognized the return address, what she had prayed and hoped for such a long time, and now it was finally here. Her hand began to tremble. The return address simply read: *"Teacher in Moscow."*

Chills shivered down Katie's spine. *"Oh, my goodness."* Katie jumped in haste from her chair. *"I'm so happy."* Katie kissed the front of the envelope that she had so patiently waited for.

"Your face is so very red, Katie," Janet chuckled.

"It's from my friend in Russia." Katie shyly smiled. But inside a rush of excitement overwhelmed her, just as she had felt at the train station months before.

"Friend? Yes, I am sure." Janet's face scrunched up in disbelief.

"Can I go to my room for a few minutes?" Katie asked.

"Of course!" Janet replied laughing as Katie began to walk in shock, her hand trembling holding the letter. *"Run along now and read your love letter, but come back*

soon." Katie nodded and zipped out into the Hawaiian sunshine and then down to her room.

"I can't believe it!" Katie looked up to the ceiling and laughed. *"Thank you, God,"* she whispered. She sat down. It had been three months since she had seen her Max, yet she had not given up, and had held the highest hope in her heart. He had not forgotten her at all, nor what they had shared months before, on those winter nights.

Taking out the letter, from the envelope. Katie read each and every word carefully.

"Dear Katie, hello there!
Today is the eighth of March; we celebrate Women's Day this day. So, my best wishes and prayers to you on the eighth of March!
For my birthday I was...guess where? At the airport in Moscow. Yeah! I was in Moscow for three days on a business trip. And I opened your letter at 7:25 a.m. the first of March. I felt so blessed that day! Thank you. I know you were praying for me that day. You're right; the Moscow Metro is really cool. Comparing it with metros in other cities, I have to say it is beautiful! The stations are decorated so lavishly.
This week my teaching in the school is going to be finished. I hope I will have more chances to show what a good teacher I can be.
By the way, Katie, my student, your teacher is sooooooooooo proud for you! (Your Russian spelling is good, and I wish you to have a speedy progress in Russian. I remember of my promise to find you some Russian books with pictures – wow!) I hope you will get this letter of mine, although our

postal system does not work very well. I'd better finish for today, but I will write again soon.
Love, Max"

Smiling, Katie peeked into the envelope once again, a bonus letter!

"Dear Katie,
Hi again! Yesterday I flew to Moscow once more. I've got a great job where I travel a lot! At least I got everything done that I had to do. Tomorrow morning, I fly back to Krasnodar. It is seven thirty p.m. and time to have some rest. I think I deserved it. So, I'm sitting in McDonald's and writing you these lines. Things in Krasnodar are going well, but I wish we had a McDonald's restaurant in Krasnodar. Ha! Yeah, it's really cool. And by the way, there are a group of English people over here. An hour ago I bought a very funny travelling clock, and you know its practical and necessary for a travelling man just like me, ha! OK, I'm going to be back to my Big Mac sandwich.
With love from Russia's heart, Max "

Katie closed her eyes, knowing Max had not only remembered her, he was also waiting for her letters as well. *"He is so sure we will meet again,"* Katie sighed. She felt his heart singing to her, oceans away. Oh, how she wished they could speak by telephone at least.

So began that night, the first of the same dream she would have of her far-away Russian boy ... Each time Katie stood underneath the gazebo, the pay-phone would ring and on the other end Max would be calling out her name. But when she responded to him, he could not hear her, and then the line would go dead.

Katie woke up, the first time in a cold sweat, heart racing. She went to get a cold drink. Standing at the sink she felt dizzy.

The next morning, she told Maria about the dream.

"Katie, I know you were destined to meet Max in some way or another, and I know if he is the one, God will reunite you back together," Maria said.

Katie smiled at her friend. *"I really want to believe that we are truly destined to be together one day."*

Even though she couldn't reach him in her own dreams, going to sleep that night, Katie knew she was in his heart and very much alive in his dreams. Frustrated that their communication was not constant, Katie knew he was indeed thinking of her, halfway across the globe.

Chapter 14
Worlds Apart

Turning twenty-one was a milestone that Katie looked forward to, being young and carefree. The past year had proven to be her best one yet.

Max was very much alive in her heart. Unexpectedly he had entered her life and she knew that her birthday would be one to celebrate as he was now a part of her, and she hoped he always would be.

Yes, she would turn twenty-one, now if only she could share this birthday with Max here in Hawaii. That would be the best gift ever.

It was yet another beautiful day, the summer warmth all around. She wondered what that day would bring. After finishing her breakfast, she headed back to the kitchen.

Laughing to herself now, Katie knew the gift of having Max, with her today was like a long-forgotten fairy tale, sealed for the moment. Minutes passed and then the payphone rang in the background. She closed the door and went into the kitchen. Janet knocked on the door. *"Katie, the phone is for you."*

"Really? Okay. Thank you." Katie walked down the steps, wondering who it could be?

"Hello," Katie said. The next instant, a trio broke out singing happy birthday to her.

Laughing, she couldn't quite place the call until she

heard his voice. *"Katie, this is Max."*

She couldn't believe her ears. *"Max? Max?"* Katie repeated.

"Max from Russia," he replied.

"Hi! How are you?" Katie asked. Her head spun a little as her heart beat faster. He remembered her birthday. Even though Alexi and Dmitri were on the other end, it felt as though she was only speaking to Max.

"How are things in Honolulu? Have you gotten any of my letters?" Max asked.

"Great, I have two," Katie replied.

"I sent you three," Max said, surprise in his voice.

"Oh, no!" Katie said.

"What are you doing in August?" Max asked her. *"Why don't we meet in Paris?"*

"That sounds great!" Katie said to him. *"I will have to see. Summer school is coming up, and I am not sure if I will have holidays."*

Max paused. *"I will call you soon, Katie."* And with that, his voice disappeared and only echoed in her head as the phone went dead.

For a moment, Katie wondered if she had been dreaming, surrounded only by sounds of geckos, otherwise only sheer quietness all around.

*

"It's going to be a beautiful summer again." Max looked up at the trees. June was the month, you could wear no coat and Mother Nature kept you warm, especially in the south of Russia. The sun had been setting as he headed on his way home with Alexi and Dmitri.

Hearing Katie's voice once again made him warm all over. *"She's the perfect girl to me."*

The three young men walked towards the trolley stop. *"It was fun singing to Katie. She's such a sweet girl,"* Alexi remarked.

"Yes. Sweeter than you know." Max smiled. *"Bye, guys."* The two boys looked at Max and chuckled. They spoke in quiet Russian among themselves.

Only two more days until his younger brother's wedding, and Max looked forward to it. The sky had turned a warm shade of red on that summer night in Krasnodar, and it had been so great to speak with Katie.

He smiled. A girl: so far away yet close in his heart. The young Canadian girl who had stolen all his glances. Katie was not forgotten in his heart, not now or ever. He loved and treasured all those times together. Running his hand through his jet-black hair, Max took his seat on the trolley. Staring out the window, he wished she could have been beside him. *"The most wonderful person I ever meet and she's gone in an instant. Katie, dear girl, you were so sweet. Will we ever see one another again?"*

Her reflection appeared as Max's hand touched the glass, sadness overcame this Russian boy. Only God knew what would happen. This he knew. He sighed and held his faith.

She could never become one of them, the girl he felt he had known forever, yet only a short time. Still, the desire to see her burned inside him more each and every day of his young life. Max smiled, looking at the row of apartments as he reached his own for the night.

*

Walking away from the telephone that summer day, Katie became overwhelmed; tears flooded her eyes. She could not stop the wetness on her face. Brushing them away, she closed her eyes and saw Max. His smile overpowering her thoughts in that moment.

It had been so wonderful to hear his voice. Her Russian boy, the one who had changed her life in an instant. As the scorching sun beat upon her face, Katie smiled, hoping Max could feel her smile even in faraway Russia. *"What an amazing birthday surprise!"* Max had sent her a message of love through the wires.

"Olivia!" Katie ran up to her dear friend, who she spotted walking out of the gazebo. A place of rest, for anyone who lived on campus. Olivia was usually found there, reading or pondering life.

"I just got a call from Russia." She hesitated, ready to burst with excitement. *"From Max!"*

"Oh Katie! Really, Katie! That is great news. How did he sound?"

"Wonderful," Katie told her friend, excitement in her voice. *"He sounded so far away, but good."* Katie went on to explain the call further. Hearing Max and his soft gentle voice, especially on a wonderful day, turning twenty-one made her swell with pride and love inside.

"Is that all you talked about?" Olivia said, her curiosity growing more obvious by the second.

With a twinkle in her eye, Katie laughed and bit her lip a little, still smiling. *"Well, he did mention Paris,"* she added, grabbing Olivia's hand. *"Do you know what this means? I have hope, more now, more than I ever had before. I mean, it could be that we are really truly meant to be."* Katie placed her hand on her cheek. *"Imagine if we reunite and something spectacular happens... like a wedding!"* Katie giggled, grabbing Olivia's other hand. She was full of more excitement that afternoon and all because of one Russian boy.

"Things are different now, the mission to Russia changed us—forever," Katie declared. *"It changed me Olivia, now you know, in more ways than one."* She smiled shyly as her secret love for Max was now completely open.

"I am so happy for you, Katie." Olivia hugged her as they parted ways.

Katie looked up and whispered, *"Someone is indeed watching over us."*

She felt her heart race with pure intensity, still recovering from the phone call and the thrill of hearing Max's voice.

Katie went to her room, found her purse and took out her wallet. Where was his recent letter, she pondered? Eyeing it on her nearby pillow, she took it and away she went. Grateful that Max had written his contact work number, it was like gold to her. Then she was on her way back out the door quickly. Katie wanted to send a fax to Max, so he would receive her words immediately instead of waiting for a letter. The print shop was nearby and she put a pen to the paper. Even as she walked at a brisk pace, she wrote to Max. The pen striking quickly and from her heart.

"Dear Max,
How pleased I was to receive a phone call from you on my twenty-first birthday. It was very special for me.

*It was the best gift I could ask for, better than anything. You sounded so well. I pray that peace and happiness will carry you through the rest of this year. I hope one day we will meet again, so I can express to you how greatly you have influenced my life. I feel so alive with the memories of last winter in my heart. I think of you often and pray you are safe, and happy. I remember back to those winter nights when I was sick in Russia. Yes, you were my angel. Thank you for being there, my friend Max, you can never know how much the love in my heart flooded me as you showed such kindness. If I knew how to tell you in Russian, I would. I mean your language. You will, teacher, one happy day! May God richly bless you, until we meet again. I do think that meeting in Paris is a possibility as well.
Love, Katie"*

Katie handed the store clerk the fax, paid and left smiling all the way back to the campus where new youth would be arriving the following week.

Soon a fresh note from her own heart would make it to her Max, in the south of Russia. *"How would he take it? I am sure he knows my heart and my true feelings for him. How could he not? My love, so far, but forever in my heart."*

When Katie passed by the library, she stopped in for just a minute. Looking on the shelf, she saw nothing new. Then her eye caught a title on the spine of a book— *"Russia: A Colourful and Magical Look into Yesterday."* She took the book. The pictures inside were so vivid and real that she reached out her hand to touch them. *"My little Russia,"* she thought, closing her eyes. *"My dear Max."* The photos became real images in her mind of what Katie had seen with her very own eyes, real life in the former USSR. *"My love is there, my sweet Max. But his world is not mine."* Tears began to well up in Katie's eyes.

"Attention please. The library will be closing for lunch in fifteen minutes. Thank you."

When Katie heard the announcement, she approached the front desk and placed her card on the counter. The librarian copied the information and then the book was hers. Only for a few weeks, of course, but still it would be all hers to explore.

Happily skipping back to the kitchen on campus, the warm sun beat down on Katie's young face. She returned and apologized to Janet, for her long absence. Janet understood, with a smile. It was hard to concentrate on work, lost in her own thoughts about him, sure that Max was thinking of her that very second too.

"Katie, there is a phone call for you," Mai called to her through the kitchen door. Mai was her forever friend from Japan. They had hit if off when she arrived in Hawaii, sharing many fun shopping trips and conversations.

Katie came outside to the payphone, surprised, and picked it up. *"Hello?"* she said. The line was dead. *"Hello?"* Katie said one more time. Strange. Katie saw Mai walking towards her. *"Who was that on the phone?"* Katie asked. Mai looked at Katie, surprised.

"I'm not sure. It was a male voice with a lovely accent." "Why wasn't he there when I got to the phone?"

Mai shrugged. *"I guess there was just a bad connection."*

"Thank you for telling me, Mai."

Katie returned to her work, disappointed. *"Was it Max on the phone? It had to be."* She had missed him and now she would leave for home in less than four weeks. Katie sat down for a minute. *"He truly misses me."* Katie smiled, as she felt Max's faithfulness to her.

He had entered her life so unexpectedly, and now she bore only his name on her soul.

*

"Krasnodar thirtieth June, 1993

Dear Katie,
Hello, my friend! It's midnight here. Dmitri and I are sitting at a friend's place writing letters. We don't have much time, or maybe we do – the whole night I would say. Two Canadians are leaving Krasnodar to return home tomorrow, and I made up my mind to write to you by all means. They made me think of sweet you. I tried to call you this morning. First, at seven a.m., the operator asked me to wait a bit because the line was busy or something – I don't know – I thought I would call you later on (as I had an exam that morning) SORRY! Anyway, I'm going to call you this week. We have to discuss some things. This summer we have many plans and I'd be very glad if you could join us or perhaps we could meet you in Europe.
The majority of the time I will be in Amsterdam/Holland. Dmitri and Alexi are planning to come to Germany in the middle of August. We'll meet each other over there, and are hopefully

going to visit Marty and Shara in Switzerland. (We are not sure since we didn't even call them yet.) Actually, there is a car in Switzerland that belongs to Lukas and we are supposed to take the car from there to Krasnodar. It's going to be fun! It would be incredibly great if we (you and the three of us) could see each other in Europe. By the way, we could come by car back to Krasnodar together. I mean the four of us. Does it sound fun? I hope we can meet once again.
Love, Max"

Yet another wonderful letter from the man she loved. Imagining Max beside her, Katie felt her heart burst with excitement once again.

Tomorrow was Friday and Katie was looking forward to Saturday already, which would mean beach day. It was the one day when Katie left all her cares behind and headed for some sun and relaxation. She decided to write to Max one last time before heading home to Canada.

"Hi Max,
I hope this letter finds you well. Please make sure that you say a big hello to your family. I still have to take a picture of my family for you. Also next time you write. All mail can be sent to Canada. Thank you! I wouldn't want to miss any letters from you. I wish you a wonderful day!
All my love, Katie"

Chapter 15
New Horizons

Returning home to Canada brought much anticipation to Katie.

She had been through much in the past year and wanted to share all she had seen and done with her family and friends. All of her dear friends in Hawaii were not going to be forgotten, but Katie had many stories burning in her heart to tell everyone back home, especially about her fateful meeting with Max—just months before. Her flight left Honolulu that afternoon at four o'clock. During the flight, she would occasionally take out Max's photo and smile.

Despite a gruelling six-hour flight, Katie tried her best to sleep, but kept having visions of Max. Eventually exhausted, she slipped into a deep dream.

"Miss, Miss." The flight attendant interrupted her slumber. *"We will be landing in about ten minutes."*

"Thank you," Katie told her. Lifting the shade on her window, she looked out and wondered what the future would hold. She couldn't help but think about things now that she was approaching her homeland.

Her eyes veered to the right, seeing the vast set of trees that surrounded the opening toward Vancouver airport. Yes, a perfect sight, her hometown, where she would soon be walking and exploring once again.

When she saw her family, Katie flung her arms around

everyone. It felt good to finally be home.

Max was far away, yet close in her heart.

That night, as her brother and sister slept, Katie and her mom talked into wee hours. *"So, what is it about this boy Max, that intrigues you, Katie?"* Her mom quizzed.

Katie blushed. *"Oh! He is everything! His spirit and liveliness, his excitement about life drew me to him."*

"Do you think you have a future with him then?" Katie's mom looked into her daughter's eyes. *"I just want you to be careful; he is of another culture,"* Sarah offered.

"I know that, I am and will be very careful. I just feel like he is a part of my future," Katie declared.

The discussion ended rather abruptly as Katie shrugged her shoulders and made her way to bed for the night, with only one boy on her mind, and running through her dreams.

*

It had been one month now since Katie returned home to Canada and she still had heard no word from Max. Yet in her heart, Katie was still convinced this was the person she would one day marry. But how could she be so sure? She supposed it was her feelings, so at ease, a deep love had grown and it still carried her each day, from when she had left him that cold winter night in February.

Katie kept her hopes up, and remembered their times together, and knew that something magical was in the air that night. She believed in this for now. For the time being, yes her Russian boy was far, yet he remained close in her heart.

*

Gold and orange leaves fell slowly that day on a quiet path in Gorky Park, Moscow, a place where Max had loved to collect his thoughts on many occasions.

He was on a three-day business trip and had risen early. After deciding on a morning walk, he began to envision Katie's face. He had thought of her often, even more so recently. Maybe because time had passed and the seasons had changed, as the days grew colder the memories came rushing back. Katie had been in this very country last winter. And now she was far away in her own.

Autumn had begun for both of them, each in their native land. Should he call her? Would it be a waste of a talk? Katie was perfect to him and now it felt as though her heart was reaching out for his. A reunion seemed like a long-forgotten dream. But he couldn't let it go.

He decided he would call her that night. He closed his eyes and ran his fingers through his hair. The timing was right. He needed to call this girl that had turned his world full-circle so unexpectedly. *"Oh Katie!"* His eyes turned towards a young couple who were sitting on a nearby bench. Arms wrapped around one another. They were deep in conversation. Max smiled, catching a glimpse of the woman, the wind gently blowing her hair slightly over the black fur of her hood. *"Blonde hair, just like my Katie."* He decided— *"It's time!"*

"Tonight I will dial her in Canada, I need to speak with her, hear her lovely voice." The girl that had unexpectedly stole his every glance, and most of all his heart. Off he walked, faster now, toward his hotel,

picking up his pace as he reached his destination.

*

Katie stood by the rain-drenched window. *"What does the future hold? Is Max in it? I miss him so."* A boy she barely knew. *"I do know how he really feels about me. His writing says everything."* Taking out a pen and paper, Katie sat down at her desk, and began.

"Dear Max,
It has been a while since we last spoke. As always, I love hearing from you. I miss Russia, especially you, my dear teacher.
The times we spent together in Krasnodar meant so much to me. If only we could re-live them.
Please write soon and take care. Love, Katie."

She held on for some kind of light from the south of Russia. If only time had forever stood still that winter. Katie could replay every word, every look, and every smile over in her mind, yet it did not bring Max closer to her; he was still so far away. He was one boy she would never forget. She remembered his words to her: *"I love you."* She felt his love in her heart, knowing he meant those words sincerely.

The wind grew louder by the second as memories of Krasnodar came flooding back. Drifting off to sleep, a twist turned in Katie's stomach. Loving Max had made her heart warmer, brighter and so full of life. Leaving him had been the hardest.

Early the next morning, someone knocked on her door. Katie's mom appeared in the doorway a second later. *"Do you have any letters to mail?"* she asked.

"Yes, mom, I actually have one," Katie said. Handing her the most recent one she had written to Max.

"Okay, I will be back soon." Her mom closed the door behind her.

Katie jumped to her feet. *"I am going to hear from Max soon. I just know it. I can feel a light from Russia already."* A new day dawned and dew glistened on the October grass outside her window. What was the future now? Katie had decided she needed to move on and perhaps forget about Max. She could apply to her local college and pursue her dream of becoming a writer. *"Nothing holds me down now. I am only twenty-one years old. I want to build my life and carry on, perhaps keeping Max as a never forgotten memory."*

Katie sensed the morning cold and dived back into bed, comforted by the warm covers. She drifted back to sleep. In her dreams, Max stepped over the stone onto the mountain. *"It's beautiful up here,"* Max said, waving to Katie. *"Come to me."* He stretched his hand out to her. Katie stepped onto the rock and reached out her hand, but could not touch him.

She turned over. It was the same strange type of dream again. Him drawing her near, but unable to connect. In all her life, her soul had never been shaken so strongly. Hopefully in her lifetime, she would see Max once again.

Waking up hours later, Katie decided to call her grandma. Dialling the numbers, she felt Max, and wondered if he was thinking of her, as she looked at her watch. It was eight p.m. in Russia.

"Hello," an older woman answered.

"Hello, Grandma," Katie said. *"How are you?"*

"Oh, sweetie! Hello there. I'm good. And you?"

"I am good, Gram."

"Well, why don't you come and stay with Grandpa and I for a few days."

This suggestion made Katie happy. *"Yes, what a great idea. I will get ready and come right over."* It was mid-morning. Katie got up and dressed. It would be nice to visit her grandparents. She always felt like it was her second home.

"Hello, Sweetie," her grandma said cheerfully when Katie arrived a half-hour later. *"How have you been sleeping?"* she asked in her English accent. *"Any new dreams lately?"* Katie smiled. She had always been close to her grandmother and had told her all about Max.

"Yes, I slept well, but no dreams."

Grandma put her hands on Katie's face. *"I wonder when you will hear from that dear boy. I'm rather excited to see what the future holds. I feel it's going to be a good one."*

"I know. I do too, Gram." Katie smiled.

Moments later the phone in the kitchen rang.

As her grandma went to answer it, Katie helped herself to some fresh coffee and joined her grandpa in the living room. It was nice to visit her grandparents. She always looked forward to spending time with them. Katie heard her grandma laughing from the other room. What is all the excitement, Katie wondered.

"Hi Grandpa, how are you?" Katie said as she kissed him softly on his cheek. She had always been his darling.

And she adored him with her whole heart.

"*Hi, Granddaughter,*" he said, embracing her.

Her grandma came around the corner with the biggest smile on her face. "*That was your mother,*" she said to Katie.

"*I was going to call her after lunch,*" Katie said.

"*No,*" her grandma did a little dance, excitement in her voice, she could barely contain her joy. Her hand on her mouth. "*Darling, you don't understand, there was a phone call for you, from Russia!*"

Katie's mouth dropped. "*What?*" she exclaimed.

"*Oh, I am so happy!*" She stood beaming at her beloved granddaughter. "*You better go talk to her.*"

Katie nodded and rushed to the phone. "*Mom?*"

"*Hi, Katie. Guess who called you?*"

"*No! Are you serious?*" Katie said to her mother, squealing in delight. "*What did he say?*"

Her mother recapped the conversation, starting from the beginning. Max had called to say he had just returned back from France and that he had missed her dearly. Katie couldn't believe what she was hearing. To make it even better news, Max was going to call her the following week.

*

On the morning he was scheduled to phone, Katie peeked her head out of her bedroom and told her mother, "*Mom, I am going to take a bath before Max calls.*" It was still a half-hour until he was planned to call.

Less than ten minutes later, her mother called her, "*Katie, hurry. It's Max!*"

Grabbing her towel, Katie stepped out of the warm

bath. She took the call in her bedroom. *"Hello,"* Katie said.

"Hello, Katie," a male voice echoed on the other end. That sexy Russian male voice that she had missed so much was now back in her life.

"How are things in Canada, Katie?"

"Good! I just returned from Hawaii a few months ago."

"I have missed you, Katie," Max said.

"Oh, Max! I have missed you as well." She smiled, clutching the phone.

"Katie, I want to know if you want to return here to Russia?" Max went on.

"Of course I do." Katie could barely blurt out the words.

"There is an opportunity for you to work with the RCCEF at a local detskiy sad (Russian kindergarten), teaching English. Does that sound like a possibility?" Max asked.

Katie smiled inside, *"I love hearing Max speak in his accent. Kindergarten, it sounded wonderful through his mouth."*

She couldn't believe she was hearing this for real. No more dreaming. *"I would love to do that in your country. What an exciting opportunity!"*

"Okay, listen. I will call you soon, about the papers you need to return to Krasnodar, and then we will go on from there."

"Oh, Max that sounds good," Katie said, as they hung up.

"Mom!" Katie ran to her in the living room. *"You will not believe the phone call I just had. Max invited me back*

to Russia! To work in the local kindergarten."

In her heart, Katie now knew Max still loved her beyond that winter when she left him. Popping into the nearby card shop that afternoon, a card struck Katie, as she picked it up. Two birds on the front with a heart in-between them. Inside, the inscription read: *"Love knows no distance." "Perfect!"* Katie was dancing inside as she made her purchase.

"October twenty-first, 1993

Dear Max,
I saw this card today and I just had to get it.
I know you're still undecided about being a teacher, but I just couldn't resist getting it.
By the time we see each other again, you will be so proud of my progress in Russian!!!
So, you can be my personal teacher, huh? That sounds good, really good! Well, even if you don't become a teacher, I will still surprise you with other things. Just know that I will support you whatever you plan to become.
Love, Katie"

After all these months apart, far away but close in heart, she knew Max missed her with his whole being and with all his heart. That day, Katie was the happiest girl on earth. She had received a fax from Max saying that the Russian officials had given him permission to send her an invitation to return to Russia. He was also allowed to fax it to her; otherwise it could take up to four months to receive the invitation. Typical of Max, he also included a special note to Katie's family, acknowledging their previous letters and photos.

"Dear Sarah, Ellen, and Jake!
Hi there! It was so nice of you to write to me. Though you don't know me well, you wrote many warm words and I was really touched by your letters. You are a great family. I want to make you sure that I will do my best for Katie. She is a very special person and I will take all the responsibility for her in Russia. Though life here is different from life in Canada, I'll help Katie to feel at home here. Our family and my friends will be hers as well. Also, I'm sure that He, who made the relationship between Katie and me possible, will make all the best for us.
Merry Christmas and Happy New Year! Max
P.S. I have no pictures on hand at the moment. I will send you some others next time."

Chapter 16
Hope

Waiting for the weeks to pass seemed to take forever. Katie was not sure if her fate was indeed to return to Max. Then the unexpected happened.

Originally, she had hoped to return to Russia the following May. But now it was only the end of December and all of her papers were ready. The excitement she felt! She opened the letter that now allowed her to buy a plane ticket to return to the boy who touched her heart one winter ago.

A few mornings previous, she received the confirmation phone call. *"Hello, is Kate Steele there, please,"* a male voice said, on the other end of the line.

"Yes, that's me," Katie replied quietly.

"We just want to let you know that your visa for Russia is ready."

"So soon!" Katie blurted out. *"I mean, I just applied six days ago. I was told it would take at least a month to get it."*

"Well, it's here and congratulations, you're off to Russia."

"Oh! Thank you!" Katie said as she hung up.

She could barely contain her excitement. Knowing that her Russian boy was waiting for her, worlds apart.

Max called her that night. *"Katie, how's everything?"*

"*I've got all the papers!*" she said, excitement reigning in her voice.

"*Really?*" Max replied. "*When will you be here?*"

"*As soon as I can!*"

"*I can't wait to see you again,*" he whispered that night, his voice carrying across the distance between them. "*Katie, listen. I want you to come to Krasnodar as soon as possible. It's been too long without seeing you.*" Katie felt her face flush a rose-red as they said goodbye, until the next phone call.

But that week, Katie's mother, Sarah, became more and more concerned. Her daughter was once again leaving home. Of course, she should feel happy for her eldest daughter. Sarah did know that Katie was very level-headed and she saw how happy she was. Yet, Sarah needed reassurance. She wondered what Max thought the future would hold for him and Katie. He did seem quite interested in Katie, and well she was going halfway across the world to him. Did this not say something? Max must have known it meant a lot, that this lovely girl was returning to him. Sarah decided to fax Max, and share her own hopes and fears for the future. She wouldn't share the fax she sent, with Katie until she heard back from Max.

He respected Katie's mother from the start, and knew how she felt, as a worried mother.

Max responded quickly…

"Dear Sarah,

Thank you for your warm fax. I understand your concerns; I assure you Katie will be taken good care of here in Russia by me, my family and friends.

When you meet someone and feelings arise, they

may disappear. When Katie came to Krasnodar last winter, I felt she was sent by God, and my feelings for her have not changed. I still feel the same excitement each time I think of her.

No one knows what the future holds. If things between Katie and I go well, I would consider a lifetime commitment to her (marriage). She is a very special girl and I treasure her and look forward to us knowing each other better in Russia.

Yours, Max"

Sitting down in her chair in the living room, she looked out of a nearby window. A cool winter wind began and made its way into their yard. Leaves began to swirl and fly around intensely. *"My dear daughter, Katie, what does your future hold?"* she thought to herself, her eyes catching the dance of the leaves outside. She took her glasses off and smiled as she saw Katie coming around the corner of the house.

Seeing Katie walk inside she knew she had to show her daughter the fax. Opening the door, Katie called out to her mom. *"Hi! I am home from my walk; it was so refreshing."* Sarah looked up from the paper in her hand. Holding it out to Katie, the stunned look on her face said it all. *"Mom! I knew it! I had a feeling. Did you contact Max?"*

Sitting down, she began to review the conversation on the fax. Reading and smiling wider and wider, Katie leaped up as Sarah hugged her daughter proudly. Things were going to work out indeed.

Katie smiled so big; her heart beamed with Max in every inch of her being. She retired to her room for the night and before she knew it, was fast asleep dreaming of Krasnodar and the Russian boy that was waiting for her there.

*

Katie made an entry in her diary that night:

"Dear Diary,
I love Max as I did last time we met. Even after a year, he feels the same. Dear God, keep him now and always for me. I just wish I could give him a big hug and kiss. I miss him dearly.
Katie and Max xoxoxoxoxo"

Katie rolled over and peeked at her alarm clock. It was only five-thirty in the morning. Two more hours until it was time to get up. And in only two weeks she would see the boy of her dreams. Katie pulled the covers closer to her cheeks trying to fall back asleep. Eventually she sat up that morning, her heart ready for the journey ahead.

"Today I will leave my home. My life will begin with you Max." Katie smiled. *"You are waiting for me—for us. Our time. To see where things will go. Where we left off, my love."* In that moment, Russia played on her mind. Soon enough she would see Marty and Shara for a short visit and then, be on her way to Max.

She climbed out of bed and began to dress. There was a knock on her door. Sarah looked in. *"Are you ready?"* she asked her daughter.

A sudden rush of emotion rose in Katie's throat. *"What's wrong?"* Sarah smiled.

Katie wiped a tear from her eye. *"I can't believe I am really leaving."*

"You are starting a new chapter in your life, and when you are in love you do that."

Katie laughed, wiping another tear away. *"You are right. I am happy and I want to see if I really do love Max."* *"I believe you have already made that decision, a long time ago."*

The spark in her mother's eye, made Katie realize how excited she was to be moving on and back to Max.

As she finished getting dressed, Katie wondered how the year had changed them both and how the time apart would determine things to come.

She was looking forward to being on Russian soil once again.

*

Embarking on the plane, Katie was thrilled to be seeing her friends, Marty and Shara, in Switzerland for a week before she headed on to Russia. They had kept in touch with Katie after their mission to Russia. It was very exciting, knowing Max was waiting for her far across the continent. Her dreams were about to become a reality. She was going to see Max again and find out more about this wonderful boy.

It was Valentine's Day and Katie had enjoyed Switzerland thus far. *"I am so happy to be going back to Max,"* Katie said to Shara while taking another sip of her coffee in the local McDonald's.

Today was the day she would purchase her plane ticket to Moscow.

As Shara opened the door to the travel agency. Katie hoped that a flight would be available for today or tomorrow. They sat down in front of an agent. Shara spoke in French and began to translate for Katie. The earliest date to fly out of Zurich to Moscow was February twentieth, the exact day she had left Max one year before. *"How romantic,"* Katie thought to herself, as she signed the documents. It was like a silent sign, that they were meant to be together.

Max had called Katie later that night and told her he missed her so, and that he was catching the train from Krasnodar to Moscow, on Friday to meet her on Sunday. Excitement flooded Katie's heart. *"I wish we could be together for Valentine's Day, yet I feel you close to my heart,"* Max declared. *"I must go, dear Katie,"* Max whispered across the lines. *"I miss you very much and will see you on Sunday in Moscow at Sheremetyevo airport."*

"I so look forward to seeing you," Katie whispered to Max as she hung up the phone that night.

*

Max made his way down Leninsky Prospekt, where crowds had already begun to move forward toward another day. He carefully opened up a Russian-style bun, and ate it with his warm coffee. Looking at his watch, he smiled and chuckled. *"Katie must be getting ready to leave Switzerland."* In just three short hours they would meet again. Katie had become so dear to him, leaving her home to come to live in his country. *"What a girl."* But he also wondered what would happen. She was so real last winter, a wonderful young lady. He hoped and prayed they would meet again with pleasure and the year would go well as they explored Russia together.

*

Waking up in the Swiss countryside felt good. The splendour of Switzerland alone made Katie love being there even more. Beautiful greenery all around her, with cows galore!

It was the big day and Katie felt in her heart that Max was waiting and hoping to see her once again with great anticipation.

Getting up, Katie picked out her favourite blue sweater. Dark denim blue jeans and a pair of silver earrings completed her outfit. *"I am coming back to you, my prince. I am flying halfway across the world back to you."*

Shara peeked inside her room. *"Hi, honey! How do you feel?"*

"I feel a little bit nervous, yet so excited to see Max," Katie declared. The girls went to have a quick breakfast. Marty was already loading the car.

So began the two-hour drive to Zurich. Katie sat in the back seat, hopeful, but starting to feel anxious. *"How would they be together? Would it feel as though they were a couple or only friends?"*

Light snow began to fall, and her whole body tingled as she knew she would see Max soon. Katie took out his photograph once more. The recent one he had sent to her in Canada.

"Please call us as soon as you can," Shara said, looking at Katie and smiling in the car mirror.

"Yes, Katie, we will be waiting to hear how the reunion went," Marty said, half-smiling and half-laughing. Katie felt her face turn a deep shade of red. Her heart fluttered.

Once inside the airport, Katie checked in her luggage. *"Bye, honey. God bless you,"* Shara whispered, hugging her friend goodbye. Katie felt her eyes well up with tears. She hugged Marty goodbye and was off to the boarding gate.

On board the plane, Katie found her seat and sat by the window. An older couple was seated beside her and they quickly introduced themselves. After take-off, Katie heard them speak in Russian.

"Is it your first time to Russia?" the woman asked Katie in broken English.

"No, it is my second time. I have a friend there."

"I see." The woman returned Katie's smile. *"Maybe he is a special friend?"* The Russian woman laughed.

Katie felt a rosy blush spread across her face. *"Yes, actually, he is very special."* Her voice cracked a little, knowing she was en route to Max.

"Katie, did you know on this Wednesday in Russia, we have a day called Men's Day?" the lady said softly.

"You do?" Katie paid close attention.

"Yes, and if you give your special friend something, he would be really impressed with you."

Katie smiled at the Russian woman. *"Thank you. I will keep that in mind." "Well, I am giving him my whole heart, I think Max already knows this."* Katie smirked to herself, glancing out the window.

Tracing her finger over the airplane window, she gasped, feeling the coldness penetrate her skin, and then Katie remembered ... It was almost like she had never even left Russia, or Max. And yet her heart was still the same, unchanged. Full of love and anticipation of what was to come.

As they prepared for landing, Katie looked through the misty window at the runway, the Russian land appeared before her eyes. Her heart warmed just as when she had left last winter. Now she would finally be back in the country and culture she loved so much, back to the one boy she had left but never truly forgot.

Before she knew it, Katie was once again passing through Russian customs. Passport in hand, she entered the corridor. Many Russian people were pushing their way through. She felt like she was the only one who was not Russian. She sighed. The passport guard stared at Katie. He was older than her, this time. His cold look gave Katie shivers. Speaking in Russian, he demanded her passport. Those were the only words she understood. Waving his hand at her, to indicate she could head through the gates now. Katie knew she had passed this test at least and was one step closer to reaching her destination.

The bags came down the chute onto the carousel fast and Katie stood looking for her grey luggage.

"Hello!" a woman's voice said. It came from behind her. Katie spun around and saw the Russian couple she had encountered on the plane.

"I can get you a cart," her husband offered to Katie. He came back with one even faster than Katie could answer.

"Thank you." Katie smiled. Piling her luggage on the cart, she left the couple with a friendly wave. Very glad to encounter Russian hospitality once again.

Pushing the cart, while trying to steady her suitcase, Katie saw that the line through customs was not very long. Her eyes widened as she spotted Max, standing to the other side. At that moment, her heart did a flip-flop. It didn't seem real. It felt like she was still dreaming. He did not see Katie, only she could see him. His eyes darted around, looking for her, searching for her.

Katie stepped back and stared at Max, feeling a little shy. *"He looked as handsome as ever!"* There was no turning back now.

In her heart Katie held no doubts. She just wanted to finally reach him and look into his eyes once again after so long. Katie knew she would be seen once she reached the last stop after her visa was finished being stamped. Katie handed her papers to the lady at the final customs gate.

Max caught a small glimpse of Katie; now he had truly seen her, once again. A smile spread across his lips. One year later, the same excitement rose in his chest as he bit his lip down. *"My sweet girl has returned, and to me alone."*

Passing the hordes of people, Max came toward Katie, and found his Canadian beauty, and lovingly embraced her in the middle of the terminal. *"Max,"* she whispered.

Pulling back, he looked at Katie. *"How was your trip? Come, let me help you with your bags."*

They began to walk past the crowds of people. She tried to glance at him out of the corner of her eye. Shyness overcame her, yet her heart was full now, and safe with Max. *"My dream has finally come true. I am here once again, back with my Max."*

An older gentleman walked past Max on his left side. *"Hello, Katie. I am Pavel."* He came up to her, his grin wide and proud.

Pavel was a pen pal of Sarah. She had made the connection through her church. Pavel had offered to let Katie and Max stay with his family on the night of her arrival. It gave Sarah great comfort, to know someone she knew, was in Russia, for Katie.

Katie, had reluctantly agreed to stay with Pavel's family, but knew it was, peace of mind for her mother.

"Hi," Katie offered. They began to walk outside into the frosty air.

"We will take a trolley to Pavel's home. It is not far from here," Max said.

"That sounds good." Katie stood by Max outside while they waited for the trolley bus. He placed his arm gently around her. Moscow hadn't changed a bit. Many people flooded in and out of the airport. The ground was snow-covered, so crisp and fresh. Katie smiled.

The night air felt cold and bleak. Usual Moscow winter weather, so she should not be surprised. Katie was glad she would be in a warm place very soon. The trolley arrived quickly.

"Please," Max said, taking her hand. He helped her up the steps. Their eyes met. Locking his hand over hers, Max squeezed it and Katie climbed up into her seat. At the next stop, the couple stood and allowed older people to use their seats.

The trio went to the nearby corner of the bus, and Katie felt herself back in the culture once again, sensing the feelings around her. Her ears became tuned once again to the language and flow of all the Russian words she had learned while in Krasnodar.

"I am so happy to be back in Russia," Katie said, excitement in her voice.

"And I am so glad you are here..." Max smiled as his eyes sparkled.

"It's a wonderful place," Pavel said. *"You will see many*

great things here." Katie nodded in amazement.

Coming to a halt, an apartment building stood high before them.

"Let's go," Pavel said to Max in Russian. *"Katie, we are here. Let me help you."* Max led her gently down the steps of the trolley bus. She felt so at ease with him.

Once inside the apartment, Max and Katie were warmly greeted by Pavel's wife, Yana and son, Anton. *"Come inside. It must be cold. Pavel hurry,"* Yana offered.

"It is so nice to meet you," Katie said speaking in Russian to Yana and Anton. Looking at Max, she saw his approval. He blinked both eyes at her and in that moment she felt safe.

"Katie, your room is in here." Max motioned her to follow him and helped put her bags inside.

Katie sat down on the bed and suddenly a fluffy golden-coloured dog came running in and his excited barking startled her. *"Hi there."* She patted him softly.

A few minutes later, someone knocked. *"Come in,"* Katie said.

"I see you have met Sasha, don't worry he's friendly enough." Max chuckled. *"Here is a towel and I have drawn a bath for you,"* Max said.

Surprised, Katie replied, *"Thank you. That's so nice of you."* She smiled at him tenderly.

He smiled in return. *"Sure thing. After you take a bath, we will have a late dinner. Does that sound okay?"*

"It sounds great!" Katie screamed with excitement to herself. *"Wait until I tell my mom. He is such a gentleman. He made me a bath!"*

"This is truly a romantic country." Closing her

bedroom door, Katie saw that Max was in the dining room talking with Pavel and his family, about their church. She slipped past them and into the bathroom. Locking the door, Katie realized she was where she had only dreamed she could be, back in Russia.

On the mirror, she saw a card with her name. Removing it slowly, a smile spread across her face. Katie opened it without hesitation. *"Oh, Max."* Every word grabbed a hold of her heart in that very moment.

"Dear Katie,
I want to welcome you back to Russia, we have a whole year ahead of us. I know it's going to be the best!
Love, Max"

Katie laughed and placed the card in her robe pocket. She began to undress, slipping off her garment and looked in the mirror smiling. Her face was full of sheer happiness. She never wanted this moment to end.

"Is everything okay?" Max called out, knocking softly on the door.

"Oh, was I too loud? Yes, everything is perfect!" Katie called to him. Into the tub she went. The water felt so soothing on her legs, after flying and all the excitement that came along with it. Katie closed her eyes and remembered. *"Those three words, one year to the day, would she hear them again?"*

After a good twenty minutes of soaking, Katie knew she needed to get out of the tub to be with her hosts. Yana smiled as Katie came into the living room feeling fresh and relaxed.

Yana spoke in Russian, *"Please sit down, Katie,"* and

then another phrase Katie did not understand.

"*She said that she hoped you had a good bath,*" Max told Katie.

"*It was nice, thank you!*" Katie said to Pavel's wife.

She felt comfortable once again and saw now that a traditional Russian meal lay in front of them. "*Katie, please come sit here.*" Max motioned her beside him. "*Would you like a syrniki?*" he asked.

"*Yes, please.*" Katie smiled.

Max smirked at this girl beside him, the one he had missed dearly. "*You will like it,*" Max offered. His eyes danced in delight at the excitement of seeing Katie try the foods of the Russian culture, his culture.

"*It has cottage cheese in it,*" he went on. Katie smiled as she took a bite and let it warm her mouth and entire soul. "*You like?*" Max asked.

"*Da,*" Katie giggled. Max beamed. "*Actually, I have tried it before,*" Katie confessed.

"*Oh!*" Max laughed. "*You tricked me,*" Max declared. He let out a small laugh.

"*I would never.*" Katie winked.

He placed his hand on her leg and the feelings deep down were warranted. He knew she would fit into the culture, in due time.

Katie savoured every bite. Caviar and lots of Russian champagne flowed.

"*Katie, please do try this jam on your syrniki,*" Max said. Katie had never heard of putting jam on a pancake, but she wanted to fit into his culture and gave it a try. She noticed that Max wore her favourite snowflake sweater. It triggered a memory of their time together last winter, when she had noticed it on him before.

After dinner, Yana, Pavel and Anton dismissed themselves from the couple. *"Have a good sleep, Katie,"* Pavel told her, and in Russian, to Max, he said goodnight.

After he had closed the living room door behind him, Max motioned her to the couch. Katie felt nervous, but she did not want Max to see how she felt. *"I am so happy you're back here in Russia,"* he said in his thick Russian accent.

"Me too. I wonder what the year will bring for us?" Katie said, raising her eyebrows to Max.

When Max started to speak again, the assurance was apparent in his voice. *"I know it will be good, because last winter, when we met, I thought you were the perfect girl. I still feel the same."* He smiled and looked deep into Katie's eyes. *"I know we will get to know each other better."* Katie smiled, speechless for a moment.

"Wait a minute." Katie jumped up and went to her room, and then returned with a photo album.

"Oh! Let's see," Max said, his eyes full of love. The couple sat together. Katie had compiled many pictures of her life back in Canada and of her previous time in Krasnodar.

Leafing through the pages, Max beamed as he gently placed his arm around the girl he had missed so much. And she could tell he was glad she was back in his life once again.

They talked deep into the night. Katie did not want the conversation to end, but knew there would be many more nights like this ahead. She was with someone who loved and adored her, and now Katie was back in Russia with her prince.

Max kissed her goodnight, tenderly on the forehead.

She knew this reunion was starting out right, and the future looked bright. Katie crawled under the covers and slept soundly that night. Alone in her room, far from home.

Chapter 17
Bound by Fate

Katie rose the next morning to the sound of Max knocking gently on her bedroom door. *"Good morning,"* he said, stepping inside her room, holding Sasha who fiercely tried to escape his firm grip. Max put his head down shyly. *"I will see you at breakfast?"* He smiled sweetly. *"Come on now Sasha, let the princess rest some more."*

"I will be right there." Katie rolled over and opened her eyes wide. *"I am in Russia! I almost forgot. I am also with Max. It is not a dream anymore!"* She stretched her hands over her head, and quickly dressed for the new day ahead.

Walking into the kitchen, Katie once again had the feeling she was surrounded by the true Russian culture. In Russia, kitchens were considered the prime place for important conversations. Max and Katie sat at the table that morning, just the two of them.

"Would you like some more chai, Katie?" Max asked. He had thoughtfully prepared plates of food for them. The Russian-style bread had various meats and cheese on it. The same typical breakfast she had enjoyed at the InTourist hotel with her group last year. Katie took another bite. It was so tasty, good for her soul. The tea was sweet and warmed every part of her.

Looking out the window, Katie was touched by the view, the stunning streets of Moscow. Little snowflakes danced and swirled right before her eyes. Max looked wonderful as usual. He seemed once again, fascinated by her every move.

"*I need to drop off some papers for my boss at the Radisson Hotel,*" he told her. "*It is not far from Red Square. Then I want to take you to McDonald's for lunch and we can sightsee around Moscow for the whole day. How does that sound to you?*" Max took another sip of his tea. His eyes gently watching her.

"*It sounds like fun!*" Katie replied.

"*Oh, that reminds me. I need to make a phone call.*" Max got up and went to the living room. "*Hello, Gary?*" she heard him say. "*This is Max calling. Yes, I will be there. Is it okay if I bring my girl?*" "*So now I am his girl? Since when?*" Katie smiled.

"*Can you be ready in ten minutes?*" Max called.

"*Yes!*" Katie said. She went into her room, a spring in her walk.

A few minutes later, she returned to the hallway to put on her brown winter boots, tying them tight. Max took her navy wool coat off the hook and helped her put it on. In that moment she felt safe, protected by the one who loved her.

Stepping outside, Katie felt a slight chill as the winter wind caressed her cheek. Katie remembered how bitterly cold the Russian winter was from the year before. She looked up at Max, who was looking at her intensely. He took Katie's hand in his own. "*I am so glad you have returned to my country.*" His eyes gazed into hers, lovingly.

"I am so happy to be back," Katie said, as she smiled and looked deep into his eyes. Her heart warmed. She was right beside him, just as she had dreamed.

The couple approached the trolley stop. When it arrived, Max helped Katie up the steps with his black glove shielding her. As she made her way onboard, she was greeted by the Russian language all around her once again. *"Thank you,"* Katie said to him, as they took a place by a window and began their journey to downtown Moscow.

Katie was in awe as she saw the various buildings pass. It was only her first full day of being back in Russia, yet she already felt at home in the culture that had so captivated her the year before. As she listened to the voices around her, the words were becoming familiar and she knew she would be speaking more Russian soon enough.

Katie felt her heart turn as the vivid memory of the train station in Krasnodar flashed before her eyes. That was when Max had first told her he loved her! And now here she was with him. She hoped his heart still felt the same, as Katie knew hers did. She had never felt happier. *"I am sure Max feels the same spark,"* she thought, quietly looking out the window.

"Come with me." Max winked as he gently took her hand. Fresh white snow dusted the winter wonderland of Red Square. She smiled, looking around at the Russian people walking to their destinations. Katie stared at the red ruby star atop the Kremlin, as the sun struck over buildings near and far.

Katie realized they had walked quite far and were heading toward the central gateway of the Kremlin. Max placed his hand on Katie's arm and then reached down and took her hand in his. He grasped it tightly. Quite surprised,

Katie felt her cheeks warm and she turned slightly and smiled to herself. Being with the boy she loved did not seem real, she had to close her eyes and blink. Yes, here with Max and together in Moscow.

Casting her eyes to the right, Katie caught a glimpse of Spasskaya Tower; it was the main tower with a through-passage on the eastern wall of the Moscow Kremlin which overlooked Red Square. Katie remembered it from the previous winter.

The ruby red star up high, shone in all her glory, down on the fresh snow, magnificent and glistening. Giggling to herself, she felt full of pride standing by her boy. Feelings of love came suddenly all over her being. Max glanced over at this young girl staring so warmly at the nearby tower. *"Katie, you are in awe of Moscow's beauty."* Max declared.

"Yes, Da! I mean. Oh, Max! Moscow is showing me once again how captivated I am by this country... and by you." Max looked at her, a little caught off guard by her admiration towards him. He squeezed Katie's hand tighter and then guided it up to his lips and kissed it gently. Taken aback, Katie smiled as she felt the butterflies flow in her stomach. *"My Max. Here and now."* Walking with her towards St. Basil's Cathedral, the world famous landmark church in Red Square, Max placed his arm around Katie. *"Krasnaya ploshchad' v Moskve,"* Max whispered.

Happiness came over Katie as she looked up and into Max's eyes. Being there with him, felt like a dream come true.

"Here we are, this is one of the most beautiful churches you will ever see, Katie," Max offered.

Katie nodded. *"It is indeed very beautiful, Max."* Feeling shy, her voice was suddenly getting very quiet. Was it because of his presence?

"Beauty is in the eyes of the beholder," Max said. Elation raced in his voice. The winter wind began to sweep over and swirl around the couple softly. He took off his scarf and placed it around Katie's neck, for extra warmth.

Katie smiled looking up at Max. A light snow began to fall, as it blanketed them in the magic of Red Square that morning.

"Oh Max! I can feel the snowflakes tickling my face," she declared. Laughing and looking skyward, Katie could not think of any other place she would rather be.

"Would this be better?" Max whispered softly into her ear. Without any warning, he gently kissed her nose, finding his way to her sweet lips. Then, the most tender moment exploded between the couple.

Feeling Max's kisses find her at long last gave Katie a feeling like nothing she had ever known. His tender lips continued to love and kiss her on that cold winter day, in the heart of Moscow.

The warmth of this beauty surrounded his whole heart.

He smiled as her eyes shone into his, bending down slowly his lips searched again for hers as they were waiting and wanting more. Feeling Max touch her lips against his own made Katie tingle all over. *"My prince, you are amazing."*

The couple moved over to the side of Red Square as they held their lips together for a little bit longer, kissing and loving each and every moment. Newness. Tenderness for a new and forever found love. Max laughed as he kissed Katie one more time before breaking away. *"I have wanted to do that since last winter."* His eyes danced with excitement and joy.

"Oh, really, Mr. Anchov!" Katie giggled, hugging him as if she had always been his only love.

"Yes, really my sweet," Max declared, placing his palm on his chest. A few seconds later, Max patted his chest a few times and reached into his breast coat pocket. *"Oh no, the papers, we must go and then we will have lunch."* They both rushed off together, laughing.

*

Max and Katie walked down towards the metro station that would carry them back towards Pavel's apartment. There were crowds of people everywhere. Katie held Max's hand firmly, afraid she would lose him among all the people. *"That would be terrible. I would be all alone without my Max. He is my protector and my love,"* Katie thought, looking up at Max as he grinned lovingly.

The lobby inside the Moscow Metro was beautifully sculptured. Off-white marble walls surrounded the escalator that led to the platform, and historic Russian paintings decorated each wall.

The Russian metro always had been Katie's favourite. So fast and free, it moved from point to point like a release on her soul.

"Max? What is the name of this metro stop?"

He smiled at her, enjoying each and everything that was so new to her in Moscow. *"It is beautiful, isn't it? – this particular station is called Komsomolskaya,"* Max offered.

Katie looked around in awe at the beauty of the station. *"Oh Max! I love it, so breathtaking."*

"Come, Katie, we must hurry— don't worry we will return here one day," Max confirmed.

Max guided her toward the door that opened onto the metro. He bent down and kissed her forehead. Katie knew he would teach her everything about his culture. She felt so safe and cared for by Max and felt that the future would only get brighter.

*

Early the next morning, Max came running into Katie's room and roused her out of a deep sleep. *"Wake up, Katie! Wake up!"* he said, shaking her slightly. *"I've slept in and we can't miss the train to Krasnodar!"*

"Okay," Katie murmured, only half-awake and still groggy. She threw on her jeans, turtleneck, and a warm sweater.

A few minutes later, Max returned. He placed his hands on her cheek and flashed a smile she couldn't resist. *"I am sorry. You must be hungry; we have time for a quick chai and bun."*

Seeing how rushed Max was, Katie understood and followed his lead. After their quick breakfast, they said goodbye to Pavel and his family and were off to begin their journey to Krasnodar. *"I got it,"* Max said in Russian to the taxi driver as he lifted Katie's luggage and started to put it in the trunk. *"Katie, you go ahead."* He motioned her into the car. Once inside, the couple sat comfortably next to one another. Katie blushed, still unable to believe she was back with Max.

Soft snow began to plummet over the city of Moscow. Katie gazed out the window as familiar buildings passed before her. She turned to the one her heart loved. *"Max, how do you say snow in Russian?"* Feeling bashful, she knew she would learn in due time. Max looked into her eyes, his own full of love, for this beauty, that had finally returned to him.

"I am glad you asked," he said. "Sneg," Max confirmed.

Katie's eyes sparkled with delight. *"Sneg,"* she said quietly.

He placed his arm around her as she moved in a little closer. Feeling the warmth of his love, Katie felt happy. And now, this is where she was meant to be—with her love. What would their future hold? The taxi sped through Moscow to bring the young couple to the train station.

The railway station was just as Katie remembered from the previous year, except that there was no saving angel who helped with her suitcase, this time around. After they boarded the train, Katie sat down on the bottom bunk only to find her ticket had been issued for the top bunk. Climbing up, anxiety came over Katie, as she realized that the bunk location would isolate her. For the first time, they were going to be separated.

Then an older Russian gentleman entered the cabin. *"Your wife may take the bottom bunk,"* he said in Russian. *"I don't mind. Please."*

Still a bit unsure of the language, Katie took Max's hand as he helped her down and told her what the man had said. His face was bright red. Katie had never seen Max blush. She felt proud to be his wife for the moment. They sat on their separate bottom bunks, and burst out laughing together. *"Wife? She thought. Is that some kind of sign for the future?"* Daydreaming now, Katie imagined being a little Russian wife to her Max. Seeing them walk down the street adorned with wedding bands, worn on their right hand as per tradition.

A little Russian girl with blonde hair walked by just outside their cabin, as Katie was still daydreaming. She gazed lovingly at her ... *"Yes, we would have at least two children. A little girl and boy that looked like Max and spoke lively Russian too."*

When lunchtime came, Max took out the package Yana had prepared for them. A napkin fell on his lap, and he handed it to Katie. She looked at the napkin. Inscribed in English were the words: *"Bride and Groom."* There was a picture of a dove and two rings. She blushed. Max placed his hand on her cheek and gingerly touched it. Then he took a bite of the chicken, still staring at her in pure awe.

After they finished their meal, Max motioned her over, *"Come here."* Katie moved closer to him, as he made room for her. They looked out the window.

"It's such a beautiful place – all of Russia," Katie said.
"I know you love it here," Max told her.
"I do," Katie declared, smiling sweetly at him.

All of a sudden, voices could be heard outside the train compartment, shouting: *"Reba! Reba!"*

"What is that?" Katie was puzzled. *"Max?"*
He pulled Katie closer to him. *"Shush. Stay still. It's just a drunk Russian."* He's saying. *"Fish, Fish!"*

"Oh!" Katie said, as she turned to lie beside Max in his bunk and buried her face in his sweater. Max placed his arms around Katie, gently kissing her forehead.

*

Katie fell asleep for a few more hours, and when she

awoke, Max was still sleeping. She stepped out of their cabin door. A few people were in the passageway, looking out the window. The vast land of Russia was rushing by farm after farm, in all its glory.

Katie was fascinated by the train's decor. The curtains were made of a soft silky material in a deep wine colour. The floor was a wonderful design with many colourful flowers in deep green and burgundy.

Happiness filled her heart as she took in and made a mental note of everything she was seeing pass before her young eyes. The time was here, now once again, in her place, beside the one she knew she was meant to be with, the one she had so longed for, a year previously.

"Max, my dear Russian boy." Closing her eyes Katie felt full of pure joy. Quietly coming back into the compartment, she was careful not to wake Max.

Several minutes later, Max stirred; he turned over and looked across at Katie. His grin invited her over and she accepted. Tucking herself beside him on the train bunk, they held on to each other as the train continued on, now passing through the Ukraine.

*

Early in the evening, the train pulled into Krasnodar. Katie awoke to Max gently placing his hand on her cheek.

"Katie, we are here. We have arrived in Krasnodar," he declared.

The sound of Max's voice made Katie weak in the knees. She loved his accent and the way words rolled off his tongue. Slowly waking, she turned and sat up. *"How was your sleep?"* he asked.

She murmured, *"Good."* Her face gently pressed into

his neck. He smelled so amazing.

After they had left the train, the taxi dropped them off in front of an apartment building, Katie looked up as she walked toward it, feeling like she was really back in Russia. All the familiar things Katie remembered from the year before, surrounded her, even the money. Max paid the driver with, Russian roubles, smaller than Canadian dollars, more like play money. She had to remind herself it was used in real life.

"Here we are," Max declared, as he guided her into her new home. He opened the heavy, dark brown, padded door to the flat. *"I will let you unpack,"* Max said. Showing Katie to her room, *"I am going to wash up now."* With that, he left Katie to get familiar with her new surroundings.

After they were both refreshed, Max prepared dinner. Their first one together, and here in their apartment. Katie was going to enjoy being flatmates. She could not see what he was doing because his back was turned. Then he placed two blue candles on the table. *"Such a romantic,"* Katie thought to herself, as he lit the candles. He looked in the fridge and pulled out a bottle of white wine.

For dinner, they enjoyed delicious Chinese fried rice and vegetables. *"This is so good,"* Katie told him.

"Yes, it is tasty." Max smiled shyly. *"I quite like it for a change from traditional Russian food."*

Katie nodded in agreement. *"I see, Mr Anchov, you do cook as well."* She smiled shyly. Max winked at her, placing his hand on her arm, his eyes full of love.

As she savoured each and every bite of her dinner, Katie wondered what the year ahead of them would bring? Watching Max out of the corner of her eye, he seemed deep in thought, even while he enjoyed the dinner. Catching her glance, Max smiled at Katie – gently placing his hand on hers while they finished their meal, as the candles became dimmer and dimmer.

Chapter 18
Reunions

Katie spent the next half of the day alone, writing in her journal. Max had left earlier that morning to go into his work, only for a portion of the day. He thought it was best that Katie have some rest and begin to familiarize herself back into the culture.

"Katie—you will learn quickly; I just know it." He beamed that morning when she had joined him in the kitchen.

Coming around the corner, she eyed his tall, slim figure. He was preparing chai, for them. Her heart swelled with pride. *"Finally, the two of us here in Krasnodar."*

Feeling slightly shy, she knew that this was the person, God meant for her to be with—without a doubt. *"Oh Max—I am beyond excited, to learn all that I can about the Russian culture, I mean, last winter was just the beginning,"* Katie declared.

Sitting on her bed cross legged she let out a chuckle. *"Well, my boy I have come back to you, haven't I? What will this year bring for us, a new chapter perhaps?"*
Inside she was full of gratitude that afternoon. Light snow began to fall outside, dusting the streets of Krasnodar.

Soon enough, she heard Max walk in. *"Katie, let me take you to get some fresh food,"* he said. They headed downstairs together. The market below had every kind of vegetable and fruit one could imagine. Once again, Katie was fascinated by the Russian language she heard all around her.

While they were walking back to the apartment, Max spoke to her quietly, touching her hand softly. *"Katie, I need to go to a business meeting later tonight. Is there anything I can get you before I leave?"* His eyes gazed lovingly into hers.

"I am good," Katie replied quietly, disappointed that Max would not be around.

"Hey, I have some videos you can watch. How about Pretty Woman? It's in English."

He smiled. Katie laughed, feeling better. *"That sounds great!"*

Heading out to his meeting, Max looked amazing. Katie couldn't help but stare. His black pants fit well and he looked so handsome in his white shirt and tie. *"I won't be too late,"* Max said, kissing her cheek, and heading out the door. He winked and she felt her whole soul warm up once again.

After Katie locked the door, she turned around and smiled, so happy to be back with him in this place. He was even more wonderful than she ever imagined.

It was after ten p.m. when Katie heard the door unlock and Max stepped in. *"It is quite cold outside,"* he said. His sexy Russian accent ringing in her ears. Taking the grey scarf from around his neck, he closed his eyes and coughed slightly. Gently embracing Katie—the hug lasted longer than expected. *"I missed you this night."*

"I missed you, too."

Max pulled back and took both of her hands. *"I'm so happy you are here with me in Krasnodar."* Max closed his eyes slowly, as if to take in the moment and make time stand still that tender winter night.

*

On Sunday morning, Katie woke up early, anxious to see the familiar faces, she had remembered from a year earlier back at church. Krasnodar had always been in her heart, the memories suddenly flooded back as they walked in together. Max and Katie took a seat on a back row pew.

Everything inside the church was again familiar to her ears: the music, the chatter of the vivacious young people all around, and their intriguing language. It was just as she had remembered from the times before. It had not changed, only added more new faces, which Katie always welcomed.

She felt like she saw herself in some of the young people, for only last year she had been here on a mission to help the Russians. And now she was here again, with the one who had cared so much for her. She was in his culture and wanted the language to flow deep in her heart, to not only hear the words, but to speak them in a way that would make Max proud. This season, this time for them, was only the beginning. She was sure of it.

After the service, they walked to the tram stop. Max gently placed his arm around her shoulders and asked Katie, *"How did you like church?"*

"Great!" Katie declared. She felt safe with him, and curious as to what the future would bring. *"I have never felt this way about anyone."*

Max's eyes were serious and full of love. *"I feel the same warmth between us."* Katie smiled coyly.

"Let's go to somewhere you have never been."

"Oh, I love surprises," Katie said. Turning a corner, the cool winter air rushed out and encircled the young couple, as they strolled down the snow-covered street. Max took her hand and tried his best to provide shelter, until the warmth of the tram arrived.

"Here," Max said, taking off his scarf and placing it around Katie's neck.

"Thank you."

He took Katie's hands in his. The gloves Max wore covered her small hands. *"Are you warm enough?"* he asked tenderly.

Max's boyish grin drew Katie's heart in and melted her very being. *"Yes,"* she said.

After several stops, Katie and Max had reached their destination.

Walking up the stairs, the building showed signs of past Soviet style walls, reminiscent of that era. It was fascinating for her to see in real-life. Striking her attention, she felt completely back into the culture, and very much a part of it.

Katie spotted a few children on the steps sitting down. They barely wore enough clothes. Not even a winter coat. Katie was startled, as one young boy turned and looked into her eyes. *"Mozhno mne priyti?"* he cried.

"Max, what does he mean?" Katie whispered touching Max slightly on the arm.

"He is asking if he can come with you."

Katie felt her heart leap. *"A young boy of perhaps only six years old is calling out for me."* Katie tried to smile, but felt a deep sorrow inside.

Max grasped her hand and whispered, *"It's okay. Don't be frightened. These orphans live here and he wants you to take him for a meal."* Katie looked up at Max and nodded. She felt the hopelessness, as they moved on, to the restaurant upstairs.

The smell of baking was all around them. *"This is the best place to get cheese bread. It is called Dukhan family restaurant, they serve acharuli khachapuri, which is very tasty."*

"That sounds so delicious Max!" Katie giggled in delight. Excited to try something new with the boy she loved. However, she was still thinking about the orphans down below. How sad she felt for them. To be in this life and not have things, it broke her heart just thinking about them waiting outside. *"Perhaps one day, Max and I can reach out to them, even give them more than they have here in Russia?"*

The image of the sweet children left a bitter sorrow in Katie's mind. It was normal to be in these surroundings again and she would adjust, yet it was not easy. Max broke into her thoughts several moments later. *"Come, Katie."* He motioned her over behind him, where he had ordered their lunch.

Max led Katie to a table in the corner near a window and placed some chai down on the table for them. Katie took her cup and felt the Russian tea soothe her throat as she sat with her prince. *"Try some."* He motioned to Katie as he passed her a plate of the famous bread. *"This Katie, is a traditional Georgian dish of cheese-filled bread. The filling contains sulguni cheese, eggs and other ingredients."*

Katie grinned at Max. Closing her eyes, she opened her mouth, it melted on the first bite. *"Oh! This is truly delicious,"* Katie said, smiling at Max. The texture was so different, very thick bread and so scrumptious! Katie was definitely impressed by Max's secret stop. She had only been in Krasnodar two days, yet it seemed as if the Russian culture had welcomed her back so easily. Katie looked forward to what was yet to come, with her Russian prince by her side.

Chapter 19
Season of Love

Fresh snow covered the window panes outside their apartment that March afternoon. Hopefully spring would make her first appearance very soon. It was a quiet day for both of them, with Katie reading in her room, and Max grading some papers for his university students; he had been working as a tutor on the side to supplement his day job.

Max came around the corner and jumped on the bed, very close beside her. *"Hi,"* he said. Placing his arm around her, he kissed her forehead. *"When will you let me kiss you again?"* Max whispered.

Leaning back, Katie let out a laugh. *"I just got here, barely a week ago, Mister A., I mean, I find you amazing, and well ..."*

The door buzzer interrupted their conversation. Max went and answered. It was merely a postal drop off, and nothing too important. *"I will take a quick shower now, before we head out this evening."* Max grinned as he left Katie to ponder her thoughts. Katie nodded. Thinking it was a bit unusual to be taking one this late in the day. Although she did notice Max had left early in the morning to do some errands, and perhaps he just wanted to freshen up. *"I do love a clean man."* She smirked, pulling a strand of hair back behind her ear.

Katie looked at her watch and saw that it was only four in the afternoon. She had two hours before the Bible study. Preparing some nice hot tea would do them both some good. It might help break the tension that had happened minutes before. Looking out of the frosted window, she saw the icy path, where new snow had formed hours before, children playing all around, dancing and so very happy.

Max finished his shower and joined her. *"How do you like your new home?"* Max said.

"I love it, Max, and I am really looking forward to tonight," Katie told him.

As he sat at the table with Katie, she remembered that his birthday was merely two days away. *"And only two more days until you turn twenty-two!"* Katie giggled. Just for fun she continued, *"What time were you born?"*

Max closed his eyes, trying to remember. *"I was born at one forty-five in the morning."*

"Are you serious?" Katie lifted her head quickly, spilling some of her chai, it began to trickle across the table.

"Here, let me get that." Max looked at her, stunned, while taking a cloth and wiping the reddish liquid as it dripped slowly near the edge of the table.

Her eyes closed for a second and then Katie said in the quietest voice, *"I have never met anyone born at the same time as me."*

"What!" Max's mouth dropped in surprise. In that instant, their eyes met as hard rain began to beat down the window, turning the snow into a soft slush. He leaned over and cupped her face with his hands and gently their lips

met in their second kiss. The sensation was like none she had ever felt before.

Pulling away, Katie was first to speak. *"Is this a pre-birthday kiss?"* Katie giggled.

"Maybe?" Max said, as he drew his lips to hers once again. It felt so warm and perfect, a feeling like no other, so real, no more long distance between them. Max lifted Katie's chin and brought her face closer to his as he gazed into her blue eyes. *"Katie, I do love you, I always have since you left Krasnodar last winter."*

Katie's eyes sparkled with love. *"Oh, Max, I have never stopped hoping for our reunion. Yes, I do love you and truly, you never left my heart."*

Their newfound, re-discovered love was sealed then and there.

*

Less than ten minutes later, they were standing outside at the trolley bus stop, holding hands. As they waited, Max wrapped his arms around Katie and buried his face in her blonde curls. *"You smell so good,"* he cooed. His words warmed her very being. As the doors opened, like a gentleman he guided her up the steps. She walked past the people around her, and made her way to an empty seat, still thinking about the kiss.

It was a nippy Krasnodar evening as they walked towards Tanya's house, a friend of Max's from the local church. She often hosted youth gatherings, Max was curious and attended most of them, as many as he could. It was where he found and met an array of friends that he could find a common ground with and in turn it made his spirit rise, in this new and upcoming generation of former Soviet youth.

He placed his arm gently around her. Katie felt her cheeks flush, so warm she almost felt as though they could melt the snow on that bitter night. *"Wait!"* Max turned as they saw the house. *"I just want to tell you that before that kiss in Red Square, well."* His head turned away and he ran his fingers through his hair. *"I have wanted to do that for such a long time. Since you left Krasnodar last winter. I knew you were on a mission, and no romantic relationships were allowed ... I just."* Max smirked. *"I knew the day would come, when I would be able to show you how I really felt,"* Max declared, as he squeezed her hand just a little tighter.

"Really?" Katie said shyly. Her eyebrows turned up in surprise. His lips gently kissed her forehead.

When they arrived and stepped into Tanya's house, she felt real warmth, much nicer than the cold street. *"Hey, Max!"* a tall Russian boy called out as the couple moved inside.

"Katie, I want you to meet someone. Come with me." Max led the way over and past people.

"Hey, man!" The tall boy shook Max's hand.

"Katie, this is my good friend, Sasha."

"Katie! I have heard all about you." Sasha reached out his hand to her.

"I hope only good things." Katie smiled.

"Oh, da!" Sasha laughed as he winked at Max. *"How do you like Krasnodar?"* he asked Katie.

"I love it!" Turning to Max, Katie giggled and whispered in his ear... *"He has the same name as Pavel's dog."*

Max's sparkle was deep in her eyes. She could only smile. Was this real? She was back in Krasnodar and they were getting along so well. Katie felt like the happiest girl alive. Being back in the country she adored, with the boy she knew she was falling in love with, as time marched on.

The young people in their group were so happy, vibrant and full of life in Krasnodar. That was one thing that struck Katie and held her mesmerized by this wonderful culture that gathered around her and touched her heart so much. She enjoyed meeting new friends.

Tanya approached Katie and they talked about her church. *"You know Katie, if you have time to spare, we need volunteers."* Katie thanked her for the opportunity, but didn't know if it would conflict with her upcoming job at the kindergarten.

*

Katie woke up the next morning, thinking about everything that had happened the night before. Meeting Sasha was so nice and just being with Max again made her heart turn in a full circle.

There was no noise, just the quietness of the morning encasing her in bed. Katie looked at her alarm. It was almost nine. Max had left for work a few hours before; having to catch the trolley was always a challenge, so he usually left at six thirty. Katie stretched her arms and stood up. *"Now where are my tapochki? Oh, yes, there they are."*

She turned the knob on the bedroom door and went into the hallway. Yes, Max had really gone. There was no winter coat left hanging by the door, only a lingering scent of his cologne. Katie smiled to herself. He loved her. And her heart was happy indeed.

Katie decided to make herself useful and started to tidy and clean the apartment. Smirking ... *"just like a little Russian wife."*

A sheet of white paper pinned on the board by the mirror caught her eye. It read:

"Today is the last day of Russian winter and I love you!"

She was stunned. Taking his message, Katie held it in her hand. She scanned the note once again. Max loved her now and always. Katie took the tender set of words and placed it in her drawer for safekeeping.

Later that day, Max came through the door. *"Hi,"* he said and took Katie's hands, taking her in his arms and kissed her.

She beamed. *"I loved the note,"* Katie whispered. Max smiled and kissed Katie once again. Blushing, she felt in awe of her Russian boy before her, the tenderness of his touch, it felt so surreal.

"Let's stay up until one forty-five – when my birthday truly begins," Max *said.* Katie agreed. A night full of laughter and tender kisses were shared between them. At one thirty in the morning, Katie took Max's photo. They burst out in hysterics and grabbed each other's hands. He reached for the chilled bottle, that was waiting in a silver bucket on the table, full of ice. Max began to open their sweet Sovetskoye Shampanskoye.

Katie, held up her hand, *"Stop, your presents first."* Feeling a bit nervous, she looked inside the red sack of carefully wrapped gifts and nodded. One small silver bag held her gift, a soft, mint-green neck tie. *"For a special teacher,"* Katie declared. Max smiled, touching her cheek tenderly. More presents; a nice black sweater—a gift to him from her and her family. Plus, an album of Katie's photos and her life before they met.

"*I love this! It's a very cool idea! You have a wonderful mother,*" Max said.

"*I do,*" Katie replied, smiling with pride. "*We are very close.*"

Max smiled in return and said, "*Oh, look! Time to pop the champagne with my girl. It is one forty-five!*"

"*Let's do it!*" Katie declared.

Taking the wine glasses, Max opened the bottle and poured Katie a glass first. She took a sip. "*It tastes amazing,*" she told him. They toasted as Max drew his lips to hers to celebrate the first moment of his twenty-second birthday.

Chapter 20
Love Haze

The next day a new adventure awaited the young couple. Katie was so excited and yet nervous at the same time as she hung on strong to Max's arm walking outside. Everything started to look more and more familiar to her, as she smiled and beamed with joy. They waited their turn, as the line-up grew longer to take the public transit. Stepping aboard, people grumbled about the heater not working. Katie wrapped her scarf tighter around her fair face. Taking a seat, she glanced out the window, excited to be riding part-way to a new city out of Krasnodar. The exterior of the trolley was completely covered in dust, a mix of Russian words barely visible on it.

Exiting, Max led Katie to a nearby waiting bus, and they lovingly boarded hand in hand. In less than three hours they would arrive in Maikop, a city not too far from Krasnodar. It was where Max's parents lived, and Katie was anxious to meet them. She twisted and played with her hair, anticipating this meeting. Max had told her that he had long awaited this day, when he would bring home a girl to his parents.

He leaned over and kissed her forehead. This was real now. They were together and only God knew what the future held.

Looking out the window, Max spotted the entrance to

the bus station and the end of the ride." *Here we are,"* he told Katie. *"Let me help you with your bag."* Max took Katie's knapsack as he led the way off the bus. She followed Max and the excitement rushed over her. Meeting his parents for the first time was a big step in their newfound love. She had travelled far to return to Max and now she was curious about his family and where this wonderful boy had come from.

At first glance, Maikop looked a lot like Krasnodar. The greenery was much the same, and Russians, young and old, flocked to their destinations. Yet smaller, and the air seemed fresher.

Katie smiled and took in her new surroundings. Max gently clasped his hand over hers and together they walked towards the entrance of the bus depot. A slate-grey car pulled up to the curb. It was a Lada, the brand of car most people in Russia used daily. An older-looking gentleman stepped out of the car. His well-defined face showed strength. His silver hair was perfectly parted. As he approached the couple, a huge smile spread across his lips. Katie noticed his partially golden teeth.

"Papa!" Max burst out as he patted the man's arm.

"Hi!" Oleg Anchov exclaimed. He hugged Katie. She smiled warmly as she felt her cheeks blush crimson.

Max and his father began to talk in Russian and Katie tried to understand some of the words. They walked towards his car, as Max's father took Katie's knapsack and placed it inside the car as he gently opened the door for her. Katie thanked him and stepped in. Max followed and sat beside Katie, and then they were off to meet Max's mother. He put his hand on Katie's and squeezed it softly. Once again that wink from Max made her feel so warm inside as she smiled at her dear boy.

The apartment building looked similar to the ones in Krasnodar. Max took Katie's hand and led her out of the car and up into the stairwell. He opened the door to the flat. The strong smell of borsch filled the air. Katie took off her shoes and took a quick glance at herself in a nearby mirror.

Max made his way into the kitchen and then returned, leading by the hand a beautiful looking Russian lady, who was small in stature and grinning at Katie. She spoke soft Russian as she gave Katie a hug and kissed her cheek. *"Please meet my mom, Lena,"* Max offered.

"It is so nice to meet you, finally," Katie declared as Max translated.

Katie was naturally nervous, and yet now she felt more at ease, as she had finally, officially met Max's parents.

The evening was full of laughter, champagne and of course a full Russian spread of caviar, various salads and potatoes. For dessert, she was served a warm blini, one of her favourite things to eat, along with warm Russian tea. Katie felt the utmost happiness flood her heart.

Soon enough it was time to go to sleep. Katie went into the bathroom and changed into her pyjamas, joining Max a few minutes later. As they stood in the living room, Katie couldn't help but smile. Max looked so happy and content saying goodnight to his parents. After she took off her slippers, Katie waited. Max emerged from the bathroom wearing boxer shorts and a white T-shirt.

She began to fidget, modestly removing and folding her robe. Katie plopped down on her own couch, but they were still in the same room. This thought alone played on her nerves. Max turned off the light. Lying in the dark, he spoke first. *"This is the first night we are sleeping together*

... I mean in the same room, me in my bed and you in yours."

"I know, Max. It is true," Katie whispered.

"One forty-five, one forty-five," Max said in English twice, then turned over into a deep sleep, no doubt dreaming in Russian, and leaving Katie to dream in English.

"We were born at the same time; this is a sign that we are meant to be together. Our destiny. Planned." Katie thought, drifting off into her own deep sleep. She felt her very soul remarking these words over and over as she clutched her pillow a little tighter. Her dreams became assuring.

Heading into Krasnodar on the bus back from Maikop, Katie and Max were intoxicated in their own world, and love. She swept back her hair, a part that dangled over her eyes, so she could glance at her beloved man. He turned and smiled, and then took her hand and gently kissed her skin, not covered by her glove. It all seemed too good to be real, these tender moments. Katie never wanted them to end.

*

Outside the apartment and back to life in Krasnodar, several days later, they were welcoming warmer weather. The sound of the market crowd grew louder as they bartered with one another. Krasnodar was a lot busier now.

Katie peered out the window, curious, as she put on a kettle of tea that morning. The journey and visit to Maikop had been incredible. Katie loved Max's parents. They were so warm and welcoming.

She chuckled about last night and the adventure on the way home from Max's office. All the time, Max was joking and pretending they had two children. He had reminded her of that tram ride, in a note to her that morning. Sitting down at the kitchen table, Katie held her cup of tea close, to warm her up while she read it.

"(04-04-1994) Hey, kids! Again reading your mom's personal notes? Your mom went to bed yesterday v-e-e-ery late and I hope she didn't dream about the drunken man after the joy ride we had together through town. I am going to wait for your mom today around four p.m. in the office where I work."

Katie smiled, he always knew how to write her the most touching words, and it always made her heart happy.

Later that same night after their joyride through town, Katie had slipped a note into his jacket. She hoped he would find it on his tram ride to work the next morning.

"April fourth, 1994, Max, darling!
I love you with all my heart and deeply! Thank you for always being there for me. Great listener, comforter, friend, and love of my life. In all my twenty-one years, I never thought or dreamed I'd meet someone as incredible as you. Your love has made me so very happy. You have captured my heart. I love you more than words! At the moment I am feeling under the weather and really wish you were here right now.
Love, Katie"

The notes seemed to be an emotional bond between

them, as if the international parting had instilled it in them, to communicate their special feelings through words.

The fun of it all, had Katie smitten. She loved the sincere thoughts from her dear Max. Always anticipating his words, with the original pen that struck his paper. A pen he had told her, that was used for the very letters he had sent when she had left Krasnodar. Holding onto these notes forever, not only in her heart, but to save, as a part of their courting history.

"Dear Katie,
I'm sorry that you don't feel well. Even the weather has changed; it's raining outside. I miss your cooking! You're on my mind twenty-four hours a day. I love you tons and tons,
 Max"

*

Katie, started to prepare the evening meal. Out of the corner of her eye, she noticed a letter on the floor, in front the apartment door. *"Not another letter from my Max."* She beamed. Seeing that it was addressed to her, she opened it. Everything was written in Russian. *"This isn't from Max."* Max eventually arrived home, after sharing their feelings of admiration, Katie produced the mystery letter. Max read it with a look of concern on his face. *"Oh, no Katie, the kindergarten is unable to offer you a job anymore. It seems they have offered it to a local instead."*

"*I was beginning to wonder, since I hadn't heard anything from them,*" Katie mused.

"*Yes, it is dated the beginning of March. I am so sorry

for you. The mail can be so slow." Max stepped forward and hugged her.

"Not to worry," Katie replied. *"I can now spend more time with Tanya, helping at her church."*

*

The May sky had a distinct blush to it like a painting, colourful with deep pink streaks dancing across the sky of Krasnodar.

Katie made her way to the trolley stop that was not too far from their apartment. It was nearing four o'clock and she was feeling homesick, just because she had so much to tell her family. She wanted to talk about the wonderful time in Russia, of falling in love with the boy of her dreams now and always. Katie stopped her daydreaming as she was on her way to pick up Max. She reread his latest note;

"Dear Katie,
They say: anyone who has never really loved has never really lived. I love you. I have now truly lived.
Max"

Katie closed her eyes. *"Oh my dear Max! How I love you so."* Reading the note again, made Katie miss her Russian boy already. It had been a sweet set of words to wake up to that morning.

Max had changed her life in such a way that she could not imagine being without him. That weekend, they had planned on going to visit his parents, so she could say her goodbyes. She would head back home to Canada for the summer. She knew it was a good and wise decision.

"Yes, my love, Russia will be your future long-term

home. *I know you hold the culture dear to your heart and of course me. We will have the rest of our lives to be among the people you love and admire. I love you so much for that, for being in my country and making it your own. My Russian beauty, my Krasavitsa."* He reached for Katie's lips on that spring night.

Her heart beamed proudly.

"You have shown me tenderness beyond any measure."

He had written on a quick note that morning.

Krasnodar's beauty enticed Katie as it softly struck her eyes. Yes, the time of her life was now, in her present youth. The beginning of summer was showing everywhere. Colourful flowers bloomed and her heart was happy. Falling in love and discovering new things with one another, was an exciting adventure every day. Their whirlwind romance scooped her up and drove her into a haze of steady love. But soon enough, Katie would leave for Canada.

All the memories of the last four months were so vivid, etched in her memory.

"I love you as deep as anyone can love," Max told her that morning at breakfast. Katie smiled tenderly at her dream come true, Max. Who was gazing lovingly into her own eyes. They were standing close on the balcony looking out at the whole city. This young Russian boy had changed her life over the entire time she had known him. Who would have thought, who could have known, they would be here together and so much in love.

Chapter 21
Love Forever

Stepping out of tram number 756, Katie walked towards Max's office. She spotted a babushka outside gazing at her chickens. *"Zdravstvuy."* Katie smiled, trying to speak her very best Russian.

Max emerged from the building and placed his arm around her. *"Hi, sweetie."*

"Privyet," Katie said.

Max smiled. His eyes danced with excitement. *"My girl—I see you have been practicing—good job,"* Max declared.

Katie returned the smile, proud of her words. *"Da—Max."* She giggled.

He kissed her cheek. *"Moya lyubov,"* Max whispered in Russian.

"I love when you speak in your native tongue Max," Katie offered.

"Good afternoon." He placed his hand softly on the babushka's arm. She didn't understand his English, but smiled at the young couple as they went upstairs to his office.

"My sweet girl," Max murmured. *"I missed you so much today. What will I do this summer when you leave?"* He curled his lip down and frowned, taking her

in his arms. The late spring evening was all they had for the moment. Katie's eyes sparkled with delight as she welcomed his embrace.

"*I'll miss you too, but I am so looking forward to seeing my family again and also spending one last weekend with your parents, before I go,*" Katie said.

"*Yes, me too.*" Max winked. They said goodbye to the staff and headed down the street.

"*I can't believe I am actually leaving next week,*" Katie told him.

He turned to her. "*I am going to be sad when your gone.*" Max took her hand and nibbled it softly. "*My beauty girl,*" he whispered.

Max hailed a cab as the sun was now setting. Darkness would blanket Krasnodar in merely a few hours. Hopefully the trams would still be running late into the night after their cab ride. Katie thought quietly.

All of Krasnodar in her glory looked as beautiful as their love, the striking sunset cascading over and directly above them. Once settled inside the cab, Max kissed Katie softly on her lips. She felt helpless in his arms. He embraced his love and they sped off into that late May night. Driving only a few miles away, Max commanded the driver to stop. He paid for the fare and the couple stepped out.

Katie grinned at him, surprised.

"*We are at our park, my love. I just wanted to take you here tonight... it's a pretty evening and why not come to our favourite park.*" Max winked lovingly at his beauty.

"*A perfect idea, Mr. Anchov,*" Katie chuckled, kissing her Russian boy on his cheek.

Walking over the bridge towards the vast park, the

couple were entwined and soaked in their love.

"I love you," he whispered into Katie's ear. Max helped her take a seat mid-span on the bridge, overlooking the river.

"It's so warm this evening," Katie said as she flung her arms around Max.

"Let's go on the Ferris wheel," he suggested. They clasped hands and walked to the first ride they had taken months before, only a little bit colder.

"I wonder if the same lady will be there?" Katie said.

"Perhaps." Max placed his arm around her waist with his black knapsack settled over his back. He paid their fare and took a seat. The Ferris wheel began to sweep them up and away, colourful streamers dangling from the seats. Lively Russian music was playing as the riders gazed out into the spring night. *"We are almost at the top,"* he told Katie. *"Come here, closer to me."* Max held out his hand to her.

She looked at him and felt a bit puzzled, wanting to see the beautiful view from her side, but complied and slid next to him.

He paused and looked straight at her and his emerald green eyes took her breath away. In them, she saw her future.

"Will you be my wife?" Max asked. Holding her hand tenderly. Love reigned in his eyes.

Taken by complete surprise and overwhelmed, Katie stared at him and felt a cloud of deep love engulf the two. Those magic words had indeed caught Katie off guard.

"Oh, yes, yes! I will," Katie responded, happiness flooded her eyes.

Max pulled her toward him as Katie felt his tender

touch and the warm breeze encompass them. Max placed his lips softly on hers as the night swept them into a soft love haze. Kissing the love of his life felt incredible.

The sunset gave way and streamed onto a lit golden ring, one that Max had taken from his pocket. He gently placed it on Katie's finger. The six diamonds, glistening with brilliance as Katie's face said it all, her happiness for the moment reflected in Max's eyes. Their lips locked for the rest of the ride down.

"*Hey, you kids, time's up! Get off the ride, now!*" The babushka was not too pleased. Max and Katie were clearly lost in their own world. Annoyed, the babushka came over and yelled even louder. "*It's terrible, these kids! Get off the ride, I said!*"

"*Oh, I am so sorry,*" Max told the babushka, standing up. "*We better go,*" he said, taking Katie's hand. "*Moya malen'kaya ptichka,*" Max declared. Planting a kiss on Katie's forehead.

"*Oh Max! I love it when you speak Russian to me,*" Katie declared.

Running towards the river, they laughed at what had just happened. "*That was kind of funny. I didn't even hear her, did you?*" Katie said, still laughing.

"*No, I was too into you,*" Max said. Squeezing their hands together.

Katie batted her eyes toward Max. "*Tonight is the best night ever!*" she exclaimed.

"*I agree, my sweet!*" Max replied.

Stopping in front of an oak tree, he took out a green chequered blanket from his knapsack and placed it on the grass. "*Take a seat, sweetie.*" Max kissed Katie once again. Giving her a tall glass, he poured some of Katie's favourite champagne.

"*The kind I love!*" she laughed, tossing her head back.

"*Sovetskoye Shampanskoye.*" "*I know you too well.*" He winked, joining her on the blanket.

Max opened a small container of food, Katie smiled. "*You thought of everything this night. It's so perfect, this moment planned for us.*" Max placed a piece of cheese on fresh bread, and topped it off with caviar. "*Oh Max! My favourite --ikra!*" Katie beamed taking a bite of her beloved caviar. The beads of red melted on her tongue as she savoured every bite.

"*First, a toast, to our future and all we have to look forward to, together.*" Clink! Max looked at her as she sipped the champagne. His eyes bubbled with delight.

"*What do you think you are staring at, my prince?*" Katie smiled.

"*You are so beautiful and will soon be my wife!*" Max jumped up and embraced Katie. They fell on the blanket, as people in the park looked on with curiosity. "*Here is to my future wife and the girl I fell so madly in love with. I love you more than ever.*"

"*I love you too, baby!*" Katie told Max as she rolled onto the grass beside her.

He grabbed her hands and scooped her up, taking her gently in his arms again. "*Let's sing, now together,*" he said, his happiness clear. The couple began to sing loudly and then quietly, as the May night guided them towards the tram stop over the bridge.

Amused stares from people young and old followed Max and Katie. Yet they didn't have a care in the world. It was their engagement night and everything was perfect. Katie stared at her new ring as her prince carried her on his back toward their future.

Seeing the arriving tram. *"We had better run, honey,"* Max said as he grabbed Katie's hand, they skipped together, carrying the half-empty bottle of crisp Russian champagne. Katie loved the taste and was hoping to share some more with her Max once they returned to the apartment.

The next morning, Katie left a note lying beside Max's briefcase in the corridor.

"May Twenty-first, 1994 Dearest Max,

Love of my life. I love you so much. Every day is a new adventure for us. I was born to love you, honey. No doubt! The boy I fell in love with that winter has made me extremely happy!

You have given me much love and I never imagined how you would touch my heart in such a dramatic way.

Always remember you are on my mind and in my dreams. When I first came back to Russia, I didn't expect us to get so close, so fast, enough to love one another in such a deep way. I feel as though I've known you for years upon years. No, it's the truth. I feel happy to say we were meant to be. I will have a permanent smile on my face all summer, remembering you and all the moments we shared.

I love you for everything you are! We will have the cutest kids because their dad is the sexiest, cutest, smartest, gentlest, greatest man I know. I love you, always,
Katie"

*

Today she was leaving Russia, and the most wonderful person she had ever known. Katie didn't want to think about all the time she would be away from Max. How she would miss him, yet knew she would return to Russia very soon. Katie would pack some more things for their life together, and return at the end of that summer. *"Are you ready to go, sweetie?"* Max said.

Katie felt the tears begin to flow. He gently turned her cheek toward him. *"Just think, this summer will go so fast, and we will be together again very soon."*

"I know Max. It's just so far and so long to be apart," Katie said. He pressed his lips gently on hers.

"We had better go." Max motioned, as he took her bags to the door. Katie looked around the apartment once more. It was the place where many wonderful memories had been made over the past four months.

Max quickly hailed a taxi and helped her into it, as their plane would be taking off for St. Petersburg in a mere twenty-five minutes. *"I hope we have enough time,"* Katie whispered as the taxi pulled away. Sunlight streamed through their window, as the driver hurried for the couple.

"I can't wait to have you back in my arms, Katusha," Max murmured into Katie's ear.

She giggled. *"That sounds sweet?"* She questioned.

"It's my little nickname for you," Max offered.

"I love it, oh Max, I love you so much." She gently buried her face in the crook of his neck, knowing he felt the same way. At that moment, Katie wasn't afraid any more, of what the future would hold. She felt in her heart that everything was going to work out perfect.

"Are you okay, sweets?"

"Yes, I am ... happier than I ever dreamed possible."

"I know. Me too," Max whispered.

Over the loud speaker came a Russian voice stating the departure gate for flight 546 on Aeroflot to St. Petersburg. *"That is us, honey."* Max lifted her bag and proceeded to the entrance. *"Now remember, no laughing,"* he said.

"I will try," Katie said, grinning. How were they going to pull this off? She had Russian identification borrowed from Max's brother's wife, to get the generous Russian citizen discount on the airline's flight.

Passing the gate, Max turned and looked over his shoulder. Next in line was Katie. Looking around from side to side, she felt her nerves bundle. She just had to pull this off and then she would be home free. Walking casually up to the counter, she flashed her best smile. The official peered at her over his steel-framed glasses, as Katie felt her body twitch all over. *"Da,"* the agent nodded. He tossed the identification back at Katie. Whew!

"Oh!" Katie ran to Max. *"I did it!"* She declared. He jumped up and down with proud relief and excitement.

After they were called on board, they quickly found their seats in the back. *"Have we decided on a wedding date yet?"* Katie asked.

Max traced her knee, and softly rubbed it with his hand, his eyes full of love. *"What do you think – spring or summer of next year?"*

"I was thinking of a late spring wedding, my love. It's about a year away, so we have lots of time to plan," Katie cooed.

"That sounds good," Max agreed.

Before they knew it, the couple were already approaching for a landing in radiant St. Petersburg. It was a quick three-hour flight from Krasnodar. Gazing out the window, Katie knew this love was for real.

The golden roof domes, adorned like crowns. Katie was captivated by the splendour of the churches in St. Petersburg, they were so very beautiful during this time of year. Despite the evening hour, the sky was bright as day. Max told her it was called White Nights. Staying light all day and night, due to the geographic location. It was amazing, the colours almost blinding to the eye.

"Russia is so magical and enchanting," Katie said to her prince. Max placed her hand within his own and squeezed in admiration.

As the taxi driver came to a halt, Max paid the fare and guided Katie's arm. *"Let's go. I want to show you all that St. Petersburg is and more,"* he said.

The sun lit their way that day. Max took Katie's hand gently. *"I want to take you to a special park; you will love it."* Turning the corner, Katie could see the extravagant Ferris wheel. Colourful ribbons streamed from the silver bars, striking her eyes as the sunlight danced off the many colours.

"Oh Max! —Look at the wheel— it's breathtaking," Katie declared.

"I knew you would like it," Max offered. *"Let's take a ride."* He helped her into the seat, as tickets were collected. *"I want to take my princess to the top,"* he said to her, as the Russian sun radiated over his young face.

"Your princess wants to go on every Ferris wheel in the Russian empire, with her prince," Katie proclaimed.

That night, as Max and Katie sat in the guest room of - Hotel Okhtinskaya Victoria, he touched the cheek of his dear bride-to-be and whispered, *"I love you more than you could imagine."* Max drew his lips to Katie's. The couple fell onto the freshly scented sheets that awaited them that night.

"Look honey, eleven p.m. and outside it's still light out. *This is the white nights I spoke about, in St. Petersburg,"* he said.

"I love it," Katie said to him, looking out of the window. *"It's so magical."*

Her eyes glanced out to where people walked and then she looked over the bridge, taking in the view. Max kissed Katie's cheek. He murmured, *"You're magical, princess."* He stroked her hair. Katie wished the moment could last forever.

The next morning Katie found a note on the mirror in the bathroom. It read so tenderly;

"Dear Katie,
I love you more than you could imagine. You're the best and sweetest girl. I can't wait to marry you!
Love forever, Max"

Katie smiled as the tears ran down her cheeks now, she truly knew dreams could really come true. She wrote Max a reply as she stood in her bathrobe.

"Dearest Max,
Love of my life. I love you so much, sweetie, every day is a new adventure for us. I was born to love you, no doubt. The boy I fell in love with last winter has made me extremely happy, and you have given me much love. All my Love and much more, my Russian boy! I love you

forever, Katie"

*

After a beautiful train journey from St. Petersburg to Moscow, the couple arrived. Glad of their timing, but sad about Katie's pending departure.

"I love you," Max whispered, kissing Katie's ear.

"Oh, Max, I love you dearly," she replied. Max paid the driver and the young couple made their way into the airport.

Katie would be heading back to Canada, but first a stop in Switzerland to visit Marty and Shara.

"It's your turn now. I will talk to you after you arrive in Switzerland." He smiled as they embraced tenderly. *"I love you, sweetie."*

Katie waved and proceeded to the front booth. The cold stare she was given indicated something was wrong. *"I am sorry Miss. You may not board this plane,"* announced the official, looking at her sternly.

Fear crept over Katie as she struggled to understand why and looked back in search of Max. *"I don't understand."*

Katie felt her eyes well up, and then a young Russian man came behind her. *"Are you having some trouble Miss? Allow me,"* he said and began to talk to the officer in Russian. Katie turned and motioned for Max to wait. *"Apparently,"* the man stopped in mid-sentence as he turned to Katie. *"There is a problem with your visa."*

"Take her bags off the plane immediately." The radio was clear enough and loud enough in Russian with words Katie knew. She looked past the gate and saw Max looking

back at her with a confused gesture. Katie turned and ran towards him, as she flung her arms around him.

"*Sweetie! What is it?*" he said with a very concerned look on his face.

"*Oh, Max! They said my visa is not valid, it expired weeks ago. I am stuck here? Shara is waiting for me in Zurich.*" Hot tears began to stream down Katie's cheeks.

"*Don't worry, sweetie. I will take care of things,*" Max assured her. Katie hung onto him as he guided her to a chair nearby.

Max approached the window confidently, spoke to the official, and showed him Katie's passport. She could see the officer getting mad and waving the passport at him. "*What is going on?*" Katie thought as she sank into her seat. "*I need to go to Switzerland; I have my friends waiting. Oh, God! Please let everything be okay.*"

A few minutes later, Max came over to Katie. "*Sorry, my love. The reason, they won't let you leave Russia, is because your visa has expired ... I thought it would be fine.*" He shrugged his shoulders. "*You need a special stamp from Krasnodar, to be put into your passport that allows you to leave Russia.*"

"*Oh! No!*" Katie placed her hands over her face. "*I am sorry honey. Look, I will call Switzerland and I can fly back to Krasnodar tonight and be back on Monday,*" Max said. Katie half-smiled. Max kissed her forehead. "*I will take you back to Pavel's. I am sure they won't mind you staying for a few days.*"

*

"*Max I called you last night, but a man answered. I asked*

for you and he said nyet, then hung up," Katie shared.

"You probably rang the wrong number was all. I was there all night." Dismissed Max.

"I'm sure it was the right number? Well, not to worry, you're here now."

Even though she had been sad to leave Max several days earlier, she felt relief seeing the stamp in her passport, allowing her to leave Russia.

"I love you so much, my sweet girl," Max whispered, kissing Katie once again after a rushed weekend back to Krasnodar.

While standing in the airport terminal. Katie looked into Max's eyes. *"Max, my love, think of me lots this summer,"* Katie said, placing her hand on his cheek. The lovers kissed and away Katie went to board her plane.

Sheer happiness washed over Katie as she saw Shara waiting at the gate in Zurich, Switzerland. *"Oh!"* Shara said, hugging her friend. *"I am so glad you made it safely. Wow!"* She looked at Katie's left hand and the ring that shone so bright. *"I see you have some news."* She smiled at Katie, pointing to her ring finger. A huge smile burst across Katie's lips. Hugging Shara, she felt the confirmation that she needed. The support of her friend for her love and life to come with Max.

Chapter 22
Summer of Letters

Flying out of Zurich was a breeze, but leaving Max was not. Staring out the window, the clouds made way to a fiery red sunset, as the plane made the journey to her faraway homeland.

When she arrived in Canada, Katie spotted her mother instantly and waved to her. She made her way through the crowd. Both embraced with hugs and smiles. Sarah took her daughter's suitcase. They walked to the exit. *"Are you tired?"* her mother asked.

"I feel fine," Katie sighed. Being back at home, she felt at ease and yet very far from Max.

The next morning Katie woke up and saw a fax that her mom had dropped off, on her bedside table. She smiled and jumped up in delight. *"My Max. He never fails me."* She sat back down on her bed, letting each and every word sink in.

"Tuesday fourteenth of June.
Hi, sweetie!
Hello from Moscow from the balcony of hotel "Ukraine". Yes, I am in Moscow and will stay here until Friday and I'll be here the whole two next weeks. I'm doing different things with Gary and one more guy from Switzerland. It's pretty interesting.

They pay me well and the hotel and other expenses are taken care of for me. I can go home on weekends and they pay for the plane tickets.
I like my room. You can see that Parliament building out of my window. (I think that the card I sent to your Grandma Veronica was a picture of the "Ukrainia" hotel is this a – sign?!) Oh, gosh, another sign – a second ago CNN weather forecast gave the weather for Canada! I MISS YOU SO MUCH! I wish you were right here, in the hotel with me.
Oh, yes, next week I'll be in St. Petersburg again. In general, the thing that I'm doing now is very important for me to get promoted, etc. SO, I'm serious about everything I do here. I am glad about how things are going now.
I love you and miss you. Call you soon. Yours, Max
P.S. TONS of LOVE…"

"*Awww, my Max.*" Katie closed her eyes, holding that precious fax in her hand. Grabbing her notepad, she began her reply, to the love of her life who was so very far away.

"June Fifteenth 1994 Dear Max,
Hi, babe! I miss you so much! It's not the same without you. Love you! So, tomorrow I am getting a perm! Yes, can you believe it? I am actually doing it, going to be a curly girl for you.
It's been really good at home. Everyone that I show your picture to, say to me, He's so handsome - Of course! I have the handsomest guy!
Da, da, the more I am home, the more I realize how much I truly love you. Being apart I miss you so deeply!

It's like a part of me is missing. I feel like you are the closest person to me now. I never ever felt so close like this before. You've changed my life – forever. You are perfect for me... but I am sure you already know that. It's been fun seeing all my friends. I've told them how great you are. The more I tell people about you, I realize how lucky I am to have you in my life. I will always treasure the bond between us. We are the match, honey! I thank God for giving and keeping you just for me. I am so happy our paths crossed at the right time. You are the best, awesome, greatest guy I know, love and adore. I want to give you a huge kiss now!
Love, Katie"

It seemed like these summer days were all about Max and Katie communicating by written word only. *"Strange,"* Katie thought to herself one morning. *"Usually Max loved talking, he insists that these letters will strengthen our love? I really don't understand."* Her eye brow curled up in wonder. *"Silly thought anyway,"* Katie decided.

Katie carried on and began to read her card from Max;

"June twenty-first, 1994
Hi, darling! I miss you so much more than you can even imagine. Being far away from you, I realize more and more how strongly I love you. I just cannot live without you! Katie, I LOVE YOU (I can keep writing this tirelessly, but the card is too small). I am still in Moscow. It seems as if I'm already a month out of Krasnodar, though it's only <u>eight</u> days...

Working here in Moscow is kind of boring for me. No friends around, no YOU...
Oh, yes! Pavel's wife and their son are at the apartment in Krasnodar now. I'm wondering what they are doing now? She is probably jumping on your bed and Anton is trying to break my VCR. Whatever... Last weekend Pavel drove me to the nearest subway station from his place in his car. Yes! This crazy driver gave me a real joy ride for fifteen minutes. I was surprised the way he drove and the car actually worked. But this is another free circus I hope you'll enjoy personally one day.
Love you, and miss you tons! Your forever, Max"

A month had already gone by and Katie had settled in nicely at home. *"Good morning, my dear."* Her mom poked her head inside of Katie's bedroom.

"Hi, Mom!" Katie greeted her with a sleepy smile. *"I was thinking we could have a picnic outside today – it's lovely weather for it."*

"That sounds great!" Katie replied. *"I will be out soon. I am just going to have a quick shower and put on my new sundress."*

"Sounds perfect," Sarah agreed.

A variety of meat, cheese and buns with several salads were strewn out on a red chequered tablecloth. *"Momma always knows how to take good care of me,"* Katie thought sitting down.

"Has Max asked you about having children?" Sarah asked her eldest daughter.

"Well, he did say four was a nice number." Katie

smiled.

"What about speaking Russian? Will your children learn the language?"

"Of course, Mom! Max is good that way; he would want his future kids to know and be proud of their heritage."

After a wonderful two hours of conversation, Katie decided to head inside for the day and write her latest fax to Max.

"July second, 1994. Dear Max,

Hi, babe! I miss you! Lots 'n lots. Tons and tons, eh! Do you know how much I love and adore you? Can you even imagine? Well, more than anything in this world! Each day remind yourself of this fact. I'm remembering all the interesting times we had in Krasnodar. It's the best being in love with you and being by your side! When I see you, I will be the happiest woman on earth!

You are so cute; we will have a cute little family, eh! For sure a little boy, so his dad can teach him to be nice to the girls!

It won't be long until I see you again and we can totally make up for lost time, eh!

Kisses, kisses, kisses, and more kisses! You'd better be ready because it will be the rest of my life long baby!

I wish you were here, one day someday, my Russian prince. I miss Mom and Dad too. Say hello to everyone for me!

I can't wait until you meet my family. You will love them! I miss your smile, touch, hands, and most of all your love!

which I can certainly feel across the globe.
Please come to me soon! I love you!
Love, Katie"

Not expecting a quick reply from Max, she had a surprise one afternoon before going for a walk, the phone rang.

"*Hi, Katie,*" her mother's voice echoed on the other end. "*I have a letter, here at the post office from your one and only.*"

Katie squealed in delight. "*Mom! Hurry home, oh, thank you!*" Katie could hardly wait for yet another spread of precious words from the man she loved.

A double bonus: Max enclosed some letters from his parents as well;

"*July seventh, 1994. Dear Katie,*
Thank you for the postcards from Switzerland and Canada. I am touched. All of us think about you often, look at the pictures, miss you and look for- ward to have you as our guest in Maikop.
As soon as you and Max arrive in Moscow, inform us in Maikop so we can meet you at Krasnodar airport. Katie, say the warmest "hi" from us to your family. I love you as my daughter.
Love, Oleg"

"Dear Katie,
How are you doing? Thank you for all the postcards. Max says you miss us. We miss you very much, too. Your "companion" promised that when you get back, he'll drive all of us to the Black Sea.

*We come on the weekends to visit the kids and grandkids in Krasnodar. We wish you were here. We miss you especially across the distance. We think of you often. You're a very tender person, and I think Max has to treasure your love and take care of you.
I am happy for both of you! I wish you to have a good summer. Love, Lena"*

"July fourteenth, 1994

*Dear Katie,
Hi, sweetie! I'm sorry I had to finish my conversation the other day so quickly. First I think that you need to rest more and clear your thoughts.
I don't care anymore about that stupid embassy. My family and friends made me forget about it right away.
I am not that desperate to go to the U.S. The only thing that I am sorry about in this case is that I'm not going to meet your family.
That really frustrates me. I love you the most of all in the world! I hate to be at a distance. So, you'd better be back soon. Sasha is going with me to meet you in Moscow. He will stay at some friend's place. And I have a surprise arranged for us. The two of us, I mean. I love you beyond any words.
You are the best thing that ever happened to me. The one I love more than anything else.
The one I adore and admire! I cannot think of myself without thinking about you. You are the best and I*

miss you incredibly. Say "Hi" from me to the family. Till next week. Love you tons and miss you a lot.
Max"

"July twenty-first, 1994
Dear Max,
Hi! How are you? I am good. I am getting ready to see you soon! I miss you more than ever. I think I'll probably fall in love all over again. So, are we going to go to the Black Sea with Mom and Dad? Way Cool! Night Swimming? Sure! I Love you.
Where are we going to stay in Moscow? Alone? Us? Maybe? Maybe not? Oh, Max, I miss you so much, but it won't be long till I see you! I hope you are good and not working too hard. Paka. Love me.
P.S. My grandma, Veronica, sends her love."

"July twenty-eighth, 1994
Dear Max,
Hi! I got your fax this morning. For some reason it was cut off after the last part where you said I may keep the baby pictures.
Max, there is one thing I've been wondering about. I have heard that sometimes a person will marry someone just so they can get into Canada. I really need to believe that your intentions of wanting to marry Katie are not at all for this reason.
Please don't think now that I have bad feelings towards you, because I still believe you are a genuine guy. Well, Max, I need to go and send this before the store closes.

Love, Sarah"

"July 29, 1994 - Krasnodar, one p.m.
Dear Sarah,
Hi! I got your fax this morning. It was interesting.
I'm wondering why people in the West think that the sacred dream of every Russian is to immigrate to your countries. I can understand you as well as people at the US embassy, because some Russians are immigrating to US or Canada or Australia by all means. People don't really have any opportunities here or any reasons or opportunity to stay here, so immigration is their way out. They will never have any opportunities in Russia. This should be considered as a key problem. Sarah, I want to assure you, I have reason to live in Russia.

I live without any despair. I have a very good job, nice and loving family, cool friends. I can buy the things I want. I can travel whenever I want: Europe, Asia, or Africa. (America is too scared I'm going to stay there illegally.) I'm sure I can make a good career in my company. Life here, even with all its difficulties, is fun. I told Katie we may live here for a while.

I want you to understand I don't mind living here. I just don't like the attitude that Russians are people of a second sort or people who don't respect themselves and desperately use any possibility (like business trip, marriage or anything else) to move to wonderful America (Canada, etc.) where they won't have any problems and are going to live a happy life. Being an ambitious man and facing this kind of attitude either at the embassy or anywhere else, I feel hurt. My feelings for your daughter are sincere and true. My intentions of marrying Katie never had anything to do with a desire to move to Canada. I think I gave you the answer to your question.

Four p.m. - I reread my fax and decided not to change anything in it. Please, don't take anything personally. I really want the relationship between you and me to be straight and open. Though fax is not the best way of communication, it might be better sometimes than a telephone talk. I'm looking forward to getting new faxes from you. It helps me to understand you and work to make our relationship better.

I love you and wish you to
have a nice day. Love,
Max"

"August seventh, 1994. Dear Katie,

Hi, honey, thank you for your fax. The following will probably help you understand some things. You remember we talked about where we would live and I didn't mind moving to Canada. More than ever, I took it as a bonus. I know in what country I live, and there's no necessity to remind me about it all the time. I told you that you would never have kids in Russia (hospitals and other frustrating things). I thought if my job finishes next year, we may move to Canada. Your mom and I seemed to have developed a good relationship, even though we have never met face-to-face. I felt as if we understood each other perfectly well. Once she asked if one day my brother and his family might

move to Canada so we could all be together. I thought, how thoughtful of her. I always had only the best thoughts of your mom. And then, all of a sudden, she asked me if the reason I want to marry you is to move to Canada?
I know some people do it. I know I should react in another way. It's hard and hurtful. My feelings towards you have only been sincere and genuine. My love cries out to you. But a week ago when I was at the US embassy, I saw this same kind of attitude. The officer at the US embassy treated me as if I were the last criminal in the world, who tried to escape and used the business invitation to get out of terrible Russia. He emphasized several times that only a few Russians deserve to go to America. I thought, what does he think of his America? If you were there you would feel "I'm sorry that I'm Russian."
I got back to Krasnodar still feeling bad.
Then Sarah sends her fax. It was just too much for me by that time. I was wondering why your mother asked me the question, that she knew was unpleasant for me and confusing. Now I realize Sarah really doesn't know me that well. By that time, I was mad. That fax was the reason for me writing to you, asking you to stay in Russia longer time as if to prove for people something. Stupid! Why should I prove anybody anything? I just don't like the emphasis on moving to Canada. This is probably the first thing people think about when they hear of a wedding with a Russian to a foreigner. So you for sure are moving out of the country! It doesn't matter if I like it or not, people are going to think those things about me, anyway.

Like about any Russian who marries from another culture. People around here are going to think different things.
Katusha, I wait for your arrival in Moscow. All my Love, Max xoxoxoxoxo"

"*August tenth, 1994*
Dear Max,
I need to clear up some things between us. People in the West have different ideas and visions of Russia. I had mixed feelings about sending you the fax, but what is done is done. I had a feeling you might react the way you did, so I tried to use the "right words" but knew there was really no right way to say what I did. I sensed you were hurt and angry. Max, my good feelings have not changed toward you at all. I will try to explain why I wrote the fax, and hope you understand. It started when Katie was in Russia. Someone said that maybe you and Katie are getting married to come to Canada.
I was shocked because I had never heard anything like that before. Max,
I seriously had never heard of the idea of using marriage as "a way out". My train of thinking is just not like that. I thought about this when I wrote to you. It was the hardest letter I have ever written. Will you understand where I came from as a mother? There is absolutely no one in the whole world that I want Katie to marry... only you! As I said before, I was not aware that some people do want to get out of the country, while

others are content there. For me freedom is important, and it makes me angry that people in Russia cannot come and go as they please; it does not seem fair that the government has such control over the people. Max, I know that you love your country and are content living there. If and when the time is right for you and Katie to come to "Wonderful Canada", I am sure everything will work out just fine. Finally, Max, I hope I have made some sense out of all of this and that we can pick up from where we left off. You are a good man, and I can hardly wait for you and Katie to be married. Love as always, Sarah"

Folding the paper, he placed it down and drew in a deep breath. *"Of course a mother has concerns. Why wouldn't she? I understand completely,"* Max muttered to himself under his breath. *"Katie is my love and my future; I can't let her go."* Shrugging his shoulders, he did not let his mood take over the rest of the day. *"Katie is my life now and the future ahead will tell all."*

That night Max sat down in his apartment in Krasnodar, smiling up at the photo of him and his love on the wall. It was their first picture together, when Katie had returned to Krasnodar. *"Memories, so sweet."* Max grinned.

He began to write a fresh new fax to his future bride, the one that truly loved him for who he was and always would, for this he knew.

"Dear Katie,
Thanks for both faxes and your cards! I loved them! I am so happy you'll be back soon! We can hang

out in Moscow for as long as you want. I found some nice places and I'm taking you there.
I love you. I am sorry Jessica won't come to Russia this time. Sasha is going to be crushed. Recently he sent a nice letter to Jessica's father where he guaranteed safe stay for her in Krasnodar.
I'm proud of your progress in Russian. This is another big thing I am going to fulfill for sure this time with you – I promise you will speak very good Russian in a year. I know you heard that before. But this time it's going to happen for real.
I just realized I want my kids to speak Russian as well as English :)
I love you more than ever! You are the best thing that has ever happened to me! I can't wait to kiss you, my love!
I had to stay in Moscow an extra night after my two-day business trip. When I returned to Krasnodar, I ran into Sasha and we decided to go and hang out for a few hours, had some good Russian vodka and caught up on life.
He decided to stay over and we had a lot of fun. Wish you were there. I miss you!
Katie, I know you don't like the thought of living here forever.
I hate the question that is far from being clever if I'm getting married for me to move to Canada. Could you consider the possibility of living here for several years after we get married? I just want to prove not to myself but to others, we can do it, live in Russia and not need Canada to make a home.
Remember, I LOVE YOU!
Always, your Max"

"August fifteenth, 1994. Dear Max.
Hi, sweetie, did you get my fax? I sent it two days ago. Anyway, I really need the list for the kindergarten. OK, how does August twenty-third sound at about eleven thirty in the morning? SAS number 730.
I am so happy to be with you again. I can't bear it any longer, without you! Less than two weeks left.

1. Are we going to tour Moscow for a few days? That would be nice.
2. I love you.
3. I got a letter from Jessica, her parents won't let her go back to Russia.

I expected that; I don't think we would let our eighteen-year-old daughter go across the world, would we?

4. I love you, need you! Want you now!

Only until August twenty-third, because watch out, Mr. A, I will definitely appreciate you, and make up for lost time!

5. Tell your parents when I'm coming back. I'm so glad to be back for Mom's birthday.
6. I can't wait to kiss you all over. Probably even more now.
7. After we marry, you will be late for work often, because I am gonna make you very happy! Maybe some Russian jam to go with our romantic night,

what do you say?

Could come in handy, sweetie? 😊 Happy face, I miss you, love Katie"

"August seventeenth, 1994.
Dear Katie,
Hi, sweetie!
Number 730 on SAS August twenty-third at 5:35 p.m.
Sure, I'll be at the airport! I might ask Pavel to pick us up at the airport, so we'll get a free joyride through Moscow!
On the train we got places on the bottom. (now you are my almost wife) No need to be scared – it's the best train available.

1. I can imagine perfectly well the way you felt when people tried to make you speak Russian. I know you understand a lot, you just don't have enough practice. So, the next time you will feel much better and even you are going to be the one who'll initiate speaking in Russian.
2. Sasha is depressed now. It's about Jessica and stuff. He loves her a lot. I will tell you about it in person. I feel I really need to help him. We have been spending a lot of time together.
3. I miss you. One more week. Last night I watched the goodbye party video. You look so good on it!
4. How's the fam? My mom wrote a letter to Sarah and I am sending the copy to her soon.
5. I love you!
6. I wish it was the twenty-third already! I can't

*wait to kiss you! OK. I'd better go.
Love you so much, Max"*

"August twenty-first, 1994.
Dear Katie, Hi, sweetie,
Sorry I didn't call you in time. I was late to the office and I kept getting a busy signal (Canadian time). I missed hearing your voice, of course, most of all I miss you.
You are AMAZING! I LOVE YOU SO MUCH!
Of course, bring your dress. Huge kiss for you. Listen, Katie, I am trying to figure out the plan for the rest of August for us: where to go, what to do, etc. Natasha said that the kindergarten starts working the beginning of September. Here is what I propose to do: I meet you August twenty-third. We stay in Moscow for three days, and leave on the twenty-sixth by train. For you not to be caught with a fake passport and get jailed, and suffer in Russia, for the rest of your life. We arrive in Krasnodar on the twenty-seventh. My parents will meet us for sure. Next day on Sunday, they will bring us to the Black Sea and stay there for a night. It's beautiful and I want to take my future bride there. I want to know what you think of all this. I would like you to go to the Black Sea with me for a couple of days in August while it's still warm.
I don't think that guy Zhirinovsky will come to power. I read his interview recently; he's just sick. Nobody's going to vote for him.
Do you want me to start making invitations for family and friends? For them to be able to come

to the wedding? If you do, please bring the names as well as addresses. Sometimes it takes three months to get an invitation.
I love you. Fax me soon. I love you and can't wait to see you in one day! Say hi to me from the family and a special kiss to Veronica (sweetie) from me! Miss you... Love you... Kiss you... Need you... Thinking of your soon arrival, I want to scream – Wow – seems as if I didn't see you for centuries! Wish my vocabulary was bigger to write you the way I feel now!
XOXOXO Max"

Chapter 23
Moscow Calling

Securing her last piece of luggage, Katie jumped in the taxi. Her thoughts were of her Russian boy, awaiting her arrival in Moscow. *"Dear sweet Max, the time in Canada this summer was good for me, to clear my mind, spent time with my family, and relive and miss you and our love, our forever love."* She imagined herself sharing these very words with him.

Opening her purse and reaching for the recent fax from Max, it read;

"August twenty-second, 1994 Dear Katie,
Hi, sweetie. Sasha's party was OK, was fun. I wish you were there. Andrew and Linda came. It was fun.
1. I tried to draw my ring size. If it's a problem finding a size, we may look in Moscow.
2. Listen, honey, I was reading about what happened yesterday with you and thought, it seems like we just have to come through it. Listen, darling, I found the remedy! TAKE IT EASY! THINK ABOUT IT IN A GLOBAL WAY!
Thinking of myself and my reaction to what your mom asked me I realized I was only hurt because I DID CARE what Sarah thought about me and my

feelings.
For me, this is the most important thing, when close people understand my intentions. Your family as well as mine know that we really love each other. Make sure you find the understanding among your close friends, and I don't think you need anything else. As I wrote you already, there's no point in being like able to everybody, let the opinion of other people stand. Don't be bothered. What do outsiders know about us? Nothing, so let people talk about us, judge the intentions and all that stuff. No need to get frustrated. It is hard. Just take it as it is. I'm sure the only way to show people who is right is to be a good example of a family all your life, living happily together, raising wonderful kids and keeping our love for years. One day we both will look back and realize how ridiculous and silly it was to get frustrated so badly of things we shouldn't really worry about.
I love you, the only one, forever. I love your family. My family adores you. The rest is up to us. And I know this "the rest" is going to be the most amazing and best time and experience in our lives!
Listen, honey, you may count on me and on ANY SUPPORT you need from me here. Take it for granted. Today I received another card from you and your cute baby pictures; I can't help smiling, looking at you as a kid! Our kids are going to be the best! I want next Tuesday to come sooner! Tomorrow is Saturday and if you want to fax me, go ahead. I'll be at the office anyway.
In case you won't fax and will be busy with packing – I wish you to have a nice weekend, good preparations before you leave "the nest", quiet and

relaxing time with the family. I can't wait to see you again and to make all your worries disappear. So, see you at Sheremetyevo airport on Tuesday! I love you and miss you lots, Max."

Smiling, Katie folded up the fax and knew her prince could not wait to see her and have her back in his arms once again. Thinking back on their love, Katie knew it was meant to be, and nothing would ever tear them apart. *"Oh Max, how I love and miss you so sooo much,"* she confirmed within her heart that late afternoon as the taxi sped on her journey to the airport.

Landing in Moscow over half a day later, Katie was full of the utmost joy. Heading through the gates in Sheremetyevo International airport, her love waved her over – Max.

After grabbing her passport, Katie ran to him. *"Oh, honey, I missed you!"* She placed her face in his neck, only to be showered by his kisses.

"My princess," Max murmured softly.

"He looks perfect," Katie thought. He wore a new green sweater and khaki pants. He always looked amazing to her. Once again he became the man of her dreams. Holding hands, they walked upstairs into the Moscow airport.

While waiting for her luggage, Max was unable to take his eyes off Katie. *"Yes?"* She smiled at him.

"Sweetie, I am just glad you are back here with me." He gazed lovingly at her as he planted a gentle kiss on her lips.

"Me too," Katie said, placing her hand on his cheek.

"I have a wonderful surprise." Max smiled at her. He playfully took her hand in his as they walked outside to

their arriving taxi.

"*Tell me.*" Katie giggled, grabbing his hand.

"*You will see soon enough,*" he declared.

The taxi sped into the Moscow evening and Katie felt at home once again. Oh, how she had missed Russia and all her beauty! A country that had become so near to her heart, now she was back and couldn't be happier. Stepping out of the taxi, Katie realized how much she had truly missed Max that summer apart.

Arriving near the Krasnopresnenskaya embankment, a row of apartments stood in awe of the warm summer evening. A Russian breeze cascaded across Katie's cheeks. She gazed up at the sky, that now cast an incredible design. A spectacular sunset, streaked in rouge, blanketed Moscow. Katie was taken by Russia's beauty.

Max took Katie's hand, guiding her into the building. They walked upstairs and into the hallway. Max opened the door to the apartment. "*It's beautiful.*" Her eyes lit up.

Max showed her the inside and then spun Katie around embracing her on that special night. "*I have missed you so,*" he said as he began to nuzzle Katie's neck.

The love she felt was real enough. "*I feel the same, it was so long to be away from you,*" Katie told Max.

"*We will never be apart again,*" he whispered. His eyes dancing with excitement.

That first night back, Katie was proud of what she had on. A light-blue skirt, not too short, freshly shaved legs and a white T-shirt, she was happy with herself and turned back to look out at the city of Moscow. Dazzling lights welcomed her back and in her eyes the wonder she saw warmed her heart, completely.

Placing her leg up on the low window sill, the breeze blew softly over her sun kissed cheeks, and she felt relaxed. Katie looked outside once again at the night lights, into the city of dreams.

Pouring the chai, Max stole a glance at Katie. *"I am so happy,"* he thought to himself. He was excited to have her back in his country. *"My sweet girl, my one, soon-to-be bride."* He handed her a full cup.

"Thank you," Katie said as she joined Max on the balcony.

Several hours later they were hand in hand as they walked downtown into Moscow's deserted streets. *"Where are you taking me?"* Katie asked softly, squeezing his hand, as Max ran his hands through her hair. He wanted this first night back to be just perfect.

"Well," he spoke coyly. *"Somewhere I have never taken my princess."*

"Okay." And they continued on.

"Wow! This is amazing," Katie commented as they turned the corner. *"Oh Max!"* Katie put her hands over her mouth. A restaurant greeted them – with the name above it *"Santa Fe."* It was located inside a gorgeous mansion, within walking distance of the Moskva River's edge.

"Amazing!" Katie spoke quietly.

"Mexican, I knew you would like it," Max whispered to Katie.

"I love you," she said to him as they entered the building. The wait would be over one hour. He always knew what to do. He spoke Russian to the waitress, suddenly Katie and Max quickly found their place. Even though they had to share with another couple.

The piping hot plate arrived and the two young lovers

dug in and enjoyed it while they could, for that night in Russia was still young. Tall glasses of champagne arrived as Max toasted Katie. *"Welcome back,"* he whispered softly, kissing her neck.

The other couple at their table had left; they were too into each other. Katie and Max did not even notice until the waitress appeared. *"I would like the bill please,"* he said. His eyes widened. Katie could not hear what was being said. The lively and loud music drowned out any more conversation between them.

Max turned to Katie. *"You won't believe what happened! The couple that was just here, paid for our bill too!"* With this they burst out laughing.

"That is incredible!" Katie said to him as they left the restaurant.

Taking her hand, they dashed towards Krasnopresnensky Park. *"Oh!"* Katie said, turning around. *"It's so beautiful here."* Strolling along the same paths, that were once graced by Alexander Pushkin. Max stopped suddenly, lifted her up, kissed her neck and then they embraced warmly. The love Katie felt in her heart at that moment made it all too real. *"It's such a wonderful dream. But it isn't, it is us, our romance and our new life ahead."* She was with the man she loved!

It was a wonderful summer night in Moscow; the stars were shining bright. *"You are so great,"* Max said, lifting her gently from the park bench. Walking back to the apartment, the couple found pleasure in the way the city just opened up to them, like a welcoming old friend.

"Everything was perfect," Katie thought to herself.

"Here we are," Max said, opening the door for Katie.

She cooed, *"I love this place; it has such a perfect*

view of everything."

"I missed your smile," he said, making his way to her. Placing his hands on her cheeks, Max gently found her lips. Kissing her, he felt once again a wonderful feeling in his heart, one of completeness.

"How does a glass of Russian champagne sound?" he asked Katie.

"Oh, sweetie, you always know just what I need, don't you?" He led her to the balcony in the kitchen. The sound of bubbly poured into the glasses and Katie once again, felt brought back into her second home.

"A toast to you and our upcoming nuptials!" Max said, beaming. "To the beginning of a wonderful evening, a wish that the time will go slow and our love be kept alive now and always." Their glasses touched and she knew that it was indeed a night to look forward to, hoping to take in every moment. Spending time together in Moscow for the weekend, felt so magical.

"I missed you." Katie looked at Max as he lay beside her on the plush living area rug. A pleasant breeze blew lightly through the open window; she turned as the Russian White House stared at her in full view. Max placed his hand on her cheek and turned her over to face him. "I can't even begin to tell you how long this summer felt for me, being apart made me realize how deeply I truly love you."

Suddenly there was no warning as lips touched and stayed that way as the lights of Moscow shone bright, and cars sped to their destinations. These young lovers were content, as the moon watched them sleep, they were still as Max slept and Katie dreamt.

Katie felt the tears begin as she tossed and turned in her

dreams. Rocking her in and out, she saw Max, yet he was behind some kind of dark shadow. One that Katie could not make out. In reality, Max saw that she was stressing and turned her cheek. She awoke. Reassuring her he said. *"Just think, this month will go fast and we will be married very soon."*

"I know, it's so far away," Katie whispered. He pressed his lips gently on hers as she welcomed his embrace and felt happy once again.

Laying side by side, time didn't make its presence, only togetherness.

"Sweetie, what time is it?" she asked.

"Let me take a look." He glanced over at the nearby alarm clock. *"It's five a.m.,"* he whispered. *"We had a lot of catching up to do, that's for sure."* He kissed her forehead tenderly.

"I am so happy to be back, finally in your arms... hmm, that feels so good," Katie cried out. He always knew how to please her and now it felt like she was about to let go, her whole body shook with exhilaration.

*

Max looked at her with even more love in his heart that morning. *"We had better go and start the day,"* Max offered. Taking Katie's hand with a spring in his step, he led her into the kitchen. It was the place where many wonderful memories of preparing meals together, had been made in their past. She looked at Max and still could not believe they were really together at last after all her hopes and dreams. It was all Katie wanted and more.

Chapter 24
True to You

This Canadian girl was with the one, who she never dreamed of marrying, halfway across the world.
"*I love this place; it has such a perfect view of everything.*" Max smiled. He gazed outside. His eyes captured the flowing Moskva River, which was merely a few streets away. "*How does an early breakfast sound to you, say overlooking the White House?*" he asked Katie.
"*That sounds amazing.*"
To him, she was everything. He had to stop, to smell the roses, to be so thankful about how Katie had come into his life, so unexpected, and in the perfect timing.
Katie got up and reaching for her robe, stretched taking a peek in the mirror to fix her hair a little, because she always wanted to look nice for Max, morning or night. "*This is like a perfect long dream,*" she thought to herself.
Max interrupted her thoughts. "*Breakfast is served.*" He gently placed a tray on the balcony beside them. Warm coffee was in the air and the aroma was satisfying to Katie at that moment.

*

Moving down the street, subtle signs were posted before them. Moscow was always much prettier in the summertime. Yet winter had a special meaning to Katie. Flashbacks flooded her mind, their first meeting in Krasnodar. She turned to Max. *"What is it, my love?"* Max questioned.

Katie's eyes fell into his, full of love. *"I was just remembering our first meeting, last winter."* Max squeezed her hand tighter.

"How can I forget, that winter path, where my girl was walking, our destiny was waiting—that night."

"Oh Max, I love you," Katie declared. He took her in his arms. Embracing the one he loved. Planting a kiss on her forehead, Max let the kiss linger just a little longer.

Katie was full of love in that moment and her excitement for their future grew. *"We are getting closer to the embassy?"* Katie asked Max.

"Yes, we are, honey," he replied. *"We will go to McDonald's afterward. How does that sound to you, Katusha?"*

"It sounds good."

As tired as she felt, Katie kept walking. She intended to make it through this day. *"Sweetie, you look quite tired."* He led her to a nearby bench. *"Yes, I am. Max, it's just ... why is it so complicated? This system, I mean."* Her voice trailed off as she looked into Max's intense eyes. *"I mean, we can't even get married now if we wanted to. I have to prove that I am Canadian and have never been married."* Katie's eyes were full of sadness. *"How can one understand us, until they see or go through all we have?"* Katie shook her head and placed her hands on her face.

"I know. I told you this life here in Russia is no way to live. Or raise a family for that matter." Max closed his

eyes. *"Hey, sweets. Remember, we are going to have a nice big wedding in Krasnodar."* He smiled and she began to feel the bitterness fade. Their lips met, Katie felt a sense of relief in his presence.

"There, I see the embassy." Max pointed to a slate-grey building in the distance. Ushering Katie towards the Canadian embassy his grasp became tighter on her hand. They passed the guards and went inside. Many Russian people lined the hallway, sure to be waited upon next. He took out their passports. His, the Russian symbol: vivid, red and distinct in colour. Hers blue and conservative. Certainly a contrast. *"Here is our number. We will soon be next,"* Max offered.

While waiting, Katie looked outside through the window. Two young guards stood outside the wrought-iron gate. By now, Katie was used to the stares. She smiled back knowing what the return would be. Hardness. Katie had become part of this life for now. Why bother to stop and stare.

After the embassy, they got a take-away lunch, then Max took Katie back to the apartment to pack for the long train ride back to Krasnodar. Finalizing and obtaining the required documents for their marriage at the embassy was a relief indeed.

The couple arrived at the railway station and boarded the heavily loaded train. A few hours later a conversation began that Katie thought would never seem to end. She had been looking in a magazine and mentioned to Max that someone had used another person to marry them in order to escape Russia. *"Are you serious?"* His eyes widened. *"Do you remember how much you mean to me?"*

"Yes, I do!" Katie cried. *"I never doubted your feelings for me. I just ..."* She stopped mid-sentence.

"No, don't ... just." Max turned from Katie and faced the window. *"Why does this suka betray me?"* He muttered under his breath. *"I need some fresh air Katie,"* and he moved towards the door.

"Max, please let me come." Katie's hand touched his back; he shrugged it off.

"I need some time alone. To collect my thoughts, please Katie." Max looked at her and she saw the pain that held him in that moment. Katie sat down on the window seat, as tears began to roll down her cheeks uncontrollably. *"What do you mean betray you?"* Katie queried. *"I believed that you honestly love me,"* he whispered, his voice shaken. The train moved on, speeding up faster. Summer trees passed them, beyond the window, fleeting in the daylight.

"I do love you!" Katie took Max's hand, just as fast, he tore it away from her own. *"Sweetie, please, try to understand me. I was only caught in the middle between you and my mom. Between a country that is notorious for mail order brides, and all the stuff that is filtered to the Western world."*

Katie tried to explain as she sensed his pain as a part of herself now. *"Do you believe in our love?"* Max whispered. Max raised his eyebrows as Katie felt more tears burning up in her eyes. *"Katie, listen to me, I have always felt something towards you, since that winter we met. It was pure destiny for me, for us, you know the truth. I have loved only you. I have no other words. My heart is true, and you know this."* The pain in Max's voice made Katie feel so broken for him. She loved him, and yet was surrounded by underlying misconceptions of their love.

"I love you!" Katie blurted out, throwing her arms around Max. Tears flowed freely. They stood with their arms wrapped around one another as the train moved swiftly into darkness that balmy summer night. Sitting down at a nearby window, Katie contemplated the conversation just as her tearstained cheeks dried, new tears began to form.

"Katie, look at me," Max said in a tone she had never heard before. Katie turned from the train's window. And she knew that was to be the moment of truth. *"Did you actually not believe I had love in my heart for you? Oh, the hurt ..."* Max mumbled as he turned and stared out the window. His hand brushed over his right cheek.

"Honey, I do of course believe you. I don't care about other people; I care about us. Max, please." Her voice softly cracked. *"As if that didn't hurt me, I love you and I know your intentions. It just was so unbelievable, I mean, when you were halfway around the world from me. And then ... oh, sweetie, I can't imagine how upset and hurt you must have been."*

Katie was abruptly interrupted by a shout. *"Young man, get out of your cabin right now!"* A Russian woman's voice screamed loud.

Katie began to run towards Max as he put his hand over her mouth. *"What is going on?"* He motioned for Katie to sit down. *"Oh, no!"* Katie had understood exactly. Someone had heard them speaking and knew she was not Russian.

Max stepped over to Katie, voice low. *"Honey, do you have your passport?"* Fumbling in the dark, Katie opened her fanny pack and handed her passport to Max.

"*I will be right back.*" He kissed her forehead.

"*No, please take me with you,*" Katie pleaded.

"*Katie, it's okay. I will be right outside the door.*" Max gently kissed her nose.

Katie tried to listen closely to the voices outside, and the highly animated conversation. She understood some words. "*Yes, oh yes. She was Canadian.*" Some people in the next compartment had heard her and Max arguing, and not in Russian.

The train began to slow, then with a quick jolt it stopped. "*Oh, God, please protect us,*" Katie thought to herself. Katie grew more curious now. Eventually the train began to move on her way again. "*Thank you, God,*" Katie said out loud.

"*Hi, sweetie.*" Max came back inside and closed the door.

"*What was that all about?*" Katie asked him. "*Oh, this system is insane.*"

He ran his fingers through his black hair and closed his eyes in frustration and sat down beside her. "*Yes, we were too loud. Some people heard you speaking in English and they told the train master. The soldiers came on board and demanded that we go back to Moscow and get a Ukrainian stamp, since we are passing through the Ukraine. It is so crazy! Can you imagine, Katie? My parents are waiting for us in Krasnodar right now, and we head back to Moscow?*"

"*What!*" Katie could not believe her ears. "*So are we headed there?*"

"*No, don't worry. I gave them some money.*"

"*How much?*" Katie asked Max.

"*Well, fifty American dollars.*"

"*Oh, the trouble of this.*" Katie shook her head. "*At least we got out of this mess.*"

Max clenched his jaw and closed his eyes in frustration. "*Sleep, princess. Another few hours and we will be home and settled in Krasnodar.*"

Soon it would be morning and Katie looked forward to seeing Max's parents once again. Turning over in the carriage the train made its bumpy way into the city of Krasnodar where Katie was prepared and ready to start her married life with Max.

A soft kiss was upon her cheek and Katie knew instantly who it was. "*Good morning,*" she whispered to him.

"*We are approaching Krasnodar.*" Max's eyes lit up. It was past five o'clock in the morning; Katie was rightfully tired. In her heart she felt bad for bringing up past concerns to Max. It would be talked about eventually anyway.

The voices outside were loud that morning as everyone struggled to load up and prepare to exit. Seeing the sadness in his eyes, Katie gently placed her hand on Max's arm. "*Sweetie, everything will turn out for the best, don't worry.*"

Max squeezed Katie's hand as he helped her down the stairs. "*There they are,*" Katie said to her Russian prince. His eyes sparkled with delight.

"*Katie, my girl,*" Oleg said, clasping Katie's arm. The warmth of his hug made Katie feel welcome as usual.

"*Oleg,*" Katie whispered, giving her Russian Papa a hug. "*Kak dela,*" she added in her best Russian.

Oleg answered happily and told her how he had missed her. Lena smiled and gave Katie a warm, welcoming hug. It was so good to be back. Katie took the back seat beside

Max in the Lada. Warm summer air blew through the window as they sped away to Maikop.

As they rode, Max began his story of the Ukrainian mix-up on the train. *"Yes, Katie, this is Russia,"* Lena told her.

"I have seen that first-hand," Katie replied to her future mother-in-law. The plan was that the following morning they would all head to the Black Sea for two days. Katie looked forward to this, and catching up with her new family.

Lena mentioned the sweet perfume Katie wore, when she walked into the apartment. *"I can just come here like this past summer and smell your scent, my girl,"* Lena said quietly. It was so much like Lena, beautiful and in her own special way. She cared for her as a daughter. Katie took her new tapochki out of her knapsack and was so proud to be back in the Russian culture.

"You look so irresistible," Max whispered to Katie. He wrapped his arm around her waist and nuzzled her ear.

"Oh, do I? It's too bad your parents cannot understand us," Katie teased.

"Be prepared tonight for a long, long, long kiss, princess." Max was interrupted by his mother calling from the kitchen. Katie winked as he went to see Lena. Max came back, as Katie was deciding to take a quick shower. *"My mom wants to know if you would like some of ... guess, your favourite summer soup ... okroshka?"*

"Oh, yes, I would love some, after a quick shower."

"I wish I could join you." Max smiled and winked at her.

"I bet you do," Katie said, kissing him softly on his lips.

"I will be finished soon," she promised.

The soothing spray of the hot water over Katie's body brought the biggest smile to her face. Being home in the place where she knew she belonged, and soon to become a Russian wife felt like a dream come true to this twenty-two-year-old woman.

Wrapping the towel over her head, Katie whirled into the kitchen. *"Katie, please come and join us,"* Lena said.

"Thank you," Katie declared. Taking a place at the table beside Max, she felt like she did not have a care in the world. Katie was with her love and their life together was just beginning for them. *"Oh, Lena!"* Katie whispered as her lips tasted the wonderful soup. *"You know this is my favourite summer soup."*

"Yes, my girl, I remember." She smiled patting her gently on the arm. Katie nodded, smiling at Max for his seal of approval. Her Russian was indeed getting better and he knew it.

"Now a toast," Oleg said, taking out a bottle of fine Russian vodka. *"To our future daughter-in-law, who has already become like a daughter to me."* Tears welled up in his eyes as he looked over at Katie, who by now had the same feelings for him. She was thankful for the love Max's family had shown her in the short time she had known them. They were very happy for their son. From the very start, it was her youthfulness and the joy she had brought to their son's face. He was on cloud nine since he had met Katie. He was a different boy because of her. He was in love.

That afternoon after loading up the Lada, the Anchov family was off to the Black Sea resort, happily carrying the newly-weds-to-be.

"*Katie, look!*" Max declared as he took her knapsack out of her hand. Stepping out of the car, Max guided Katie out onto the sidewalk. "*Yes, my love Max.*" Katie smiled up brightly at her fiancé. Max pointed towards the beach. It was so beautiful. The seaside. The incredible view. Russians flocked to and from the shore, as Katie kicked pebbles. Sunbathers gathered aimlessly to bask in the hot, late August sun. In a few short weeks, she would be at her very own wedding. "*It's going to be wonderful,*" Katie declared out loud. Her toes felt the soft warm sand pouring through them.

"*A seashell for your thoughts,*" Max whispered, into Katie's ear. He clasped his arms around her, surprising her. "*You smell so good. As always.*"

"*Why, thank you, Mr. Anchov.*" The young couple walked over the sand and across the pathway.

"*Let's go this way, sweetie,*" he said. Katie held on tight to his hand. Climbing up the rocks, Max took off his shirt. "*Sit down here,*" he commanded Katie. Reaching and holding on steady, Katie sat beside him.

"*This beach is stunning,*" Katie remarked.

"*You are,*" he said, cupping her face in his hands. The sounds of the sea were lost as the lovers kissed. She placed her hand on his back, moving slowly downward. Caressing him softly and tenderly, Max moaned as the love of his life guided him to passion and then a sheer explosion, in a matter of minutes.

*

Being back in Krasnodar for a few weeks, Katie had begun to feel homesick one afternoon. She decided to call home, knowing it would make her feel much better.

"Mom! Hi, it's Katie," she said in a soft voice. Her mom was so happy to hear the sound of her oldest daughter over the line. Worried about her as of late, knowing Katie had made choices that somehow she did not quite understand and maybe never would, she was chipper. On the other end, Katie detailed her upcoming wedding to Max and shared her good spirit. Her mom told her that she had received a letter out of the blue from Max's mom and it was a pleasant one.

This made Katie happy, knowing that her future husband's mom had indeed reached out and shown interest in Katie's family. Katie listened as the letter was read to her over the phone.

"Dear Sarah,
Here is Max's mom, Lena. Though we never met each other, I thought I'd write you. I wished I spoke English. I'll ask Max to translate this letter. I am so happy for Katie and Max! I love Katie and I'm sure she was sent by God to Max.
When I look at Katie and Max's pictures, tears of happiness set in my eyes. Thank you for the way you've brought Katie up. She is tender and amazing.
She is the best! Max tells me that all the time. (We miss her as a part of our family. I hope to meet you personally one day. Maybe I will speak a bit of English by that time.) My husband says "hi" to you and your family. Love, Lena"

Max had also reached out in his own way to Katie's little sister and sent a lovely letter that made her jump up and down with delight;

"Dear Ellen,
Kate and I are going to have our wedding on the last day of this year. New Year's Eve! Isn't it cool? (Well, like everything that is happening with her and me!)
I also got my hair cut. Believe me; it's much shorter than yours! Katie and my mom like me to have it this way. OK, I'm game. I'm going to take a lot of pictures of Katie and me next weekend, so we'll send some to you soon. I know we'll meet each other one day!
Anyway, keep in touch, OK? Love, Max"

*

A Russian-style wedding would soon be underway in just two weeks. Their pastor friend and his wife were being called back for some urgent missionary work, causing the wedding day to be bumped up significantly. Many things had to be taken care of before September twenty-second. It was an exciting time for the couple, the preparations just beginning.

"*Max, sweetie, tomorrow we need to take Nadia to look for her dress,*" Katie told him that morning at breakfast. The dear little girl who had touched Katie's heart last winter in Krasnodar. After Katie had returned to Max the couple had tracked little Nadia down in Krasnodar months before. Having the proud honour of being their flower girl, put a sheer spark of joy in this Russian girl's eyes. She beamed with happiness at her involvement at their upcoming nuptials.

"*Yes, of course, my love, we can do that.*" Max smiled sweetly at Katie, with his handsome grin. One that she was going to live with for the rest of her life.

Happiness glowed all around the couple as they anticipated their upcoming joining. Max closed his eyes for a longer than usual time. Katie looked at him in dismay.
"*What is it, Max?*" Katie asked, curious.

"*I don't know, Katie. I just ... Well, my thoughts are going wild with things right now; don't worry everything is good ... We will be Mr. and Mrs. soon.*" Running his hands through his jet black hair, he looked up at the kitchen ceiling and sighed.

Katie laughed inside. "*Maybe Max was getting cold feet? No, it can't be. We're on a happy cloud of love right now and nothing is going to change that for either of us.*"

"*Max, I don't understand, why can't I be Katie Anchov when we marry?*"

He looked deep into her eyes. "*Well my love, this is a part of the Russian culture. You will be Katie Anchova - such is the way when we will marry.*" Max nuzzled her neck whispering "*I know sweets, you just want to be the same, and I promise we will, when we arrive in Canada. Then you and I will have Anchov as our last name. I love you, angel face,*" Max said.

"*Oh Max!*" Katie smiled. "*I love you, even more now that our wedding date is getting closer.*"

Hustling down the street, Max and Katie made their way towards little Nadia's house, to pick up and take her to the nearest store for dress shopping. Knocking on the door, Katie saw the conditions in which this little girl lived and knew she was not among one of the fortunate ones in Russia. Her mother, young and single, had two other boys to care for. She seemed very happy that her daughter was chosen to be a little flower girl. Nadia came out of her room and ran into Katie's arms. Her bright cornflower blue eyes gazed into Katie's, and she was full of happiness. For the joy she brought to this four-year-old child was precious.

Speaking in soft Russian, Nadia beamed up at Max. He gently took her hand in his as they walked outside towards the trolley stop. Katie followed, elation burst in her heart, on that late summer day. Max once again, became a hero in her eyes.

He offered the little girl a chocolate ice cream cone down on Krasnaya street. *"Spasibo,"* she shyly whispered. Laughing in delight, he picked her up and carried her to a nearby bench. Katie smiled knowing how wonderful a father Max would be to their own children one day. Running along the streets together, the trio happily accepted the wonderful warm day, despite it being September.

In the first store, they had no luck finding a flower girl dress. The next store, however, brought them more luck than they had ever dreamed. *"Oh, Max!"* Katie squealed in delight. *"This dress is absolutely perfect for Nadia."* She beamed with approval as the dress adorned the little Russian girl. Nadia smiled sheepishly as she modelled a light gold dress with flecks of green. It was the one she really wanted, so Max and Katie agreed. Her mother had given them a certain amount of roubles to cover the cost. However, Max paid for the dress out of his own pocket, knowing that Nadia's mom had probably saved all month, for the little amount, she gave to the couple. They were happy to buy the dress for their wedding, as it was an honour they had found Nadia once again and treasured her role in the ceremony. Katie hugged Nadia, whispering in Russian how beautiful she looked. *"My sweet Russian girl,"* Katie thought. *"How I wish you could have a better life someday."* She hoped a brighter future would welcome the young girl one day and she could lift her eyes, towards a better tomorrow.

"Katie, please take Nadia's hand; we are heading into a busy part of the market. I don't want my two beauties to get lost," Max declared, his face full of joy and warmth. He certainly knew how to care for women young and old.

"Yes, Max," Katie said, taking little Nadia's hand as they headed back home for the day.

*

Running out to the place to be free, this was the dream that circled Katie's mind as she slept that night. She was in a large field in Krasnodar dancing in the daisies. Max came behind her placing his hands upon her extended belly, his eyes were so sparkly, with vivid colours of dark and light beams. She did not understand. He was laughing so hard. Max smiled and kissed her deeply. Katie woke up, startled, in a cold sweat. *"That must mean that we will have children sooner rather than later?"* She thought and then fell back into an even deeper sleep.

Over and over she counted the days ahead. She was ready to become Mrs. Anchova, officially, forever.

Turning the key in the lock to their flat that morning, Katie saw that Max was gone, the lights were dimmed. In one more day they would be married. Happily and always. Eyeing the note on the counter, Katie took it and began to read Max's last words to her as a single man;

"Katie,
I bought bananas and drinks and took Nadia with us. I will drop her off tonight to you and my parents. The snacks are for the rehearsal later at the church. And we are now standing waiting for the tram. I picked up our cake for tomorrow. Now I am headed to civil hall to bring your passport there. (No faxes today.) I will meet you and Dad at the rehearsal at four thirty. (Get my camera in my knapsack.) Love you tons and tons! After rehearsal, I'll leave with you and my dad will drop me off at Sasha's tonight. Love, Max
P. S. Am I dreaming? Or will you be my one and only forever tomorrow? Yes, my girl, my love, you will. For that I look forward to, holding you in my arms, but always in my heart."

Katie's face beamed as she knew that soon enough she would be marrying the love of her life, and she could not be happier.

Chapter 25
Love Sealed

Being late September, it was cooler than usual. Hushed voices came from the kitchen, as Katie turned over on her pillow. *"What time is it?"* From the darkness that surrounded her, she knew it was early. Turning over she was careful not to wake little Nadia. The clock read five thirty. It was so early! She lay awake, unable to sleep. *"What will our future hold?"* Katie pondered on her last morning of being single.

Today was the big day. She smiled. In six hours, Katie would be walking down the aisle, forever into Max's arms, to become his newly wedded wife. The only heaviness in her heart, was because her family and friends were back in Canada. At least she had the devotion of Max's parents. They loved her like a daughter.

The door opened slightly. Katie shut her eyes. Max walked over and gently kissed her forehead. *"Hey, you,"* she said.

Somewhat startled, Max laughed. *"So you are awake, princess?"*

"It's bad luck to see the bride before the ceremony," Katie said.

"I know. I just came to have some quick breakfast with my parents," Max said, heading out. He looked back and

mouthed:

"I love you, Katusha." He smiled gently at his bride to be.

"I love you too," Katie said, turning over and wishing it was time.

Little Nadia was still fast asleep, her hair in curlers. *"She's such an angel. I do wish she had more of a life here. Sweet little soul,"* mused Katie.

She decided it was time to get up and start the day. Wedding day. She smiled with her warm cheek pressed into the palm of her hand. Standing up she ran her fingers through her blonde hair. Gazing out the window Katie pondered. *"What will life bring us Max? Much joy and happiness I do know that."*

Her wedding dress was displayed vividly through the closet door. Nadia turned between the covers and mumbled something in Russian, probably dreaming. Yesterday, Nadia was so excited and chatting like a happy little girl, about her dress that she would be wearing. Katie smiled over at the little Russian girl now fast asleep. A true sweetheart.

Putting on her housecoat, Katie went to join Max's parents for breakfast, by now Max had left. Feeling nervous, she barely finished her bun and cheese that morning. Lena smiled at her future daughter-in-law. *"Max waits for you, dear girl."* Lena was happy that her son had indeed found the love of his life.

"Thank you, I love Max very much," Katie offered.

Around the corner Oleg came, he happily sat beside Katie. Placing his arm around her, his smile said it all. *"I proud, you joining family,"* he said in broken English. Katie smiled and felt her soul burst with joy and love in that moment. *"Now, to you and Max!"* Oleg declared.

Behind his back he was hiding two little shot glasses. He placed them firmly on the table and poured some Russian vodka that he had taken out of his jacket. Katie's eyes widened. Cheering with Oleg made her a very contented bride-to-be, on that morning. The burning sensation as the vodka slid down her throat was sure to cure any pre-wedding jitters.

*

After completing the civil ceremony at the Zags, a former Soviet legality carry-over for marriage. Max, Katie and his family then transitioned to the sanctity of religious marriage. The front of the church was surrounded by many Russian people of all ages. Ready to welcome the young couple into their new season of life.

Soon, Katie would look into Max's eyes and give herself to him. *"On this day, my hero, I will become your wife."* Katie looked up at the entrance and her life ahead, smiling. Max was just past the doors, waiting for her and longing to see her once again. This was the day they both had waited for, and one that Katie once thought would never happen, even in her wildest dreams.

The chapel door opened, Katie entered the sanctuary and after a quick search she saw Max's dad. He walked over and kissed her on the cheek. *"Hi, Oleg,"* Katie whispered.

Oleg winked at his future daughter-in-law. *"Are you ready?"* he asked Katie in Russian.

"Da," Katie replied. They linked arms and began the walk away from her single life to Max. Katie did wish her family and friends from Canada could be there at that

moment in time. Friends from the local church, and youth that knew them stood as Katie walked down the aisle, and deep inside, her excitement grew. She grinned, looking ahead at her future husband. Max looked as handsome as ever. He caught Katie's eye and smiled warmly.

Their vows were soft and tender; Max said his in Russian, and Katie said hers in English. At once they became husband and wife. Mesmerized by the gold bands that now adorned their fingers, Katie smiled proudly. As per Russian tradition, they were worn on the right hand, on the ring finger.

Katie was prepared for the whole toasting ritual. One Max had suggested beforehand. A wonderfully ornate tray was waiting in the corridor for Katie. On it, six glasses filled to the top with a clear liquid. Vodka, a good one, Stolichnaya of course. Giggling with excitement, Katie carried the tray as steady as she could. Katie knew it was the best, as her and Max had shared this brand of vodka on several occasions. *"Who shall be first?"* Katie's eye-brow curled up in delight as her eyes danced around and over the guests.

"May I?" Oleg offered. Her new father-in-law was beaming as he made his way to the tray and dropped a few rubles in Katie's hand.

"Oh, Papa!" she exclaimed. He kissed her cheek.

"Welcome to the family, sweet Katie," he whispered.

"Gorko!" Katie declared, as Oleg downed the glass, to the roar and cheer of the others. Looking at Max, he smiled lovingly at her, his mark of approval was apparent.

Max carried his new bride down the stairwell and toward a waiting car, decorated in tradition. Crossed golden rings symbolized a wedding and marriage in

Russian culture. They were greatly adorned atop of Oleg's Lada, held by a blue sash, flowing faintly in the breeze. Well-wishers gathered outside the church and cheered for the newly-weds. Pastor Andrew and his wife Linda hugged the couple. *"We are praying for you and your new life together."*

Less than one hour later family and friends gathered around the table in Max and Katie's apartment. Toasts were offered as they ate and celebrated this Russian wedding on that cool September night. The guests began leaving before nine o'clock. Katie kissed her new husband tenderly. Max whispered to her, *"You are the most beautiful bride ever."*

"I love you," Katie cooed as they fell onto the bed that had their luggage, waiting to be taken.

Just before midnight, steam rolled off the train tracks as Max wrapped his arms around his new bride; he tried his best to keep her warm. The train would be coming soon, one that would take the newly-weds to Moscow for their five-day honeymoon. Boarding the train, Max led his bride down the passage and into their compartment. Katie smiled at her new husband as he took her gently in his arms. Now it was only the two of them, love and more love, as Max kissed his bride.

Once they settled into their compartment, Max made his wife's bed nice and cosy beside him. Heading under the covers, Katie looked over at her new husband with pride. It was finally the day she had become Mrs. Anchova. How happy she was to be on her way to Moscow once again, for their honeymoon and then to begin their new life together back home later on.

"I love you, Mrs. Anchova," Max murmured to his new bride. Katie looked up in adoration. Tickling her feet

under his, he felt the touch of Katie's, he was in his happy place. Running his hands through her hair, he kissed her soft lips and placed his hand over the small of her back and pulled her closer to him. They both evolved into the pleasure of intimacy, as husband and wife.

Falling fast asleep, the couple each in their own land of dreams, Katie with hers, Max with his. A new life together had begun for both, as the pastor had said when he presented the couple to the parishioners. Beaming with joy, Max showed it on every inch of his youthful face. My bride, so beautiful, so mine.

*

Glancing at her watch, Katie turned over. *"Good morning,"* Max said, gently kissing Katie's forehead.

"I love you, Mr. Anchov," Katie whispered, kissing him in return. Max put his arms around her.

"My new wife," he whispered back as he nuzzled on Katie's ear. The couple began their morning in each other's arms, quietly enjoying each other, as the train travelled on its way to reach the capital of Russia. Katie was so excited, she had always loved Moscow. She could not wait to spend her honeymoon there with her now husband. Her Max.

Gazing out the window hours later, Katie let out a laugh full of happiness, tossing her hair back, she playfully grabbed Max's hand. *"Sweetie! We are almost in Moscow."*

"Yes, beauty, soon. I would say in about one hour. Come back to bed." He gently took his bride and fell onto the bed that had kept them warm and full of love throughout both nights.

*

Max's boss had let them stay at his private condo in Moscow as a wedding gift. It was wonderful to be there again. Max turned the key and in the couple went. To their surprise, they were greeted by a vase of flowers and a *"Happy Wedding"* card. There were also three bottles of champagne and a huge box of chocolates, including Russian caviar, all set in a wonderful wooden crate.

"Just beautiful." Katie smiled.

"It really is a nice gesture," Max said, taking Katie into the living room. *"I just can't believe that we are really married."* His eyes scanned the apartment. Looking over at the nearby window, it was as if he were in a trance.

"Why do you say that, Max?" Katie felt a little stunned.

Max stopped in his tracks. *"I—well, I mean—it is just—I am so happy, Katusha, and yet it is still so surreal; we are married now, and forever."* Taking Katie in his arms, she felt lost in his lingering kiss and forgot about his sudden dazed moment before.

The next morning of the honeymoon, Katie woke and felt Max's hand on hers and smiled. He gently kissed Katie on the forehead. Plans were made for the day to relax and walk downtown.

"Are you all warm, honey?" he asked. Katie nodded, taking Max's hand and holding it to her cheek. A first snowfall over Moscow, greeted them.

After hours out on the streets and catching a few sights, tired, the couple headed back to the apartment. *"It is too cold to be out. I would rather be with my new bride in a warm place."* Max winked at Katie. Evening fell and Katie looked out the window as the smell of warm roasted potatoes filled the air. They had decided to stay in, eat and have lots of Russian champagne that night.

"I have had the best time ever, on our honeymoon," Katie said to her husband.

"I agree," Max replied. Pouring the champagne, he seemed deep in thought, and clearly happy.

"My favourite," Katie declared. Max winked.

"I know you well." Katie smiled as she toasted with him. *"To the best-rest of our lives,"* Max said.

The honeymoon flashed by. The next morning came quickly and the bags were packed as Max and Katie prepared to catch the train back to Krasnodar that evening. Katie loved every moment with her Max and looked forward to what the future held for them, starting their lives as husband and wife. It was a dream come true for Katie.

Running to catch the train. *"Come on, let's go."* Katie motioned, as Max followed her. *"Here I am, on my honeymoon, with my hero!"* Katie kissed Max's nose, he nibbled on her ear in return, a deep love now blanketed the couple in the heart of Russia. Lifting Katie up, he spun her around, like a ballerina. Her head jolted back as she burst into hysterical laughter. *"Happy five days, Mrs. Anchova,"* Max said, helping her onto the train for their journey back to Krasnodar.

Katie was glad she fitted in, for now she was one of them, in the true sense. Her new husband was pure Russian blood, therefore she had a part of him now, since they had become one.

*

Katie stood behind Max as he opened the door to their apartment. The honeymoon had been incredible and now they were ready to begin life together. Settling into the regular routine was easy. Her work days at the kindergarten were less than anticipated. Despite this, she filled her time with learning Russian, volunteering at church and taking care of their home. She chuckled to herself, *"I'm now a little zhena."* Max had his work days quite steady. Looking forward to seeing his wife at the end of each day brought him much joy.

"*Mrs. Katie Anchova.*" His eyes twinkled as he held her in his arms most nights.

"*Max, I could not be happier,*" Katie whispered as he stroked her hair one night. Looking into her eyes, Max was intoxicated by Katie's beauty.

"*Your laugh, and smile, warm me,*" Max cooed. Katie reached for his hand and gently placed it on her cheek.

Some evenings were different. Katie would wake up with Max missing. He would be in another part of the apartment. Talking in fast Russian in a low voice. Muffled. Katie wondered and then she would fall back into a slumber. She trusted Max with all of her heart, so it was nothing to really worry about. Newly-weds. Love here and now, that was all that Katie cared about.

"Dear Katie,
Best wife in the world and best cook. This is just a note to remind you how much I LOVE YOU.
You are the one who makes me the happiest man in the universe! Being your husband, living with you, sharing good and bad things is the most exciting thing that ever happened to me. Every day with you is like a first date. I will never get enough of you!

*In my wildest dreams I never imagined I would love my wife so much. Thank you for being there for me and being my wife.
I love you, Max"*

Calling back home to Canada the next afternoon a familiar voice picked up. *"Mom! It is so great to hear your voice,"* Katie declared.

"Hi, Katie!" Her mom sounded like she missed her very much, across the distance. They chatted for close to one hour and saying goodbye was bittersweet. A few hours later Max appeared.

"Max!" Katie looked at him in shock as he was all dishevelled with a slightly swollen eye. *"Let me, please,"* Katie cried.

Max turned away from his wife. *"No, I am fine,"* he said sternly. Going into the bathroom, he was nearly gone for about twenty minutes, he came back fully clean. The bruise seemed to be a bit faded. *"My sweet, don't ask what happened or worry about me. I can take care of myself."* Katie didn't know how to react. It was almost like Max was hiding something.

"Oh stop, Kate," she thought to herself. Max sat down at the kitchen table and opened a new bottle of Russian vodka and poured as the silence grew more awkward between them.

Climbing into bed that night, Max was fast asleep. Staring at the bruise on her husband's eye, Katie touched it softly. *"I wonder what happened and why Max won't confide in me?"* She shrugged her shoulders, kissed him softly on his cheek and tucked herself under the covers for the night.

*

"*Chuda, is that you?*" Katie called the next evening. Max had told her in the morning he would be working late that day and not to expect him home at the regular time. "*Okay, I understand, Max,*" Katie said, saying goodbye to him that morning.

"*Katie, some things in this Russian life you will never understand. Please just stay innocent and sweet.*" Max closed his eyes as he kissed his love goodbye.

That evening Katie was on a little hunt. "*Come on, kitty.*" Katie's voice became quiet. "*There you are, sweetie.*" The cat was a present from Sasha. He was delighted at Katie's excitement when he gave it to her a few weeks earlier. She picked up the kitten and gave it a small cuddle against her face. Chuda jumped out of Katie's hands and into her favourite hiding place. "*What was that?*" Katie opened the curtain in their bedroom, thunder and lightning streaked across the November sky. The crackle seemed to grow louder with each shake. The night was getting darker and Katie had to get things ready. Time to prepare a late dinner for Max; he will be so tired after today. Knowing how much he loved borsch, she had practiced and had become pretty good at making it by now. It was a ten-hour workday for her husband.

Tomorrow, Max's parents would arrive for their weekend visit. Katie looked forward to seeing them, as always. Plans were to be made for the up-coming Christmas holidays.

It had only been three months since her departure, yet Canada seemed like a world away. Max had been so sweet the night before his bruised eye incident, bringing her a single red rose in honour of their two-month anniversary. In reminiscing about the gesture, Chuda jumped up on her lap. Katie brushed a piece of fluff off her furry face. Suddenly, it dawned on her that Sasha had a fresh graze on his face, the night he had given the cat to her. *"Was his injury related to Max's?"* She pondered.

Katie found a wonderful surprise, when she woke, a little under the weather that late November morning. Max had left a note on the table for her. She took a sip of her sweet chai as she began to read;

"Dear Katie – the best thing in my life,
Please stay in bed all day (tea and honey etc.). I will be home around three p.m. I love you. I will bring good medicine. This morning when I woke up, I felt overwhelmed with feelings towards you. I am so happy you became my wife, and I will always treasure this.
Love you lots and tons. Max"

One year ago, the future had been a fog of uncertainty. And now they were living a wonderful life in Krasnodar with talk of having children during the latest discussion. She beamed with pride, knowing that soon enough that would happen and a little Russian baby would be on the way. Katie dreamed of that day when she could give Max the love of a child.

Over the past month, Max showered her with the most love she had ever seen or known. She couldn't be happier. They began to talk about moving to Canada, perhaps in a couple of years, knowing that their life would hold more opportunities outside of Russia. Katie agreed knowing in her husband's heart he wanted to make life better for both of them, especially if they wanted to have children soon. She placed her trust in Max and knew he would be able to care for the both of them. *"Max's now and forever bride."* She laughed. *"What would the future hold?"* Looking at Max that morning before he left for work, she thought he seemed at peace and content with himself and life in general.

Drinking his warm chai, he smiled at his bride and held her hand at the kitchen table. *"I love you, Katie. Princess."* Max kissed her hand. Taking one last sip of his tea, Max stood up and declared that he was off to work for the day and would see her very soon.

Standing up Katie felt obligated to walk Max to the door. *"Oh stop Katie, he doesn't want to interact,"* a little voice whispered. Gently taking her in his arms, Katie felt safe once more. He bent down, a soft kiss gently crossed her nose. *"Paka,"* Katie whispered.

"I love you Katusha," Max said.

"Da, I do the same to you," she replied.

*

Red and rustic, the apartments were worn well beyond their years. The many blocks of them Katie knew like the back of her hand, for she had taken this route home, so many times. Krasnodar was beauty in itself. She loved where they lived, where they loved. Max had made their nest so cosy and loving, since the first day she had arrived a few years before. Knowing their apartment held so many memories now, like gold. Or far greater. Those would mean more to her than anything else. Katie walked up the steps into the very old building. The cracked cement and shattered steps were from past Soviet times, a shame, she thought. People spoke Russian all around Katie. The smell of freshly baked bread caught Katie's nose, stopping her at the entrance. This Russian staple had quickly become one of Katie's favourite foods. Especially since that first winter in Krasnodar two years before.

Looking down on the steps, a broken flower vase caught her eye. Then she remembered. It looked the same as the broken vase in their apartment. It stung her, and pained her to think about it. The previous night's incident had come as a complete and total shock to Katie. It was as if their love had completely changed because of one terrible night ... so unexpected.

Taking Katie's arm and holding it in a fierce grip, the heated argument had come out of nowhere. Max looked stunned. *"Oh, sweetie! Oh!"* Max's eyes widened. *"I am so sorry."* Katie marched into the kitchen and felt Max hover over her as she tried to dismiss what had happened between them. *"Katie!"* Max screamed. Staring in a trance, she could not believe this was the man she had just married.

Touching the vase of yellow roses, Katie smiled. *"I still have these, I can forget about what just happened."* Max placed his hand on her shoulder as Katie cringed. Glass began to shatter on the table as Max struck his hand faster than Katie could blink. Cursing in Russian, Max slammed his fist on the table, as the water poured out of the vase and across the table. Only fragments of the glass were left at Katie's feet. Hot tears flowed out of Katie's eyes. Max left the kitchen, and Katie sat down, trying to understand what had just happened. The shock on her face was almost as if she felt frozen. After Katie looked in the mirror, she brushed a tear from her face. She heard the blare of the TV. Max was in the living room. Katie got into her pyjamas and went to sleep alone that night.

The next morning Katie woke to hear Max fixing breakfast. Katie dressed and went into the kitchen to join him. She dreaded facing Max and hoped he would be in better spirits. *"Good morning,"* she said.

Her husband turned around. *"Oh, hi, sweets."* He placed his arms around her waist. *"I don't know what happened last night?"*

"Let's just forget it. Okay?" Katie said, sitting down. She felt numb. *"What did I just get myself into, marrying a man who now seems upset and out of place as of late?"* Sorrow passed over her face as she tried to think happy thoughts of their past together, not this present life.

"You know how much I love you, don't you?" Max said, looking into her eyes.

"Of course," Katie replied. Max gently kissed his wife and out the door he went.

Katie closed her eyes remembering that morning. *"Never mind, just forget about it,"* she thought as she approached the tram and paid for her fare. Greeting Max at his office, he seemed to be in a better mood. *"My sweet,"* he whispered into her ear. Katie looked into his eyes with question. Like a little bird, scarred by a side of him she had never seen before. Perhaps it was just a onetime thing, she thought, kissing the man she truly loved.

*

Several hours later the couple started a conversation in their kitchen that never seemed to end. *"I really don't mind living in Russia."* Katie smiled, sipping her chai.

"What!" Max's voice became louder. *"Katie, you can't be serious!"* Max declared. *"This is no place to raise kids, if you want them to have a decent future."* He turned away from her. His hands tightly clutching his mug. *"I mean—this is not the future place I want to be. Sorry, for us to be."*

"But, I really do love it here," Katie said to her husband, surprised by his mood, on the subject.

"I don't Katie—really, we will leave one day," Max declared. Standing up, Max placed his mug in the sink and headed into another room. Katie knew the conversation was over. *"What is wrong with him?"* Katie sat in disbelief as tears rolled down her face. Her heart raced faster than she could stand up.

"Why can't you stop being upset?" Katie asked Max the next morning. Max stood with his hands on his hips.

"Because, you are the only one I can take my frustrations out on, the one who actually listens to me." He stormed off to work.

Katie lay on the bed sobbing. *"We had the perfect love, what is happening to us now?"* Maybe Max would change once they moved to Canada. *"I think Canada will be better for us, Max,"* Katie told her husband that night.

He smiled. *"I know you're right. I just ... just want to do the right thing for us,"* Max offered as he gently kissed Katie.

"If only he could be like this all the time. Where is my old Max?" How could she have lost him in the wake of

their developing marriage? Sorrow came over Katie. How she wished she could rewind the clock of time. Where on earth had her Max gone, the boy she had fallen in love with all those years ago? It seemed like a long-forgotten dream, one that she so wished to rekindle in present day.

Shaking her head, she prayed to be part of that time, where Max held her and loved her in his strong Russian arms. *"I won't take any more of this mood from you Max. No way,"* Katie cried.

Max's eyes raged bright red as he stared at his bride with defiance. *"What do you mean?"* Max grabbed her arm.

"Let go of me," Katie commanded. Max turned and went into the kitchen. She heard him putting on the kettle.

As she awoke the next morning, Katie got up and listened. Yes, Max was just leaving for work. He had come in their room to get a shirt. Katie had been hurt once again, Max didn't kiss her that morning, telling her he was still mad from their intense argument the night before. After the door locked, Katie went into the bathroom. She started to feel a slight pain in her stomach. Two hours later, she and Ivan, her brother-in-law, stood in line, waiting at a dreary local hospital. Translating for the doctor, Ivan told her the results – a possible pregnancy. Elated, Katie smiled between the tears and hoped Max would be happy about this sudden news.

He smiled solicitously at Katie as they went up the elevator. *"Thanks for taking me, Ivan,"* Katie offered. Ivan smiled, knowing he had been of great help to her, on a day when she had needed it the most.

"Take care," Ivan declared.

Later that night, Max came home. Inside their kitchen he looked at Katie, then walked away. *"Ivan took me to the hospital today,"* she whispered. His response? She did not know what to expect. Deep down she hoped and prayed he would be excited at her impending news.

Max spun around. *"I am sorry, sweetie. You know I really do love you. I didn't mean for our argument to get out of hand last night ..."* He put his arms around Katie as she barely returned his embrace. Her whole body froze and she felt like there was no love left inside.

Where would she go? Where could she escape? Krasnodar was her home for now, and she had agreed to live there forever. To say she had loved and lost was correct. It felt like that anyway. They were drifting slowly apart, and Katie was not sure if Max would be coming back to who he used to be.

Chapter 26
Love Cracks

"September twenty-second, 1996. Dear Max,
Happy two years! I love you so very much. Being your wife has been the best! The best days of my life. I love and appreciate all you do.
You are the greatest! Don't ever forget, I love you. All my love, Katusha"

After Katie put down the pen, she realized it sounded almost as if she was hoping to win back the old Max. Yes, the words rang true on paper. Yet in reality, they were hard to prove. Her love for Max was slowly beginning to fade. She picked up the note from Max, off the kitchen table that morning, as she sat in silence. Smiling, she soaked in each and every word.

"Dear Katie,
My sweet and desirable girl. I have loved you from the first night I met you. Max"

"It was really a lovely letter," Katie thought, placing it down. For today was their second wedding anniversary.

"Morning, princess," Max said to Katie, coming

around the corner and into the kitchen. *"I see you have found my latest love letter to you."* He bowed his head in silence as some guilt passed over him. Katie stood up hoping his mood would set a normal tone for the day ahead.

They embraced. *"Just wait a minute,"* he told her. Behind his back Max produced a sort of offering, a second chance? New hope. Katie could not decide what it could be. At her place on the kitchen table, Max placed a heart-shaped box down.

Opening it, Katie saw a beautiful gold ring inside. *"Oh Max, it's just so wonderful and simply stunning."*

"Sweetie, let me put it on. I love you." He placed the ring on Katie's finger, it fit perfectly.

"Please don't hurt my feelings anymore," Katie said.

"I can't help it at times," replied Max. *"I will try not to anymore, because you mean so much to me."* He smiled almost shyly at his wife. The couple sat in silence as Katie admired her new ring. *"Do you love it?"* Max asked.

"I do, I really do, Max."

Children had been on Katie's mind in the recent weeks as well. Knowing she would potentially live in Russia for years to come, made her feel at ease with things. The culture had welcomed her years before and she knew that she was well adjusted to living in it.

Katie sat unable to speak, words were just not there. Max placed his hand over hers as she looked out of the window. *"Our anniversary and my beauty seems full of sadness."*

"You know why I do, Max; things have not been the same lately." Katie looked into his eyes.

Max cleared his throat unable to look at his wife. "Things will get better, I promise," Max declared, his eyes now glazed over. A sign that Katie had seen before, when he was not pleased with something. "Let's have a pleasant day together and just forget about things." He stood up quickly and grabbed his coat off the hook. He looped his blue scarf neatly and quickly, as he prepared to venture out into another early autumn day in the city.

Katie stood up and was unsure of what to do. "I just feel something is not right." Deciding then and there to follow her husband's lead, felt out of the normal, however, she went and joined him on the street.

Krasnodar her home, had now become questionable.

*

Days later, that flutter in her belly came again. Katie knew her way to the hospital. It was on the opposite side of town, which meant one hour by trolley. Katie remembered from when she had gone there previously, including the visit a few weeks before with Ivan. "Let me think," she thought quietly as she wrapped her grey scarf around her face. "Katie, think, and hard, you remember the way to the hospital. Okay, yes I remember, it's in the part of town I like." She had to go, to find out for sure. Walking up the stairs, now needing a rest, Katie sat down on the bench and waited. Nurses walked the halls with patients and pregnant women.

Approaching the counter, Katie tried to explain in her best Russian. "I think I might be pregnant." The two nurses smiled and spoke to each other. After the exam, they told Katie, with concern; *"Girl, be careful and come back in one week, for another test."*

"Spasibo," Katie offered to the women. Happiness radiated across Katie's face, she carefully buttoned up her jacket and in minutes she was on her way out of the building. Excited to share the incredible news of a possible pregnancy with Max.

A cool breeze blew over her, as she exited. *"Oh!"* she placed her hands on her face, bursting with joy as any expectant mother would be. Maybe? No, she felt the wonder.

Katie looked at her watch. It was already four o'clock. She needed to meet Max in less than one hour. This first visit to the hospital alone, made Katie hope for a positive outcome. Now she had more concrete information than expected. The nurses seemed sure that she could have a baby on the way. Tram number 123 came quickly, and Katie found an empty seat. The ride through the city was fast. Katie jumped out at her stop.

She knew her way to Max's office, around the path past the gate and to the top of a flight of stairs. Before she had a chance to knock, Max opened the door, looking surprised. *"Hi, sweetie. I was just going to go outside and look for you. How are you?"*

"I am fine, Max," Katie said. He gently lifted the loose hair from Katie's face.

"My blondie," he whispered. *"Okay, I am ready to go home now,"* he offered. The couple started to walk out of Max's office. They silently continued their stroll down the pathway.

Birds hovered above them. *"You're so irresistible,"*

Max said. His smile curved over the outline of his mouth. That smile she loved so much. It burst across his face.

"*I love you too,*" Katie told him. Looking up into her husband's eyes, it was now the moment of truth. "*Max ... I ... well ... I decided to venture to the hospital, on the opposite side of Krasnodar. The one that has the highest standards, you know what one I mean.*" Katie's eyebrows arched up fully now. Max glared at his wife standing before him, he was speechless. This sudden news caught him completely off guard. "*Max—say something—I wanted to be sure—that is why I ventured out to the hospital. I mean—I wanted to see if there was any truth to my feeling sick these last few weeks.*"

"*Yes, Katie, do tell, you were feeling ill ... is everything fine now?*" He asked curiously. Katie's eyes began to fill with tears of joy and sorrow. Hope would and could be their future.

"*Max, I am carrying our child,*" she whispered with a shyness in her voice, one of a young and proud wife, who would soon have a baby in her arms.

By now Max's face was bursting with delight. His lips had now turned into a fully-fledged smile. "*Oh Katie!*" Max declared. "*Are you sure?*"

"*The nurses told me to come back for another test and to take care, but I can feel it inside,*" Katie gushed.

Grabbing his wife and spinning her around in the chilling air of Krasnodar, Max placed his warm breath over Katie's eyes, reminding her of happy times past. "*My dear wife, I love you. I do!*" He gently kissed her lips and Katie welcomed his kiss in that second. "*Follow me, princess.*" Max ran a few steps ahead of Katie.

Two men were raking up leaves in the nearby park.

Max winked at them and spoke Russian. They made a small clearing on the grass. *"Close your eyes, Katie."* Taking Max's hand, she slowly eased herself down. A soft green blanket was spread out and it made Katie feel nice and warm, as she sat on top of it. *"Now, you can open your eyes."* Two candles on a wooden box lay burning in holders from their wedding. A bottle of her favourite Russian-style summer drink, mors, was standing between the candles. A smaller closed box was displayed in the middle of the blanket.

"Oh! my favourite drink! You are just amazing," Katie told Max. *"How could I even dream of this?"*

He sat down and placed his arm around her. *"Please open the little box."*

With a mischievous look on her face, Katie carefully unwrapped the box. As she opened it, tears began to flow down her cheek. *"It's so beautiful,"* she said, holding up a delicate necklace. Katie was in awe. The rose gold tone twinkled in the setting sun. The pendant was a miniature Fabergé style egg, embossed in pink gold. *"Thank you, sweetie,"* Katie cried. His eyes looked at hers with love. She never wanted this moment to end. He fastened the necklace around Katie's neck. She fingered it in astonishment. *"Just perfect, oh Max, it is breathtaking."* Putting his arms around his wife, Max kissed her gently on her forehead.

The couple hailed a taxi and headed home. It seemed like their old love had returned. Or had it?

Max opened the door to their flat and ushered Katie inside. *"My love, let us now move on, and never look back ... I mean—"* Max stopped in mid-sentence. *"The future is bright; I can just feel it."*

Katie wondered. *"Oh, really, Max. Okay, time will tell."* She nodded in agreement. *"Max, I will love you no matter what,"* she said, twirling her new necklace as she spoke.

Max grinned at her. *"Well, that is kind of a funny thing to say."* He chuckled, taking her hand.

"Oh, Max!" Katie replied. *"I just mean, you know our future is going to be full of greatness and new hope. I will always love you."* Katie could not even believe her own confirmation, that she just spoke of, to her beloved Max. It was almost like she was convincing herself, he had changed back into the old Max.

Early the next morning, she felt an unusual twitch in her stomach. *"Max, wake up,"* she whispered to her husband. *"I feel really ill. Something is not quite right."*

He opened his eyes and rolled over on his side. *"Okay Katie, I will get you to the hospital,"* he offered. He dressed quickly. Then went to the telephone. Katie could hear him in the other room, arguing in Russian. She could understand, that he wanted Ivan to take her to the hospital, as he had a business meeting this morning with Sasha. Max slammed down the receiver, then made another call. This time he was pleasant and apologetic to Sasha. She dressed a bit warmer and put a long navy scarf around her head and neck, barely showing her fair face. The tram came quickly and they were soon in their seats alongside the rush of boarding morning commuters.

"Da," one of the nurses confirmed, once they were at the hospital. *"We told this young woman to come back and check up again with us."*

"Yes, I know my wife is possibly pregnant," Max declared. The nurses nodded in agreement. Katie lay on

the nearby examining table. Minutes later, a doctor appeared. They spoke quickly in Russian to him. A huge smile spread across his face. *"Da! Spasibo,"* Max said and shook the doctor's hand as he left the room. Then he began to plant kisses all over Katie's face. It took her by surprise as she looked up into Max's emerald green eyes. *"Princess! Momma-to-be!"* Max was in awe and could not stop showering his wife with affection.

"Yes, it is confirmed, my love!" Katie giggled, grabbing her husband's hand. *"Oh, Max!"* Katie beamed, her heart full of complete happiness at the news.

"We have to just watch your pregnancy now, just take steps to make sure you get lots of rest ... As we already know there is a little Russian baby on the way, with a future in Canada!" Max kissed Katie's forehead. Her heart quivered. *"I am so happy and yes, I will be careful,"* Katie said, placing her hand on her stomach. Love and joy overcame her in that tender moment. *"My sweet baby, I must protect you now and always." "Let's send a special telegram to my parents, to announce our happy, happy news,"* Max said. He began to walk out of the hospital, and down the street with Katie, the stride in his step was blissful. *"Great idea, sweetie."* Katie nodded in agreement.

She began to show and grow a little more each day. The flutters began in her ever changing body. Katie smiled proudly and placed her hand on her belly. *"My dear baby, how I love you so, I will be so happy when you arrive. How much joy you will bring, that I can already feel."* Katie was immensely happy that a new life was growing and soon would be in her arms. She could not wait for the day to come. Each opportunity, Max started talking in Russian to the baby, gently placing his hand on Katie's stomach and kissing it softly.

*

Deciding to stay in Maikop for three days was a nice little break from city life in Krasnodar. Oleg was so happy for his daughter-in-law and son at the news of a baby on the way. He proudly walked around the kitchen drinking his tea and smiling ever so gleefully at Katie. The moment she arrived he hugged her, then placed his hand on Katie's bump and kissing it declared, *"Otlichno! Excellent news."* Katie had always loved Oleg like a father and was so pleased at his reaction. His grandchild would make him so proud and so happy. And she was sure Max would love a son to carry on the Anchov name as well. This child was going to be so loved by everyone.

"I'm going to miss this," Katie said to Max. They sat with his mother in the kitchen, talking about what the baby would be like, look like. It was a very exciting time for all of them.

"I know what you mean," Max told her, nodding with a big smile. All their talks with Lena would come to a close soon enough. When that time would come to leave Russia, Katie had no idea. Hopefully one day, when their baby was older.

The sounds of birds could be heard the next morning. A dazzling sun peeked strong and hot through the window. Katie turned over and noticed that Max had already risen. She heard his voice coming from the balcony as she got up to use the bathroom. *"Good morning, Katie."* Oleg peered around the kitchen corner. She hugged him tightly, feeling comfort from him.

Katie went back to bed to read her book, and then suddenly Max entered the room. *"Morning, princess,"* he said, kissing Katie.

After a quiet trip back to Krasnodar, there were very few words spoken between them.

Max had slept on the couch the previous night, unable to connect with his wife. He seemed more restless after returning from the visit to Maikop. Katie heard him on and off in the night dreaming, almost having nightmares. *"No, I can't, please,"* Max cried in his slumber. He had left early for work the next morning.

The card perched up on the shelf caught Katie's eye. She walked towards it. *"My God, how could things have changed so drastically the last few years between us?"* Katie pondered. She rolled her eyes. *"Another plea to keep me in his life."* Another sign of weakness on how Max had failed her royally.

"Katie, what can I say in this card? You mean more than the world to me. I never in my life felt that close to anybody like I feel to you.
Well, I hope you see a happy face in that mirror as well. I love and adore you ...
My love, my angel, my golden girl! My Katie, I love you. Your Max."

Katie threw the card down, walking away. *"Sometimes things can turn around, can't they?"* She thought, staring out the window of their apartment. She sipped her chai that morning, glancing out at a group of young Russian children that had now gathered and were playing in the nearby schoolyard.

*

It still felt like yesterday. So much they had gone through together. Almost two and a half years had passed since they were married. Max and Katie reached their destination, a beautiful, beige sand dune area. It was a popular one, yet a secret spot in Krasnodar on the outskirts. *"Let's go sit near the trees,"* Katie suggested. Max followed her as she showed him the spot. *"It's such a beautiful day, chilly, but warm in the sun's rays,"* Katie helped him place the blanket in the grass.

"I wonder what we have in here?" Max opened the basket and took out a package. *"Oh, Katie, my favourite banana bread! You're the best! I am so happy you are my wife."* Max took her hands and gently kissed her forehead. He took out his book on women expecting and began to read. Katie opened her coat and looked at her newly expanding tummy. She was only in her first month and wondered when the baby would really begin to show. Her morning sickness had finally passed.

*

Spending two days in Moscow was relaxing indeed. After Max's business meeting on the outskirts, they headed back to the city. The last memory of their honeymoon in Moscow was full of happiness. Katie could only wish this time would be sweet with Max, again.

Katie brushed the thought aside as she held on tighter to her husband. The wind blew slightly against Max's face, causing him to turn it towards Katie. He smiled at her, like he used to.

Now on to a new beginning, just as a new life was starting in Katie. Walking along Arbat Street, they turned a corner where sheets of plastic were flagged and marked all around. *"What's down there?"* Katie grasped Max's hand tighter.

"It's an archeological dig... part of the old city, they have discovered." Men, young and old, were digging and talking, measuring this unearthed mystery. Rubble and wire fences encased the scene. The ground was slashed in all different shapes. It was fascinating for Katie to see this. So many holes all encrusted together.

"Let's go have some lunch, the baby's hungry," Max whispered, as he took a nibble of Katie's ear.

"That sounds good to us," Katie declared, as his lips touched hers.

Clouds began to separate as Max and Katie walked towards the Arbat McDonald's. *"I see the red star, it's so beautiful. I remember when I first saw it two years ago."*

"I love you, angel," Max murmured softly. His eyes glimmering with a new hope, of what their baby would bring.

He seemed to be changing back to his old self, but different somehow? He patted his pocket, where he kept a poem Katie had given him the night before.

"Look into my eyes, they are shimmering with love.
Overtaken I am by your very being.
Now I realize that you have been the one all along.

Finally, I have found my best friend and soulmate for life.

As we begin the journey down "our" road, let's not speak a word, rather let our lips touch and inside we'll both give so much.

Forever, I am yours until the end of time.

Whereupon the ocean meets the sand, and I feel the touch of your ever-loving hand.

Love, Katie"

When Max looked at Katie, she still felt those previous love butterflies, yet she was concerned about how he seemed to be changing in front of her very eyes.

"Katie, our baby will be so sweet, just like you," Max said. His eyes glistening through hers on that autumn afternoon.

"Oh, Max!" Katie placed her hand on her cheek. Sorrow fell over her as she held mixed emotions towards her husband.

"What is it, Katie?" Max fumbled for money from his jeans, paying a street vendor for a small teddy bear. A gift for their baby-to-be. Finishing, he turned to Katie, anticipating her response.

"Life is sometimes like a mirror; it can shatter then it will reveal the truest of things within your heart." Katie silently thought. Suddenly these words just came to her mind, seemingly out of nowhere. *"He seems to be more in love, with the future of our child, than me."* Thinking quickly, she replied to him. *"Going through life and now this pregnancy with you, has made me so much more happy."* He smiled, handing her the toy bear. She smiled

back shyly. *"He just confirmed it!"* Raced through Katie's mind.

*

A few months later, Katie had come full bloom. Her belly was reigning. *"A reminder of our love."* So she thought. Carefully whipping up a meal of roasted potatoes with grilled onions, Katie smiled. *"What is it about him? Am I missing something? Did I not detect the right thing? He has been very mysterious lately. I want to be there for him, always. I have to get through to the man I fell in love with, and I will."*

Hushed voices caught Katie's attention, as the sound of feet shuffling became loud, then sheer silence. She walked out into the hallway, making her way to their heavily locked door, a typical kind in Russia. Peering through the hole, Katie saw that a letter had dropped, waiting to be picked up off the cement floor. Opening the door, Katie felt a warm draft of the changing seasons. It is probably a letter from his boss, she thought. Bending down she winced slightly. *"Oh, the baby is moving so much today. Ah!"* Another twinge of pain grabbed her as she tried to steady herself. Her due date was a mere six weeks away.

Touching the beige envelope, Katie took it inside. Sitting down at the kitchen table, she wondered. The return address read: *"S. P. from Moscow."* *"Hmm, initials only?"* Katie thought. *"Sasha was Max's best friend. Could it be a letter from him?"* A date and time could be seen on the bottom. *"Hmm ... strange"* – Katie thought quietly. *"So hard to know. I can't open this; it is none of my business."* However, curiosity caught her that spring morning. Holding up the envelope to the sunlight steaming through the kitchen window, Katie tried to read the Russian words, with a few happy faces. "Hmm," she thought. *"It is probably just a greeting for my Max."* Setting it down on the table, Katie finished her tea and decided to go have her afternoon nap. The baby sure needed one.

Several hours later she heard a key opening the door to their flat. Katie's eyes opened wide as she immediately woke up. It was Max. Walking out into the corridor, she smiled at her husband, with a little bit of suspicion about his letter. Max spun around taking Katie in his arms. *"Hello darling, I am sorry I was later than I thought, working tonight."* His eyes seemed hazy, and his disposition out of character. *"Likely drinking,"* Katie thought, quietly dissecting her husband's behaviour then and there. Katie nodded, hugging him. Something felt very different about his touch now.

Walking into the kitchen, Katie followed Max and hoped for some answers. *"How was your day, my girl?"* Max asked, sitting down at the table. Katie looked at him and began to speak.

"It was nice and I do feel the baby will be here soon." She half shrugged.

Biting her lip, she knew it was now or never. *"There's a letter, it came for you today,"* Katie declared. Taking it from under a nearby book, she pressed it towards her husband.

Max glanced at the envelope in front of him; he nervously looked away. *"Oh, this, it is so nothing... Katie, don't worry about it."* Max shyly tossed it across the table.

"Max!" Katie shrieked. Her voice grew full of

impending anger. *"I feel like you are hiding something from me lately."* Her eyes widened with fright and courage at the same time.

"Forget it, I told you," Max muttered, pushing his way past his wife. The look in his eyes, a burning red told Katie her time of questioning was up. Ignoring this, Katie persisted with her questions. The night grew on.

Max finally broke down. *"Okay, you want the truth, you are going to have our baby in Canada. I have bought you a ticket and you fly back this Friday. I don't want our child to be Russian!"* Katie couldn't believe her ears.

"Why would you do that?"

Max asserted. *"You're going, that's final."*

Katie ran to the bedroom crying, her feelings mixed. *"Could this be the chance to leave him? He wouldn't be there for the birth?"* She fell asleep sobbing. Awakening later, Katie heard Max in the other room, the TV was loud, a Russian movie was playing. Max and his laughter grew dim, suddenly he was sleeping. Katie wept. Their lives seemed too far apart now, how could their past love ever be restored.

*

That morning, Katie placed her hand on the sheets and felt wetness. Her water had broken! Now she knew it was for real. *"Mom!"* Katie looked at her standing in her old bedroom doorway. *"We have to go to the hospital. The baby's coming."*

Sarah jerked into action. "*Keep calm*," Sarah said to Katie, her voice half asleep. She gathered the nearby hospital bag that was all ready to go.

Lying on the hospital bed, the pain was more than Katie

could bear. Nurses swarmed around her. They told her to relax as she tried to concentrate on pushing. Sarah held her daughter's hand in support.

"*She is eight centimetres,*" one of the nurses declared, with a look of confusion. "*The baby is also breech.*"

When Katie heard that, all she could say was, "*No!*"

"*We need to do an emergency C-section now,*" the nurse said. The head doctor nodded as he prepared for the imminent arrival.

Katie yelled, "*No, I need to push now.*" The excruciating sensation Katie felt was now at the top of her mind as she tried to concentrate. The pain was getting more and more intense as she held a firm grip onto Sarah's hand. She knew the reward would be here soon, her sweet baby. In that she found comfort with each passing burst of pain.

With that, a little baby boy was born bottom first and crying into the arms of his mother. "*He looks like an angel,*" Katie whispered, looking up into Sarah's eyes.

"*Yes,*" Sarah agreed, beaming, then kissed her daughter on the forehead. The baby's soft skin touched Katie's as she cooed over her son.

Max was ecstatic, as the news was shared with him. Katie put her son to the phone. Max spoke to him in Russian. Despite the distance, the love they both felt was apparent.

*

Just as a new dawn had begun to stream through the airplane window that morning, so had a new life begun in Russia for Lev.

Born to a Russian father and a Canadian mother, this

boy would be loved and treasured. Katie smiled, beaming with happiness as she softly stroked her son's tender face. *"He is just perfect."* Her eyes rested on the tiny miracle that she now called her own.

"Da, Katie, he really is, there is no doubt about that," Max replied. His eyes sparkled with delight over his new born son.

"Lev! We shall call him Lev," declared Max.

"Da, I agree, what a wonderful name," Katie said proudly.

Chapter 27
Love Lost

Late November, 1999. Happily set into her routine as a mother, Katie cherished every minute with Lev. She looked into his chocolate-brown eyes with joy. The quiet times with her son were the most rewarding as she smiled at him and he in return. *"I will protect you always. I promise,"* Katie whispered to Lev. She put him down in his crib, after he fell asleep in her arms.

Katie smiled as she gazed out the window, it was another beautiful day. Snowflakes swirled in all shapes and sizes outside on the street, the hustle of Russians transported Katie back to a few years previous.

Rolling over that afternoon in her own nap, Katie's throat felt very dry. She smacked her lips together and thought about what had gone on last night, a very late talk into the wee hours. Max had tried to come to an agreement with her about how and where Lev would ultimately be raised. It would have to be in Canada. That meant, within a couple of years they would have to move. *"Oh, how times have changed,"* she thought to herself. *"No sense in dwelling on things."*

The sound of the phone jolted Katie's thoughts back to reality. *"Hello—yes, I can hear you. Olivia, is that you?"* Katie asked. *"Yes, Hi Katie—it's me,"* Olivia confirmed.

Happiness came over Katie. *"Oh Liv—it is so good to hear your voice,"* Katie blurted out with excitement. *"How are you doing?"* Katie pressed her friend for a full update.

"I am well my friend," Olivia said. Her voice full of excitement. *"Los Angeles is treating me very good – so very different than when we were in Russia – I miss it at times, the mission, the people."*

"Yes Liv, things do change and I am living among what I never even imagined would be my home," Katie replied.

The girls chatted for a bit longer, talking about past times and memories they had encountered in both Hawaii and Russia. The call ended with Olivia promising to call soon. Placing the phone down Katie was full of complete joy at hearing from her friend.

*

"Do we even know each other anymore?" Katie whispered. Max was a man she felt she no longer knew. Had she lost sight of who he used to be? Turning over on her pillow, she saw the jet-black hair as bold and striking as ever. *"Wonderful,"* she thought. *"He is home now. I had no idea."* He had snuck in that afternoon early from work. Unusual, since he seemed to have many late days at work. Pretending to sleep, she hoped Max would not try and wake her. But sure enough, Max kissed his wife on her lips. Katie slowly opened her eyes and batted them just a little. He smiled, unsure if Katie wanted that kiss.

"Good afternoon, Katusha," Max whispered. Katie felt her stomach turn.

"How long will this last?" *"Max,"* Katie murmured, placing her hand on his cheek. He closed his eyes and

scrunched his face up, knowing he had been the real cause of Katie's sorrow as of late.

Max stood up and lifted Lev, from his crib, in the nearby hallway. Lev, had awoken and was being a monkey, trying to climb out of his bed. Max kissed him tenderly on the cheek, and then went to his laptop to check his email. Katie heard him connecting to the phone line, then log on and type away at the keyboard. Having access to the internet was rare, Max was fortunate enough to have his American boss take care of that. It seemed that, it was this luxury of the company laptop that kept Max happy these days. The door opened slowly and wider. Katie's eyes danced into Lev's. He smiled at his mother, waved his blanket at her, and ran into her arms. *"My joy. My sweet pride."* Katie kissed her son's head and closed her eyes, praying that the future would be a bright and happy one for him.

Hours later, with Max out at the local market getting some fresh produce, Katie began to do some laundry. He had offered and Katie did not protest. It was helpful for her in that dark evening anyway. She settled Lev down for the night. *"Oh, my poor little one."* He must have heard it all. The arguing last night. This is his refuge. Her young infant, clutched his tiny bear as he slept.

Returning to the laundry, she noticed a faint sweet smell on one of Max's shirts. Not Max's, but familiar. A nice scent.

Suddenly the phone rang, quite loudly. Katie picked it up. *"Hello?"* A male voice on the other end piped up. *"Is Max available?"*

Katie's eyes opened a bit wider. *"I ... no ... he is not home right now."*

"I see. Well, okay. We missed him at the party for Alex and Sasha last night."

Katie turned her nose up in surprise. *"I don't know if he knew about it,"* she said. There was heavy breathing on the other end, then laughter, a click and the phone was dead. *"What party?"* Katie thought it was strange, and just when she thought things were not odd enough around here.

"I wonder how we will do in Canada?" Katie closed her eyes as a tear began to trickle down her cheek. *"No,"* she whispered. Walking over to the kitchen window she peered out into the darkness. A nearby lamppost was lit. Snowflakes began to swirl intensely, holding a young couple on that cold night. They huddled together, full of love. Biting her lip down, Katie pondered. Flashbacks of the past came over her in that moment. *"Oh Max, what changed? My questions can't even be answered now."* Eyeing the lovers outside, she smiled and bowed her head. *"No, not us, not anymore. Well, guess what Max, I am not going to wait for that day to come. I am going to make my way out of Krasnodar, before you ever take us to Canada."* She decided right then and there. Tears began to well up in her eyes. *"No!"* She slammed her hand down on the kitchen counter. *"I won't let you get to me, Max Anchov,"* she thought.

Katie eyed Max's leather jacket. It was the one he only wore for special occasions. He had slung it over the chair last night before he had gone to sleep. Katie went over and fished around in the pockets of the dark black garment. She felt a thick piece of paper. Katie took it out and carefully opened it up. Scribbled on it were directions and a few different male names. Including a few names of women, she was sure she had met. In the corner of the paper was a happy face, a flipped over one, that Katie knew only Max had the talent to draw. He had sent Katie many of those same faces, when they were young and dating. *"Some drunken Russian get-together most likely."* Her mouth gaped open in disbelief. Katie felt a sea of emotions flood over her. All her suspicions were coming true. She put her hand across her mouth and bit her finger. *"Perhaps women were there? Russian ones? With Sasha?"* A sudden pain passed over her and in that minute she began to understand, just a little bit more.

She heard Lev calling her and returned the paper to the original pocket.

Sorrow fell over her body that night as she tried to fall asleep. Max had not elaborated on what she had told him about the mysterious phone call, he simply crawled into their bed that night and fell into a deep sleep. Several hours later Katie put her hand on Max's back. *"Max!"* she whispered.

He stirred a little. *"No, please. Katie, don't. Haven't I hurt you enough ... you were the love of my life, I can promise you that much. I just want you to be happy."* He looked into her eyes. *"The longer we stay together, the more I will feel trapped into someone I cannot be to you."* He rolled away into a silence, slowly mumbling in his own sleep. His demons shook him and carried him deep into his dreams over and over.

*

"Liv, I know you mean well, I ... just can't imagine life without Max at the moment." It wasn't the call that Katie

was expecting that early day. Katie's voice lowered. She bit down on her lip a little harder now. Her friend could not see her through the wires, what did it matter now anyway.

Olivia stalled. Persuading her friend, would take more than just a small challenge. *"Yes, I know Kate, but do you realize the longer you stay with him, the harder it will be to break free, I mean really free."*

"Damn it Liv! I made a vow to him, I— you don't understand, I just can't walk out on that promise, our life—Lev." Katie paused, the reluctance in her voice gave Olivia all she needed to know.

"So—what you are really saying Kate, you don't need Max, he needs you."

Closing her eyes, Katie wished her friend was right there, so she could cry on her shoulder. *"Oh Katie, I know, that of late, from what you have told me, he is not the same person you met years ago in Krasnodar."* Katie winced.

Glancing out the window her fingers nervously fidgeted with a strand of hair that had fallen over her eye. Staying with Max would be far from easy since her heart and mind had changed. *"What you are saying—you still love Max?"* Olivia closed her eyes.

"I—well Liv, you know our history, our story, I can't at this point even think about leaving him."

Leaves and snowflakes began to fall, dancing endlessly in that new morning, Krasnodar was about to welcome a new season soon enough. Katie tried to distract herself from Olivia's truthful words. *"You do know that I will help you with anything you need, Kate. I have ways and means, contacts,"* Olivia offered.

"*Yes of course I know that—Liv, you have been there for me, any time I have needed your help. I appreciate that so much,*" Katie whispered intently. "*Okay, I need to go now, I will be in touch soon.*"

Katie pondered over her conversation with Olivia and knew she had to decide fast. A few days later the phone rang, Katie quickly picked it up. "*Hi, its me.*"

"*Oh Liv!*" *I have been thinking, and I know you are right about things. I am ready,*" Katie whispered.

"*Katie, I know it will be hard, but I will be there for you!*" Olivia paused.

A sudden rush of tears began to form in Katie's tired eyes. "*I hear him coming! Max, he's home.*" The girls said a quick goodbye as Katie turned into his wife once again.

"*Hello Katusha,*" Max declared. Katie walked to her husband placing her hand on his arm, lovingly. He smiled. "*Were you on the phone?*" Max slid his fingers over her hand, Katie closed her eyes in fear.

"*No, Max. I was just talking to Lev.*" Feeling like she no longer knew him, his touch on her skin made her flinch.

"*Katie? What haunts you? Your eyes seem different; I feel there is a distance between us lately?*" Max questioned.

*

Reaching over to her cellular phone, another perk from Max's American boss. Katie touched the keys lightly. "*Hello?*" the lively voice answered.

"*Liv, its me.*" Katie went quiet as she knew not what to say. Tears began to form in her eyes. She pushed them away.

"*Oh Katie! It is so good to hear your voice my friend.*"

"*I miss you, very much,*" Katie replied. "*How is Los Angeles treating you?*" Katie spoke, trying to control her emotions and sound happy.

"*It is amazing, I enjoy the sun, just like our time in Hawaii. How are things going since our last conversation?*" Olivia responded.

"*Liv?*" Katie paused.

"*Katie, what is it? You don't sound yourself,*" Olivia asked.

Katie bit her lip down nervously. "*I am leaving Max.*" Confirming her plan, Katie felt a sad sigh of relief.

"*Oh Katie! I support you—I just want you to be happy and safe,*" Olivia offered. "*I know Liv, I do too.*"

Tears gushed openly now. "*I—I don't even really know what I am running from? I can't ... Oh Olivia! I do wish you were here. I made a vow to Max, for life—how can I truly break it? Am I the worst person? I did love him, I loved us, what we had. But ... things are different now.*"

*

The next morning, rushing and speeding like a bullet through their bedroom, Katie knew it was now or never. She had to take heed and pack up Lev and be on her way. Max had left for the day only a few minutes before.

Not saying too much, he was coming down with a cold. He had sat at their kitchen table with a light wool scarf, wrapped around his neck. Katie prepped his usual, meat and cheese on a bun. The whistle on the kettle blew, his chai was ready. *"Oh, don't you worry Max—I am leaving, for good."* Pouring the hot drink into a mug, Katie made sure her nerves were not that obvious. She had to pull it off. *"Oh, Max."* Katie placed her hand on his shoulder. *"You have caught a cold, I am sorry."* She bowed her head with a little bit of guilt pressing on her.

"Da," Max whispered. *"Don't worry about me Katie. Concentrate on keeping yourself healthy."* She smiled, turning away from her husband. Unable to connect with him.

"You seem very quiet this morning, Katie." Max looked out the window. The years had grown on him; at twenty something, he had become a completely different person.

"I, well, no, Max ... I am just a bit tired today," Katie offered. Max began to cough and cough. He winced and closed his eyes very tight.

"Shit," he mumbled. Shaking his head, it was almost as if he were in another world. Katie cringed. *"He's probably just hungover from another damn party."*

"Maybe I should just stay home today?"

"Nooo!" Katie screamed in her head. *"Think fast Katie ... I have got to get him out." "Won't you miss that business meeting, you mentioned? I know you have had so many lately, it must be important?"*

"Da, you are right, I must go." He rose from his meal, dressed for the weather, then kissed her cheek. *"Okay Katie, I am on my way. You know, I am happy. We seem to get along better these days."* He smiled.

In a trance and without any emotion, Katie nodded. *"Oh really Max, how dare you say that to me,"* she thought. Staring at a man, she no longer felt she knew.

Max departed, closing the door. Katie counted the

minutes to ensure he was well gone. Now, she was truly ready to head on her way with Lev by her side. She looked out at the now overcast sky, dreary, but inviting.

Knowing time was precious, Katie opened the door to her closet and quickly dressed. *"Not that one,"* she thought to herself, grabbing the wrong turquoise blouse. It was snowing lightly. How could she be so careless? With a bundle of nerves in her stomach she was tripping over the bed, almost hitting her head. *"I have got to leave. Should I call Olivia? No, that will have to wait. Time is precious and I must take advantage of it. Max will be home in just a few hours from his meeting. I can't leave any trace of our departure, he will notice any faint mark of us being gone. I can only take the essentials."* With Lev fast asleep in the next room, Katie went into the kitchen and grabbed some snacks and drinks for their journey ahead. *"Lev... darling,"* Katie whispered, as she shook him gently.

His boyhood locks fell over his tender eyes as he blinked, slowly opening them and seeing his mother's face before him. *"Momma, ya ustal,"* he whimpered quietly. Katie frowned and kissed her son's cheek, assuring him that he could sleep longer, once they were on the train.

Lifting her son into her arms, Katie smiled and hugged him close. *"I promise you, everything will be okay. We are just going on a little journey,"* Katie declared.

"Papa?" he cried.

"Da. He will see us soon. I don't know when? Don't you worry, my sweet Russian treasure, all will be well." Lev nodded at his mother's deep blue eyes, they were his every comfort.

"Ya lyublyu tebya," he whispered.

"I love you too, my dear son. So very much." Katie assured him. She felt the tears well up in her eyes. Things would indeed work out for the best, for the both of them.

Katie directed the taxi driver to the main railway station, a place where Max most likely would think to look for her and Lev. Perhaps, it was in the back of Katie's mind to pass here one last time, the same train station where Max had first declared his love. Running her hands through her hair, Katie held back tears that were ready to trickle down any second. The snow began to slide down the window of the car and change to slush. She knew, that this would be the last time she would ever see Krasnodar again, in her lifetime. The memories would only be etched in her mind. That was where they would stay.

"Oh, Max, how could this life have come to such a turning point?" She shook her head and held her son closer. There was no way she wanted Lev to live a life any longer in Russia, she certainly did not want her boy to be drafted into the military, when he was older. That thought alone scared her and she did not want that for their son. Moreover, it did not sit well, about what Max had done to her and could possibly do to Lev. She had to leave Russia. And it was now or never.

*

"Katie? Katie? I am home," Max called out. His eyes looked around the apartment. Checking in the bedroom, he found that they were not at home and assumed she was at the market with Lev. Resigning to this, he made himself some chai and watched TV. As time went on, Max started

to get agitated about her absence. *"Where is my meal,"* he ruminated. He decided to prepare his things for the next day's business travel to Moscow. Walking into their bedroom, his emerald green eyes saw that the closet door was ajar. Reaching in to get his suitcase, he quickly noticed that Katie's rucksack, the one she used for travel was gone. Ripping open the door, he scanned in one glance. In horror, he saw that some of her clothes were missing. Running to the chest of drawers, his suspicions were confirmed. Just like that.

Max slammed his fist on the bed and flung his head down in agony. His anger gave way to the clenching of his teeth. *"Katie, damn you, where did you go and where have you taken our son?"* Fumbling for his cellular phone, Max dialled his wife's number. He was glad of the technology; most Russian people did not have access to at that time.

No answer ... Max tried again. *"Answer you suka!"* His mouth opened in shock. *"She won't get away with this,"* he thought to himself. *"No one does this to Max Anchov. No one."*

*

"Yes, two tickets to Moscow, the train departs at six o'clock." Katie paid and thanked the clerk, then walked over to the bench and sat down with Lev. She looked at her watch and saw it was near 5 p.m. Her phone began to ring. The number indicated that it was Max again. He was still trying to call her. She wasn't going to answer. People around her, were beginning to wonder why she wouldn't answer the phone. Sensing this she turned down the ring

tone. Closing her eyes, she remained calm, pushing in the numbers, she knew who she had to call—Liv.

Olivia had pondered about heading to Warsaw? She could make the trip for business or pleasure? Yet on her mind, Katie, her friend who she wanted to help, knew this could be the perfect way out for her, when she was ready. An exit plan was in place.

"Hello," Olivia answered her cellular phone on the second ring.

"Hi, it's Katie!" she shrieked, almost out of breath.

"Hello, my friend!" Olivia declared.

"Olivia, we need your help and real soon." Katie explained that she had finally broke free, from Max.

"How did you get away?" Queried Olivia.

"I packed up, left with Lev in a taxi and we're here at the train station, waiting for the six o'clock to Moscow."

Olivia's voice took a serious tone, *"Katie, you must listen very carefully. Do not get on that train. Max is not shy about bribing officials and could also use his father's connections to track you down. You must not use any more public transportation. The train to Moscow will be a good diversion. Go hide in the toilet and I will call you back, as soon as I can."*

Olivia eventually called. Instructions were given and off Katie went with her small son in tow. But before, she took the battery out of her cellular phone and dropped each piece into a separate garbage bin, as directed. This way, no one could answer or call from the phone, if found.

Darkness was upon them. A long tram ride and a short walk, led her and Lev to a vacant lot on the outskirts of Krasnodar. Nearby was a kindergarten. Katie smiled. She would always have fond memories of helping the children.

But now it was time to build a new life, one without Max.

Standing in the cold night, trying to catch her breath, she knew she had to remain calm for both of their sakes. A dark Lada pulled into the lot. Stepping out of the car, an older man walked toward Katie. *"Miss, Olivia sent me. I know her well."* He smiled in confirmation and Katie nodded. Katie smirked. *"Liv did have a way with people and connections in places that most didn't."*

He didn't provide his name and ushered them into the warmth of the running car. *"Do not be afraid, you are safe now,"* he assured and drove into the chilled evening. *"Poland, here we come."* She smirked to herself. Now they would be off to Warsaw. No looking back, not now or ever.

*

She knew what he had been up to. An array of Russian women adored Max. As striking and seemingly loyal as he was, Katie had no doubt he had fallen into the arms of another woman. At this point, she didn't even care. Their love had been lost a while ago. Yes, the memories were there. Yet they were not enough to hold them together. Katie was moving on and that was that. Her son was coming with her, no matter what the cost. Making sure their passports were in order, Katie felt a burst of relief come over her. Thinking about how she had secretly updated them without Max's knowledge months before. Flashing back …

"Where do you think you are going, my sweet?" Max had glanced over at his wife as she prepared lunch that autumn afternoon. Katie nervously looked around the

kitchen, fiddling with the curtain above the sink.

She put her head down in guilt. *"Max, I have to go to the market, I ran out of baking soda for one of the dishes I am preparing."*

Max pushed his lips up in disbelief. *"Very well. I can keep Lev with me, then we can go and take a walk to the park."* Katie agreed and off she went about her business. She made way to her church. Weeks previously she had sent all the required documents and photos to the Canadian embassy in Moscow. The replacement of her expired and Lev's own new passport, had hopefully arrived. Delivered to the church and not their home. She needed some kind of relief in her heart and most of all her mind. Opening the package, she withdrew two valid passports and clutched them to her chest and whispered. *"Thank you God, for providing these."*

The Lada arrived at its destination. Katie glanced at her watch and noted it was almost ten at night. Not to worry. *"Spasibo,"* Katie said, nodding her head at the gentleman, for giving them a ride. They began walking towards the small dacha he pointed to. She held the new passports firmly in one hand and Lev's hand tightly in the other. His future was all Katie cared about. She didn't want him to live in a society, which would dictate or tell him who to be or where to go. Catching her thoughts, she realized that was not true. The country and people of Russia had been good to her. It was Max's own little society they couldn't live in anymore.

They slept that night Nina's house. A good friend of Olivia's. Katie was happy that Olivia had kept in touch with her Russian people after the mission had ended. Nina had graciously offered to let them stay with her before they left for Poland. She welcomed her and Lev and understood somewhat the situation. Katie did not go into great detail. She felt comforted in the fact, that soon they would be out of Russia for good.

Pulling the covers over herself and Lev that night, she tried to fall asleep. A few hours later Katie awoke to sweat soaking her nightgown all the way through. She was moving in and out of dreams, Max, Krasnodar, trains, past memories. Suddenly her eyes widened. Katie thought about how Max must be sitting in their apartment miles away, wondering and hoping. *"Your wife and child are gone and you need to face the fact,"* Katie whispered. Rolling over, her mind gave way and she fell into a deep slumber as heavy snow began to fall outside. Safe, secure and exhausted.

The next morning, Katie murmured, awakening from a dream. Except it was more like a nightmare that rocked her out of her sleep. Max was looking for her and she was running down the street crying, and there was no place to hide. Feeling foolish, she ran back into his arms, looking in his eyes, but they were cut out. Hollow. Jaded. Just like their love had become. She wiped the bead of sweat that had just dripped off her brow. Crawling out of bed, she was careful not to disturb Lev as he lay sweetly sleeping in his own land of dreams.

He missed his father, no doubt, and of course Katie did want them to reunite once she got her life together and started fresh back home in Canada. *"Oh Max! What have you become to me?"* Anger ruled her eyes.

Stepping into the shower, the hot water seeped over every inch of her young body. Katie felt free and happy, to now control her own destiny by the choice she had made only a day earlier. It would be best for everyone.

While getting Lev dressed, a sudden knock came on the bedroom door. Nina peeked her head inside. *"Dobroye utro, my girl. Are you ready for zavtrak? You two must be hungry?"*

"Yes, please," Katie replied. The warm chai soothed Katie instantly. Nina nodded in approval as she offered a selection of cheese, Russian salami and freshly baked buns. *"Thank you very much,"* Katie offered to Nina.

"My pleasure, and God be with you and your son on this journey." Nina winked, clearing the table.

Lev ran to Nina and hugged her saying, *"Ya lyublyu tebya, babushka."* Nina smiled, holding back tears.

As time ticked on, Katie tried to fend off her anxiety by reading. *"What is the next step in the plan?"* She wondered. Moments later the telephone rang. Katie could hear Nina talking in the next room. *"Da, da,"* Nina motioned Katie to the phone.

Katie spoke into the receiver cautiously, *"Hello?"*

"Hi Katie, it's Greg, I'm a friend of Olivia's. I'll be brief. A couple from our mission, Boris and Irina will be leaving for Kiev tomorrow morning. They are picking up a load of donations from a group of Canadian charities. They will stop by Nina's at about six, to pick you up. They will be in a blue truck. Take care." The sound of the phone hanging up, answered Katie's previous worry. Another night of waiting.

"Come Lev," Katie motioned to her young son. The truck arrived on time, stopping in the darkness. Despite the early hour, Nina had prepared breakfast and food for their travels. Katie and Lev said an emotional goodbye and thank-you, before heading outside. Bundling up her scarf

around her face, Katie felt the warmth encompass her that morning. *"We just have to make it to Warsaw, and then we will be that much closer to Vancouver."* She shut her eyes, pain burning through them. Feeling the sting, the guilt inside for leaving Max.

As they approached, a truck door opened. The next step to freedom. On board, it moved into the quiet morning. Boris and Irina, a mid-thirties couple spoke little English. Katie expressed her appreciation, in her best Russian. The trip would take about two days, because of the snow covered roads. Boris and Irina would alternate driving, limiting the stops to just fuel and toilet breaks. Despite the language barrier, the time was enjoyable. Food was shared and Lev laughed a lot.

As they saw the Ukrainian border come into focus, Boris told them, that he would do the talking and for all to have their passports ready. Speaking in Russian, the border guard conversed with Boris. He explained their travel plans and that Katie and Lev were friends heading to Warsaw. The guard picked up a phone and spoke rapidly. Katie began to descend into a pit of fear. *"Did Max, call the authorities?"* The minutes began to build up, a long line of vehicles formed behind them. A female guard directed Katie and Lev to come inside. Her English was fluent. Looking at their passports, she asked why there were no entry stamps into Russia? Katie explained that they were newly issued from the Canadian embassy.

"What are your travel plans in the Ukraine and where is the boy's father?" With those questions, the official closed the passports and placed them on the counter and waited for Katie's response.

Katie, getting nervous, dismissed this feeling and

found strength. *"We are traveling through to Warsaw—to meet a friend, then flying back to Canada. My husband has to work and can't come with us."*

"Where in Canada do you live?"

"Vancouver," Katie confirmed. "I have relatives in Vegreville, Alberta," the guard shared. Katie was holding back tears, the guard somehow understood her situation. *"You may go, have a safe trip back home."*

Katie and Lev climbed aboard the truck once more and it moved ahead. They were out of Russia.

Entering Kiev, the truck moved at a steady pace, the traffic building. *"Boris knows the city well,"* Katie thought. Hugging Lev just a little closer, his chocolate brown eyes smiled with excitement, looking into Katie's eyes. His mother, his protector. Suddenly the vehicle stopped in front of a busy structure. People were moving in and out of it.

"Train station," Boris declared, pointing. *"You must hurry please, I no park here."*

"Spasibo," Katie offered stepping out of the cab with Lev and their belongings. *"Thank-you for your kindness."* The truck quickly moved away into traffic. Lev held her hand tight. *"Don't worry darling, you will love our little adventure, and you will see your father very soon, I promise."*

Lev nodded, his small fingers curled around Katie's. He giggled. *"Papochka?"*

"Da, my son, soon." Katie scooped him up and was on her way.

Dusk was now present. *"What time would the train to Warsaw leave?"* Katie mused. *"The train system should be similar to Russia,"* she said to herself, pulling her backpack straps tighter. Walking over the sidewalk, between the masses of people towards the entrance, she turned to her boy. *"Now, we must move swiftly and I want you to follow me and no questions asked, Okay?'*

"Yes, Momma." Lev beamed. They giggled together.

"I want you to be adventurous when you are older too," Katie winked at her son. She leaned down and quickly kissed his forehead with a burst of love. This little treasure was the reason she lived each day to the fullest. Her son, her love, the keeper of her heart.

Checking the departures time table, Warsaw bound would leave at seven the next morning. They ventured outside and looked for suitable accommodation for the night. Katie found a small hotel, booked in, had a nourishing meal, then tucked Lev into bed. His eyes looked into his mother's, as she serenaded him with a Russian lullaby. Slowly he became drowsy, then drifted off to sleep. Warm, safe and protected.

Katie busied herself, sorting and preparing for tomorrow's early leg of the escape. Done. She called Olivia. *"Hello?"* Olivia's voice was a comfort.

"Liv, it's me, we made it to Kiev. Thank you so much, for getting the help for us." Katie went on to provide details of the past few days and the upcoming train trip.

Olivia confirmed, that she was already in Warsaw and would meet them upon arrival. *"Katie, there is something else, I have to tell you,"* her tone had changed. *"I received a phone call from Max. A cleaner found your cellular phone and the battery while emptying the bins, and the station master was able to trace it back to Max's work. Max asked me if you called? I told him, yes we had spoken a few times and downplayed the conversation to just old*

friends chatting. *Don't worry, I didn't tell him, you were meeting me. I convinced him, that I'm in LA."*
Katie went numb and quiet. *"Do you think he will track me down? Does he know where we are?* Katie trembled as she spoke.
"I'm not sure, you know he has connections and his ways. We're not taking any chances. Your train will arrive about seven thirty in the evening. I will get you guys on the next available flight out."
Katie, emotionally and physically drained, fell into bed. She couldn't sleep. *"Your love is all I will ever need, Katusha,"* Max had told her a few weeks before. How could she even think or believe him now? She had to be strong and escape. Pushing away her thoughts of Max and his words, the time was now. Soon, she would only be a memory for Max.

*

"Yes, Sasha, I know," Max cried into the phone. *"I just want my wife and son back home with me here in Krasnodar."* Max slammed the phone down. *"Where on earth has she gone?* Living in this city, Katie knew her way around quite well, so he was not surprised if she had found a way out. *"Are their passports updated? I don't know! Did they go to Moscow? Her friend is lying!"* Max hung his head down in disbelief. *"I just can't think right now!"* He slumped down on the chair feeling a wave of anger and sorrow rush over him. *"Maybe she has gone to Canada? No, we have discussed it and decided it was best to stay in Russia. I am doing well at my company. She would not do that to me."*

Opening a nearby cabinet, Max pulled out a bottle of vodka. He sadly poured himself a shot of the clear fluid. He knocked it back with pain that hovered in his mind, then poured another one. This time with much more in it. The power of this liquid gem seemed to soothe him for the moment. His flecked green eyes swirled as he gazed at a wedding photo on the closest wall. *"Chert yeye!"* he shouted, throwing his empty glass at the picture; the frame with the happy couple fell off the wall and smashed before his very eyes. *"Katieeeee!"* he cried, throwing himself on the nearby couch. He slowly huddled on it, his eyes flinching and blinking through tears. Spots of blood trickled down his hand, the crumpled wedding photo still cupped in his grasp.

*

Blowing out her own breath, the bitter air formed before her. Although moonlit, it was a dark cold evening. *"Almost there,"* she said to herself standing outside the Polish train station. *"Come,"* she motioned to Lev. She knew it had been tough the last few days, but it wouldn't be too long until she and Lev would be in a whole new world. *"Keep your scarf on fully now my sweet, so that it covers your neck,"* Katie whispered to Lev. *"Momma does not want you to catch a chill."* she winked. Lev nodded. His eyes sparkled with love for her as he anticipated their adventure ahead. Curious as any young boy would be.

A sign appeared and Katie knew she had made it. *"Yes!"* she cried. Pulling Lev along, she saw Olivia, in the distance, waving them over. Running now and picking up her son as her strides became faster, the tears began to trickle down her cheeks. Freedom. Max gone.

"*Oh, Olivia!*" Katie fell into her friend's open arms. Relief and happiness flooded Katie now.

"*Hello, both of you,*" Olivia welcomed them. Behind her was a waiting taxi. "*Get inside, we will be on our way now.*" Olivia helped Katie place her backpack in the trunk of the car. Driving away, new snowflakes trailed behind the car. Katie rested her head back on her seat and finally felt free at last.

Then all at once emotions came flooding over her. Max was gone and this was what she had wanted. Yet, it felt strange, leaving the man she had once loved so much behind, in the country where they had fallen in love so many years before.

After arriving in Poland, they would be there for a very short time, then leave for her homeland, Canada. Max would never find them. The city lights streamed across the window as the car began to speed onto that next leg of escape, the airport.

Katie pressed her hand on the window and traced over a hint of frost that had made its way there. She had to make a new life for her and Lev and not think about Max any longer. Olivia peered in the rear-view mirror at Katie. Pointing at Lev, "*He doesn't have any idea, does he?*" She knew how Max had treated Katie as of late. Her eyes, once full of sadness, now danced with joy at the thought of her friend building a new life for herself. Katie nodded in confirmation. Gently pressing a finger to her lips, she hushed her friend in the hopes that Lev would not hear too much conversation. She wanted to shield him from any harsh words about Max. Even if he had hurt her, he had always doted on his son.

*

Just over three days had passed; her quest was almost over. Katie nervously purchased two tickets that evening for Vancouver. That flight could not come any sooner. No word of Max. Hopefully he had gotten the message; she was out of his life and not ever coming back. Their life was only a past memory now, time to move on. With a sigh of relief, she held their boarding passes tightly in her hand. Right now her priority was Lev, her angel.

Katie and Olivia said their tearful goodbyes, fraught with thanks from Katie. Time was precious and it marched on.

Boarding the plane hours later, she looked out the window and thought to herself, *"Goodbye Russia. You have been wonderful in so many ways. My life there with Max had a great beginning five years ago, sometimes life changes in ways you do not expect. Time to say farewell... Do svidanya."*

*

Deplaning with Lev, her eyes glanced around quickly. Katie felt a bit stunned, almost as if Max were watching them from afar. Impossible.

*

Settling into a new routine with Lev, life had become carefree. Walking down the hall a few weeks after returning home to Vancouver, she made her way back to their apartment. *"Yes, I will move on and yes there will be life after Max."* The building was quiet at this time of night. After dropping garbage down the chute, she glanced at her watch, it was nearly one a.m. and Katie felt she was ready for bed. At least the next day, Sunday, she would rest and catch up with Lev and perhaps take him to Stanley park and go for a ride on the Christmas train. Katie chuckled to herself, *"More trains."*

Chapter 28
Destiny Calls

Weeks past and a new year had begun. With that, her fears subsided slowly. Falling into bed that night, Katie pulled the covers closer, her blonde hair cascaded over her arm as she fell into a deep sleep. The next day brought much joy with her little Lev. Watching him, melted her heart. Having her son was the one experience in this world that had never been anything but pure light and happiness.

Katie picked Lev up and kissed his cheek. *"We will go now and visit Nana, she would like to see you overnight,"* Katie said. Lev nodded to his mother. Katie needed a night to prepare all of the required documents, to change their identity, so that Max would never find them, ever. Katie would make sure of that. *"Your little Katusha is now finding her own way. Away from you."* Perhaps one day she would go to Max, when she was ready to face the man she once loved. Katie bit her lip thinking. *"Forget the divorce. I would have to contact the officials in Krasnodar."* There was no point in worrying about that for now. The main thing at stake was where they were, and how she could eliminate any signs that would lead Max to her in Canada.

Katie had become used to living in secret and hiding from Max. She became even bolder when she thought of their escape to Poland. Knowing the consequences of course, but that didn't matter. If she went back to Krasnodar, Max would surely find them and she would have to bear living with him once again. Katie was willing to take the identity of a new name, in order to stay away from Max. Love used to matter, but not now.

The phone rang, faintly. She declined to answer, fearing it could be Max. Katie was clearly still afraid.

No time to lose. Katie began to make files of all their documents and resisted the urge to stop and take a break. However, around five o'clock, she was getting a little hungry and decided to go to the grocery store down below. Katie stretched out her arms and grabbed her jacket and went down to the place that would give her some comfort food and fuel, more energy for the night ahead. Eyeing the bottles of red wine in the liquor store window, Katie smiled. *"Why not,"* she thought. *"It's a celebration of sorts, Katie Anchova is moving on."* Laughing to herself, she placed the bottle of wine in her shopping bag along with her grocery store items of tuna and salad, to make a light dinner later. Satisfied, she paid for her libation and was on her way. Time would march on. It had to. It was meant to be this way.

A hollow echo could be heard as Katie walked toward her apartment with her bag in hand. She was eager to get back to work. The key began to turn in the lock. Her life was happy and free now. Memories of Max played on her mind, and yes, one day she would see him again, when she was ready. Happiness filled her heart as she breathed a sigh of relief.

"So, you thought I would never find you?" a voice whispered in the dark.

Katie dropped her bag, it fell out of her grip without warning, the wine trickling like tears across the floor. *"No, it can't be!"* She closed her eyes. Her body froze. In that instant, she could no longer hide. Two hands reached out like flames and gripped her arms. Katie faced her Russian reality. He was here. Max's silhouette danced over her and she became his once again.

*

Several hours later Katie woke up and looked over at Max. He was sound asleep. Katie closed her eyes wishing she could erase last night and Max's arrival. His surprise one. I have a feeling Oleg is behind this. His ties to the police have sent Max looking, and he would make sure his son found a way to come and find her and Lev. There was no denying it, they would be tracked down eventually.

Sunlight streamed through the nearby window. Katie quietly rose and draped the curtain across to block out the sun's warmth, it surely was not in her heart, even the sun could not put a smile on her face that day. A new morning was about to begin in the city of Vancouver.

"Papa!" Lev came dashing around the corner, excitement reigning in his young eyes.

"Privet moya malen'kaya ptichka!" Max declared planting an array of kisses on his son's forehead. Lev squealed in delight hugging his father.

He jumped into his lap placing his hand on Max's cheek. *"I love you Papa,"* Lev whispered. His adoration for him apparent.

"We are here, all together in Canada, just like I—sorry, we, planned," Max declared twirling Lev around in a hug.

"*Morning,*" Max whispered.

"*Yes, Max let's hope it will be for everyone,*" Katie offered. Twisting her finger through her slept-in hair, her eyes had a distant look of love in them. "*Things have to change, Max, I mean it.*" Her voice was hushed. Hoping to shield Lev from any talk that he would not understand.

"*I know Katie, believe me I knew that, from how you left Russia, I am no fool.*" Max gripped his mug tighter, the dark liquid trickled through his mouth like a hot fiery brick, even on that chilly morning. He turned from Katie's gaze. "*I know that Olivia was somehow involved in all of this, the plan to come to Vancouver,*" he said. "*It's true, isn't it?*" Max questioned.

Katie frowned, knowing he had put the pieces together. "*Yes Max—you obviously had your suspicions about Liv.*"

A puzzled look came across his face. He was staring at the pile of documents on the desk. "*Damn it Katie, that is your real name, is it not? I never trusted her,*" he offered.

Katie turned from Max and departed at a quick pace into their bedroom. She sat down on their bed feeling unable to break from him. "*Max—this won't last long—Oh yes, the vow, the one made long ago, will it still stand now?*" she whispered.

*

His love. That was a distant memory. But a part of Katie still thought they should stay together for the sake of their son. The true part of her was unable to trust him beyond any degree. "*How will I ever escape again from Max? I will find a way and soon,*" Katie thought to herself, brushing away any past reminder of Max and their life in Krasnodar. *"It still baffles me that Max has come all the way to Vancouver, to find us? Why? I thought he was over with me and our so-called love? Hmm ..."* Katie began to rethink Max and his actions. *"There has to be ..."* Suddenly it dawned on her, those calls from other men, inviting him to Russian laced parties. And what about Max's involvement? What was going on right in front of Katie? She was surely no fool. Crawling out of bed that morning, Max had already left for the day.

Now, time alone to think about their future.

Pouring herself a cup of coffee, the aroma and warmth soothed her in that moment. Setting the mug down on the end table, her eyes caught sight of a piece of paper that had fallen between the table and the side of the couch, where Max's satchel had been. Reaching down to pick it up, Katie noticed a slight tremble in her hand, she unfolded it and read three simple sentences;

"I miss you. I need you now. Your Tishina one."

Katie took a sip, then slammed her mug down as the coffee splattered everywhere, across the carpet, on Lev's toys, a cat's toy, and Katie's new flip flops. Placing her hands in her face, she buried the pain instantly. *"Another woman I suppose, Max, you devil. How dare you? Canada has been good to you so far. I see, you came all this way for her, not us."* Hot tears began to well in Katie's eyes. Folding the paper, Katie carefully placed it where she had found it.

Not even realizing that many hours had passed and it was now turning into early evening. Katie decided to make this her night. Taking a longer bath than usual. Neatly finishing up in the tub, she poured herself a glass of red wine. This was out of the ordinary, but she thought it was warranted after her earlier discovery. With Lev sound asleep in his room, Katie hoped her husband's arrival wouldn't be too long. She would surely have words with him indeed. She managed to glance a peek at herself in the mirror. Her face was full of sorrow, from years of being around Max, wishing he would be the boy she had once met so very long ago. Now it was time to take care of herself. Katie put down her glass, on the night table. Out loud she spoke, *"I am happy with my night and really enjoy being alone."*

Opening her closet, she chose a light-blue spring dress. Max's favourite colour. Perfect. Slipping it on, she looked in the mirror, the dress neatly shaped her curvy figure. Max had come to Vancouver to make things right, and now Katie said to herself, *"The fight is on, this Russian woman, whoever she is—maybe I even know her? I have to face her. I worked hard to be with Max years ago."* The wine was providing false courage. Max didn't know what he was really missing with his beautiful wife. Katie spun around, admiring herself, looking in the mirror one last time.

A few hours later, she heard the turn of the key in the lock. He was home. Katie quickly went and sat on the couch, waiting nervously for her husband. *"Hello there,"* Max declared, walking over to Katie. *"My, you look stunning Katusha ... special occasion? It certainly is not our anniversary yet?"* Pursing his lips, his gaze was distant. He looked up at the clock, stating— *"Sorry I am late ... Uh, I ... well, the work meeting went on longer than expected."* He looked away as his eyes suddenly glazed over.

Katie smirked at him, knowing she had just unlocked his secret at last. Another woman. Probably a gorgeous Russian one, too. Her husband was now facing the sink and pouring himself a glass of the most expensive scotch they had in their apartment. Katie followed his every move. He never drank unless it was for something special, or he was under stress. *"Ah!"* Max declared, taking another swig and wiping away the last bit on his sacred hand, the one that so long ago had soothed her and loved her. The hand that had once made her tingle all over long ago, seducing every inch of her body. The hand that had also caused her pain.

Now, the two of them were simply strangers.

Max cleared his throat. *"So ... uh ... why the fancy dress? Why do you have to look so beautiful for me? Why now?"*

"Max! I just thought maybe we could be heading into a fresh start. Here and now. Forever."

Max's face became pale, like a ghost haunting him in that very second. Ghosts of yesterday, of Katie, beloved wife of his youth.

Max began to weep. *"Katie, you really don't know do you?"*

"I found the note from your secret silent one," Katie whispered. Her husband's eyes tried to escape Katie's. *"Max! I am so tired of your empty promises and lies,"* Katie cried. Feeling as though she was coming out of her own body.

"I will always love you and Lev," Max cried. His eyes were now tainted by sorrow. *"I can't keep things inside any longer."* Max's voice began to crack.

"*You have lied to me, Max! You lied—I can just feel it ... about things, I mean what else? Tell me! Forget it Max!*" Katie stormed out of the room. She looked back at Max, the tears began to build by the second. Placing her hands over her face, she turned away from him.

"*Katie, come back,*" Max pleaded, following her into their bedroom. Grabbing as many clothes as she could from her closet, she threw them in a pile as the tears began to spill down her cheeks in full force. Max winced at his wife's agony. "*Where are you going?*" Max asked. Katie did not answer him, her mind by now was in a steady fog, with mixed emotion, she did not feel strong, yet she carried on. The anger began to bubble, and courage began to soar through Katie, she threw her suitcase on their bed, and walked out of the bedroom, away from Max.

"*Far away from you,*" she muttered. "*I mean ...*" Looking into Max's eyes, she saw his pain.

He guided her into the living room, and they sat down once again on the couch. "*The same as he always does, when he talks about his guilt,*" thought Katie. This time the conversation progressed with deeper anger and frustration. A shattered wedding picture lay nearby, along with a few empty glasses that held the leftover aroma of scotch. Shards of glass were strewn on the floor.

"*I will always love you and our son. You know this, Katie,*" Max promised. His sad and distant eyes met hers as his lower lip began to quiver slightly. "*I have covered you with a blanket of lies for too long, Katie.*" He leaned over and placed his arm around his wife. "*Katie, look—at me.*" His voice began to split.

Katie shook her head "*Max, you have fallen back into our lives, and yet I know damn well what is going on!*"

"*Katie—look at me. Just—oh how can I make you understand?*" Max squeezed his hands just a little tighter together.

She slowly looked away from the man she had once loved. Her eyes now searched the room for anything, some past happy memory that could comfort her in that moment.

"*You don't understand!*" Max cried. He put his head down in shame. In front of the woman he had so-called loved for many years, his mask was starting to come off, clean and free. He could no longer hide the truth.

"*No matter what you tell me, I am not leaving you. My vow remains true,*" Katie whispered. "*I may be hurt and angry, but Max—I know you can explain things to me. And you will.*" His face became paler now, his eyes turned away from Katie, unable to face this woman who had now become a stranger to him.

"*Being straight is more accepted than not in Russia.*" Looking ahead without emotion, Max knew his words could not be pulled back.

Tears began to burst out of Katie's blue eyes. Wrapping herself around what Max had just told her would take more than just a minute to sink in. His eyes danced with pain. "*My—well I need to find myself, see who I truly am. Katie, please.*" Max winced as he looked away trying to stop any tears. He was older now; he could control pain.

"*How dare you! Why didn't you tell me years ago? Damn you!*" Katie now felt stronger and bolder than she thought possible.

"*Katie, I am truly sorry,*" Max said. His hands covered his face as he was unable to look at his wife. "*This was supposed to be forever!*" Katie cried. More mad than ever, she slammed her hand down on the cushion that lay on the couch. Was this real? It felt like a nightmare, and one from which she could not escape.

Katie slumped on the couch helplessly. *"Look at me, Katie,"* Max cried. *"Please let me."* He walked over to her and placed his hand on her back, taking a wool blanket, he gently draped it around her shoulders.

"Don't you dare touch me!" Katie screamed. Standing up, she almost fell backward. *"You knew this day would come Max! This conversation, you knew, you just knew! It would be a talk we would have to face, and you prolonged it?"* Her eyes were a blur now, tears raining down her face. *"Just how long were you hoping to conceal this from me?"*

Max looked away in misery, his jaw clenched. He began to walk from the back of the couch around to his wife. *"Katie, you were my saving grace, I mean, I know, yes, I should have told you ... I don't think I even knew myself for sure. I have had endless thoughts about everything."* He stonewalled.

"You said that you would love me forever," Katie whispered.

"I can't Katie, not anymore. How can I, if I don't love who I really am first. I lost you, to something buried deep inside of me. I need to do some soul-searching," Max whispered.

"I devoted my entire life to you! You used me and Lev, to get into Canada and to support your charade of a life. I loved us, but not anymore—what we once had is over. You've just dealt the final card Max," Katie whimpered. She looked away, as her hands began to tremble.

"Katusha, let me," Max reached out to her.

"No!" Her icy stare told him, he was now defeated. *"You need to go Max."* Katie's body now shook all over, for some reason, unable to handle everything.

"Katusha, you are shivering," Max said with concern.

"Don't you dare call me that anymore!"

"I didn't deny you of our life, Katie, or our love, at least in the very beginning," Max offered. Her clear blue eyes looked over at the teapot. That was exactly what she needed – a fresh cup of tea. She felt too weak to stand up even to reach for something to drink. By now, Katie had sat down on the floor feeling very alone. Sitting down beside her, Max gently took her hand in his and kissed it one last time. *"For us, for Lev, time marches on and we have the memories. That is all that really, truly matters."*

Katie turned her face to her husband, the man she felt she only now was really beginning to know. *"Yes, my dear Max, you are right. I ... I just need time ... to let this all sink in. We will go on, each in our own ways. It was fate that brought us together and destiny calls now. To each our own. I can't change who you are, Max."*

"Katie, I just need to find myself, to seek out who I am and what I truly want in this life." In that moment she knew she could be strong and understand the love of her life. His tears began to pour over her hands. *"Katie, your love truly saved me, when I thought I could not save myself. I have had struggles for years deep down, yet with you by my side, life felt more free and easy. That is why being around you, I felt happiness."* Max bowed his head, his lip shook slightly. Max whispered in-between sobs. *"Katie, I want to be free, just as you are here in your native Canada,"* Max cried. *"Can't you see?"* he continued, *"You gave me love, and patience, beyond*

anything else. *A future hope, that one day I would be able to open up to you. I—you, it was you Katie, coming into my life, so unexpectedly, I loved you—I truly did. Being around you made me feel happy. It made me forget what was going on deep down inside—that changed when I met you—you took me by surprise, your love. It sheltered me."* Max began to cry. His pain now became her own.

Katie looked up into Max's tear-filled eyes. A man sitting before her, whom she felt she would always love, despite his revelation. At that moment a tide of sadness passed over Katie, her hand reached out to Max. She became calm for the both of them. Underneath this man, he truly was trapped in a culture, that perhaps he could not be, who he really wanted to be. Now she knew. He needed her always, for the love and understanding. She started out years before; she would be there, in the years ahead.

Setting her hurt aside, Max needed to feel her acknowledgement. And now Katie was right by his side, as from the beginning. *"Max, I do know you now... all of you, and I will always love and be there for you, despite what you have just divulged."* Katie turned away clutching her sleeve, that was now soaked with fresh tears.

"Oh God, save my wife from any more of what I have put her through," Max said. *"The pain that I have caused her..."* Max began to weep harder now. Suddenly he looked over at Katie. *"Did I hear you correctly? You still love and understand me for who I am?"* Max whispered. Katie nodded. Max placed his trembling hand on his wife's face and in that moment wept like a small child. Katie embraced Max, the distant sound of a train erupted outside their window that telling night. Before long, they

were fast asleep, in each other's arms.

Dawn broke, as the glorious sunrise gave way through the window of their apartment. Katie's tears were completely dry now, she looked over at Max. He was still fast asleep. She touched his arm tenderly and reached down and kissed his cheek. *"My love spell, you are gone now. The boy I met so many years ago, now a grown man, able to seek his own life. A new chapter is about to begin for both of us. I will move on despite anything I have ever known with you."*

*

Getting into a regular routine, Katie had made a life now for her and Lev, while Max pursued his self truth. Katie had committed to being supportive, but also knew her patience would wear thin, if he took too long. Essentially, they were living at the same address, but had separate lives at this point in time. She prayed that Max would come back to the man she once loved and knew. *"I have to be there for him, he will come back to me."*

He was a businessman now, who travelled all over the world. Often venturing out of their apartment for days and weeks at a time.

The warm breeze that summer night held Katie in a trance as she slept soundly; her dreams were a jolt from the past with every scene she saw in front of her. Beads of sweat began to pour down her face just a little, as she turned over. She moaned, *"Max."* Her eyelids fluttered in that moment of soft breathing. Katie swooped back the blanket that gently covered her body. She was lifted out of sleep. *"Your deep blue eyes, my beauty."* Max had once told her in their youth. Now wretched by this thought, her eyes glanced at the one not sleeping beside her, Max. Lives had changed, the past was now all that was hoped for.

After preparing some morning coffee, Katie held the cup, as it seemed to warm her soul. Most of all, clear her thoughts. Flicking on the TV, it blasted loud and clear. She sat down on the couch. Her grasp tightened on the mug. The headlines shot straight out at her. A Russian airliner had crashed near Kharkiv. The flight information streamed across the TV screen.

"Aeroflot #987." Reality reached out, and clutched Katie in. *"No, it can't be Max. I hope that wasn't his flight,"* she whispered. Changing the channel Katie focused on other things. *"He will call. He said he would, once he reached Krasnodar."*

*

Glancing at his watch, Max smiled. In less than six hours the warmth of Hawaii would welcome him. Tired from all the stress, he drifted off into a restful sleep. It was a gamble, yet one Max knew he could do rather than divulge his new life, out of Russia. Telling Katie he needed to visit, just one more time, his motherland. The place where their fairy tale had begun. This story would buy him time. Many hours later, feeling the shift in direction, he knew it was only a matter of perhaps twenty minutes or so until the capital of Hawaii would greet him.

Max held a steady gaze through the window. Honolulu was in clear view. Although Moscow bloomed in his heart, he was ready to move on. This trip was indeed a good start. *"Just like Katie described, so many times. Captivating beauty all around."* A grin burst across his lips.

After a swift inspection through customs, Max rented a car, made his way into the city and checked into his hotel. After preparing, Max drove out to Makapu'u beach. Pristine blue water, gave way to rich white waves, lapping the sand. *"Sands of times past,"* Max thought quietly. The beach was busier, than he expected. He bided his time, eating and soaking in the sun. Heavy waves cursed the shore that afternoon. Sunbathers began to gather and pack up for the day. Darkness crept in. Max waited.

*

Piled belongings lay in the sand. Chestnut coloured sunglasses poked out, on their side, entwined by men's touristy clothing. A sharp corner of a leather wallet showed, just underneath the oatmeal sand. Glinting in the moonlight, a gold wedding band held its strength against the fierce wind, that had now picked up. If one could see clearly on this beach tonight, it would not be without flashlights or any kind of headlights.

The helicopter hovered and boats floated in their final pass of the search. It was a known dangerous beach. Another naive tourist, had been taken by the ocean, an unfortunate routine for the officials.

Officer Kapahu finished interviewing the lifeguard, who had found the items that morning, as he walked the beach. Turning he started to fill in the report. *"I'd say this is a done deal,"* he thought to himself. U.S. Immigration confirmed the arrival. The hotel and car rental name matched. He brushed sand off the document and filled it in; *"Name - Max Anchov ... Male... Russian...*

Vancouver... Missing person, presumed drowned ... Notify next-of-kin." He sealed the evidence bag, that contained the belongings. *"Rest in paradise, and may the Hawaiian gods surround you Mr. A."*

Outside their apartment, the airport was not too far away, and planes could be seen, flying to their various destinations. Katie busied herself, cleaning and doing laundry. Lev had gone to Grandma's for the day. Katie took advantage of the break and caught up on things. *"He will call,"* a little voice reminded her, *"Max promised."* She moved away from the window, after watching a plane go by.

A heavy knock on the front door, startled Katie. Answering it, she saw a police officer fill the frame. *"Good afternoon, I'm Constable Grant Tucker, of the Vancouver Police Department. Are you Max Anchov's spouse?"*

Katie felt Max's touch, shock through her without warning. *"He's dead, isn't he?"* Katie screamed.

Constable Tucker, looked at her questionably. *"Why would you say that?"*

"The plane crash, Max was on his way to Russia. You're here to tell me he's gone." The police officer suggested, that there may be some sort of misunderstanding and it would be best if he came in and talked with her. Katie made them tea and they both sat in the living room.

"We were contacted by the Hawaiian police," and he went on to explain the circumstances with their investigation around Max.

*

Balmy blue skies grazed over the numerous sunbathers that afternoon, the beach never disappointed. One striking man in particular, lay nearby, soaking up, as many rays as he could. *"Ah,"* Max remarked. *"Coming to Hawaii was the best idea."* Weeks previous, Katie had supported his new business venture, as he fell into a routine of working and travelling. Katie would do any-thing, to help him find himself.

His green eyes pierced around him, as he contemplated his time. A solution would soon present itself. Cascades of wave bubbles, crashing against the golden sand, foams of frothy white liquid spilling over everywhere. He admired all the beauty around him, with crowds of locals and tourists enjoying the later part of the day.

Max knew he could try and get lost in this flock of people, yet all he wanted was some peace, a place to clear his thoughts—paradise. Where better? Yes, Hawaii, in a sense, where the romance had begun for him and Katie, many, many years before. She had left here to eventually make her way to Russia and him. *"Dear, sweet Katie,"* Max reminisced. *"Always there for me, no matter what."* His lips turned up a curve; he smiled. *"The love and understanding of a woman, Katie. Back in Canada, she makes me feel at ease. It really is in her nature. I would not expect any less of her."*

Two days prior … *"All set!"* Max made his way to his assigned seat, fastening his seatbelt. The flight to Honolulu was departing on time. Taking an envelope out of his bag, his finger glided across the front. The recipient and address were clear. Inside his profound words. Licking the seal, he could taste the bitterness of glue and lingering double vodka. A small indulgence, he had ordered in the lounge, at pre-boarding. *"Katusha—perfect. Once I have checked in, I will post this to you."* His eyes veered out to the sky. Cloudy skies here, would be made clear, once he reached his final destination.

*

Katie sat up, fear encompassed her. Her eyes closed for a second. Not sure what to think. Max was confirmed, not to be on board the plane that had crashed. *"That was good news."* But the unknown fate of what happened in Hawaii, would haunt her for years. She looked over at the alarm clock ... it was 1:45 a.m. locally. Their birth time.

Several days later, Katie stood outside, watching Lev play with the other children in the park. She clutched a light blue cardigan around her shoulders. The air was crisp that day; a soft breeze blew gently. Her eyes still felt sore and tired, from endless days of crying. Max gone, barely able to grasp the news, it did not feel real. When and what would she tell Lev?

A thin white envelope welcomed her as she opened the mailbox. Walking back through the lobby, she slowly read the front. Standing out in bold handwriting, it read— *"Katie Anchova."* How can this be? It was in Max's hand. All Max's belongings were returned to her accordingly. However, this was a few days ago. A letter addressed to her? But how? The return address read, *"The Royal Hawaiian - 2259 Kalakaua Avenue, Honolulu, HI, USA, 96815"*

... She stared at it in disbelief, her tears flowed freely. *"No!"* she whispered. It still felt like a terrible dream, one that would now be her forever reality. She would be the one to pick up the pieces, only her, right in that moment.

"Open it Katie," she nudged herself. Lifting the letter to her lips, she tenderly kissed her handwritten name. *"Oh Max, dear you, distant you, are you really gone from this life?"* Releasing the letter from the envelope, Katie began to read every word, as her emotions danced high;

"My dearest Katie,
When you read my words, remember I am with you, in heart and soul. Please know that our love was changed, in all ways. I know I failed you. I hope you can forgive me.
One thing I do know I won't let our past ever be lost. It was planned from the beginning, and yes it was true. It was us. Completely. Our love was shaped, from the day we met. What could be against us?
We knew the timing was right, at our first meeting. It was in that magic, moment, that winter night when our paths crossed.
I know you may find that hard to believe now, I understand, I really do.
My dear, you were the one who always trusted and loved me until the very end. For even then when our love became broken, I knew. Truly knew, that I had found in you, a love that would always love me. A love free of judgement and without conditions. We changed. In good ways, we grew, and triumphed in the end. Being able to express things to you, my sweet Kate.
You never let me down, for that I will always be utterly grateful.
Oh Katie! My heart cries out for you, standing by

me, and fully understanding me, I feel this is the truest form of love. How could it not be? For that I can't even begin to thank you. My Krasavitsa, my Katie. Forever loving me. Now, you have these words from me. I speak from the heart to you. Cherish them, as I will always treasure you. I will return. If not in this life, in your dreams, always.

I am truly free now.
All my love, forever Maks xoxo"

    Katie closed her eyes, as Max flashed before her. Feeling broken by his words, the tears began to stream uncontrollably down her cheeks. Flashbacks of snowflakes in Red Square, tickling her nose, Max gently holding her, kissing her. No, he was gone. Yet, in the corners of her heart, he remained. He always would. Trembling harder now, the pain incessant, Katie fell to her knees in anguish. "*Max!*"

~The Lost Chapter~ (Un-Edited)

In his faintly dark room, Max slept deeply. A vintage Vostok Soviet Russian Submarine clock was near him, sitting on his night table. A gift from his uncle Vanya, one who he had heard about often, yet never had the chance to meet.

The clock read twenty minutes past two in the morning. He was slowly stirring in the middle of a deep dream. In a short time, a brand new day would welcome him. Now, only his night visions opened his eyes, just a little, half-way.

Katie walked towards the train that was bound for Moscow—"Max I love you too," she said, turning from him. Her eyes were full of hope for their future.

"Hold me in your soul, forever," he whispered gently in her ear.

Max felt his heart fall towards her, and then back as the train pulled away into the cold winter night. Seeing fresh tears well up in her eyes, Max knew that Katie wanted to stay in his Russia forever.

His pillow now soaked, fresh moist, indicated only tears, from this dream he had been having all too often.

Sitting up and staring out the window, light dew masked the window pane. Max closed his eyes for a mere moment.

"What a dream—the same one," he whispered to himself in Russian.

In the kitchen he placed the kettle on the stove, a

warm cup of chai was just what he needed. Wrapping his robe around him, he slid his hand over his cheek, half slumping into a nearby chair.

"Why do I even think of this woman? Someone who is not of my culture or could ever be, I think of her so often, and now she haunts my dreams? I feel as if she were my wholeness, yet now, I am only half complete."

*

The next morning arrived several hours later as Max slowly began to wake up. "How did I get here?" he murmured to himself. Laying on the couch with a letter half covering his chest, it was a letter from Katie, the one she had sent him from Moscow. "Oh yes, the dream." Max stood to his feet. Shaking his head, he tried to wake himself up to a present alertness. "I feel there will be news from her today." It had been several months since the last letter from Katie. The postal system in Russia was extremely slow, especially from international countries.

Crowds lined the bus stop as Max walked outside, the warmth of his jacket encompassed him. Stepping onto the tram he stood in the far back. Before he knew it, he was at his stop and opening his office door to his work.

Strong smoke filled the air. Gerry his American boss walked towards him. "Good Morning Max, a fax came for you this morning. It is from Honolulu."

"Da?" Max's eyes widened. What had aroused him in his dream, had now become a reality. Could it possibly be news from Katie? He made his way upstairs into the office and headed right to the fax machine. Max smiled and looked out the window. Today he was going to read precious words from the love he had let go months earlier. He placed his hand on the machine. It was still warm and Katie's was the last fax to come through.

"Dear Max,

I hope this fax finds you well. Life in Honolulu is going well and I do enjoy the beauty here. I hope one day you will see the islands and let the wonder of them touch you as well.
My mind is dreaming now of the day we will see each other again. I have memories stored in my heart, of us. Of the wonderful times in Krasnodar, our meetings. I know you are right, they were all planned.
I love that this indeed was our destiny, to meet that winter. I hope and truly know that someday we will see each other again.
Your country, oh so dear to my heart, and soul.
Knowing that you are in Russia, thinking and perhaps dreaming of me makes it that much sweeter.
Be well, be happy, and always think of me, when you step out into the streets of Krasnodar, the place where we first met.
Much Love, Katie"

His heart leaped with joy as he read *each and every word*. Glancing at his watch, Max pursed his lips together. Eight thirty in the morning, perfect he thought sitting down at his desk as he began to write, and then *stopped.* "Nyet, I will come here tomorrow after Ivan's wedding." Rain lightly covered the ground with barely a person in sight. It was in the very early morning hours in Krasnodar—the south of Russia. In these quiet times, Max loved the peacefulness that surrounded him. It was almost six o'clock in the morning, he had just left his flat. Friday had arrived and he looked forward to his days off. The next afternoon he would be attending his younger brother's wedding. Max pulled his knapsack tighter over his shoulder. He had admired the way Ivan had taken a serious liking to Dasha.

They had met at the local state university. A couple so inseparable, always laughing and so much in love. Max knew how happy his brother was just at the mention of Dasha's name. His breath drew a cool cloud in front of him on that cool morning. One amazing girl had indeed made him smile, yet she was so far away now. That girl was Katie. It was as if she had never left his heart. Four months had already passed; a smile came to Max's lips. She was so right for that time in his life. "I bet she thinks I am just a silly Russian." He cursed himself, remembering how she had smiled at him more than anyone else around them. That girl just haunts my daydreams right now. "You are wishing for something you will never have Max," he thought to himself. "She's not of your culture and never will be. What does that matter?" He mumbled. Reaching **his destination, he opened the heavy steel gates and allowed himself past the young Russian guards and went straight up to his office. Another day was about to begin in the city of Krasnodar.**

*

Max decided he would send Katie a reply to the previous day's fax he had received from her, one that lay underneath his pillow. One he tenderly treasured.

"*Unbelievable.*" Katie thought taking the fax, she placed it underneath her pillow for safekeeping. What would the future hold for them now? She was in Hawaii, and Max was in faraway Russia. She didn't expect to hear back from him so fast, less than one day. Her heart was beaming stronger than ever now. He had not forgotten her in the least. Becoming her prize, her treasure. That one letter, a small hope for them, for the future, his precious words.

"June 17, 1993

Dear Katie, Hello! How have you been? I am sorry I didn't fax sooner; I have been away at my brother's wedding. I am sorry we didn't speak much of us while you were staying in Krasnodar. I prayed and thought a lot about you. I just want you to know that you're very special to me. I really consider myself to be blessed to have met you last winter in Russia. And I remember all the words I told you in Krasnodar at the railway station. Be sure, they were told sincerely. I pray and know that we will see each other pretty soon. And I know we will have enough time to know each other better. OK, I will write or phone you soon. Love, Max."

Katie's fingers trembled as she held the paper in her hands. The reality was that Max did indeed love her; nothing had changed in his part of the world. It had only gotten stronger, for her a present hope.

Katie smiled slowly, stroking her fingers over the fax. Gazing at the words from the man she loved, the one so very far away.

Were they destined to meet? Only time would tell.

CPSIA information can be obtained
at www.ICGtesting.com
Printed in the USA
LVHW040137120623
749200LV00001B/1